W9-CMF-495

Joe R. Lansdale

This special
signed edition
is limited to

1500

numbered copies.

This is copy __817__.

DRIVING TO
GERONIMO'S
GRAVE

DRIVING TO
GERONIMO'S
GRAVE

and Other Stories

Joe R. Lansdale

Subterranean Press 2018

First Edition

ISBN
978-1-59606-890-2

Subterranean Press
PO Box 190106
Burton, MI 48519

subterraneanpress.com

Manufactured in the United States of America

For Scott Cupp

CONTENTS

INTRODUCTION

Stories are created in a variety of ways. Some come to a writer like a flash of lightning and are birthed as if by magic. Others arrive in bits and pieces, and over time, and can be a struggle. I am fortunate that much of my writing is comfortable. I get up, the story is there. I write for about three hours, finish for the day, then rise the next morning and do it again.

Most of the time it's that way. Some gestate, and as I said earlier, arrive more slowly, in bits and pieces. I may have a flash of an idea, a character, and I'll write the opening of a story, and then...it may go away. That is rare for me, but some stories are like that. I suspect that the stories that show up each morning are in fact from a deep well of information, myth, and observation. I suspect the story I choose is working itself out along with many others all the time, and it is only necessary for me to throw the bucket down the well and start cranking one of them up.

Much of what I write about comes from my past, or the past of relatives, or at least elements of their past that they have given me. If the background feels right, if the voice feels right, the story usually appears.

Elements of my day to day life ooze into my stories as well. Not necessarily the things I do from moment to moment, but the things I hear, see, or am concerned with. Social and cultural issues, politics, and pop culture; inspiration from books or stories or comics I've read, films or TV shows I've seen. They can all be fodder, something to stimulate the imagination.

I love writing. I love being a professional writer. I love these stories. They are a mixture of stories that came in a flash, and those that nibbled at me bit by bit over time. Some of them I forget I'm writing from time to time. I'll look back through my computer files and discover one of them, and say, "What is this?"

Closer examination will reveal a story I've started, or even finished, and forgotten about. It's like I have another self that writes them and leaves them as presents for me to find. I am certainly not one of those writers who loves having written. I love the actual writing of the stories, and I love having written equally as well.

These stories are recent work, and most of them deal with young people coming of age, finding their place in the world, or merely surviving it. "Everything Sparkles in Hell" is an exception to that, but the others fit that concept pretty well, or at least, like "The Projectionist," flirt with it.

Instead of writing a lengthy introduction, I'm going to save my comments for the individual stories, touch on some of the things I've mentioned here. If you are not a reader who cares about introductions or story notes, feel free to jump right in. But be prepared, these stories are not all of one ilk. They vary. I like it that way. When I go shopping I like a variety of foods, not one thing that I have to eat over and over. I want to have different culinary experiences, even if they are simple. I want to see if I can take standard ingredients and make an interesting meal. These stories are my meals. I've prepared them just for me with a hope you will like them too.

Joe R. Lansdale
Nacogdoches, Texas

Introduction to

DRIVING TO GERONIMO'S GRAVE

When I was young I heard a lot of stories about the Great Depression. The reason for this was simple. My parents had been through it when they were young adults. It was never far from their thoughts.

They were older than most parents when I was born, my brother and I having nearly seventeen years between our ages. They were impacted by the Great Depression in a way many who went through it were. They, like other relatives of mine, were careful about wasting anything. They were certain everything and anything could possibly be used at a later date, so it was saved.

Food was an exception.

"Clean your plate," was a constant admonition, frequently followed by "there are kids in China who are starving."

I don't know for sure about the kids in China, if they were starving or not, but I'm sure cleaning my plate didn't fill them up, if indeed they were hungry. Still, the idea of not wasting anything was part of our day to day life. I remember my uncle telling me once that they lived off a large bag of onions for a month. That's all they had to eat. They either grew them or bought them cheap. I don't remember. They ate them raw, fried, made into onion soup. One day someone in the family shot a squirrel and they had it with the remainder of the onions. That was a big day.

When I was growing up my mother had drawers full of rubber bands, unused stamps, paper clips, hair pins, pieces of paper, stubs of chewed on pencils, and all manner of paraphernalia that might somehow, at least in her mind, relate to survival should another Great Depression hit. They feared the idea of another Great Depression the way Superman fears Kryptonite. They always thought a fresh one was around the corner.

Guess what? My wife and I have drawers filled with the same junk my mother hoarded. We're doing it too. You laugh, but what if you need a pencil? I have one. I have several. Ball point pens, you name it. Are you that prepared?

Problem is I'm not sure where they all are. A problem my mother also experienced. She always had something you needed, but could never find it. Which meant we had to buy a new something or another to replace the something or another we couldn't find. My mom had a lot of something or anothers. My wife and I have a lot of something or anothers as well, and we too can't always find it.

What I collected most were stories I heard about the Great Depression, about how people felt, what they feared, and about the way they got through those old bad times. I listened and saved those stories in the back of my cranium next to all the books I had read, the films I had seen, the comic books I had gobbled up with my eyes.

Years later I used the Great Depression stories as inspiration for a number of novels I wrote. The most prominent of these is *The Bottoms*, but they also supplied background and ideas for *Sunset and Sawdust*, *The Boar*, *All the Earth Thrown to the Sky*, and *Edge of Dark Water*. I'm sure there are other books or stories I have written on the subject that haven't come immediately to mind, but the bottom line is my mom and dad's Great Depression experiences were so much a part of me, they were almost like my experiences.

This story was inspired by that same background, but it was birthed when my friend Patrick Milliken asked me if I would like to write a car story for his anthology, *The Highway Kind*.

I have a hard time sticking to any topic, but this one that had cars as a story catalyst, I thought I could do. Using that one element, I felt I could write any kind of story I wanted, and believe me, that's the only way I know how to do it. Write what I want and hope for the best. I can give the anthologist the germ of what they are after, but I have to find my own way. If it's too structured an idea, I'm out. It's why I'm generally not drawn to anthologies where all the stories tie together. I have to be too conscious of the other author's creations, and when it comes to fiction I'm not a great team player.

I want to write the story I want to write. In film I'm more flexible, same with comics, but prose, not so much.

This one is a Depression era road story. I've always loved road stories and books. Jack Kerouac's *On the Road* comes to mind. I also like tales that are really a series of adventures, and do not require a clockwork plot. That's not my strength. I like to capture the sound and feel of what I am writing about with the prose style, characters and dialogue, more than a carefully worked out plot. It's kind of the difference between a comedian who tells jokes, and one that tells stories which are humorous. I'm more drawn to the latter.

Driving to Geronimo's Grave was almost called *Driving to Sitting Bull's Grave.*

My brother and I, a few years ago, drove from East Texas to Yellowstone Park, as well as states and sites along the way, came down through Wyoming and South Dakota on our way home. Had a very interesting experience in Nebraska with a goofy deputy who seemed to be right out of *The Andy Griffith Show*, but far less charming. He decided my brother and I were drunk. We don't drink.

We had clothes in the backseat because we were traveling and fresh underwear seemed like a good idea, but the deputy decided we had stolen the clothes. If we had, I think we would have picked snazzier wardrobes. I would have certainly stolen a jaunty hat. He almost pulled his gun on us. He had me recite the alphabet, then accused me of having letters out of order, since with my accent t and d sounded the same to him. I told him to give me a breathalyzer, take me in, do whatever, because I was fed up with his shit. He finally let us go with a ticket for forgetting to turn my headlights on after leaving a well-lit filling station on a well-lit street. I noticed they weren't on almost the moment he hit his lights and gave his siren a whoop. He could have given me that ticket thirty minutes earlier, before he decided we were hardened criminals on the prowl for old clothes.

But before Deputy Dawg pulled us over, we stopped at a lot of historical sites. When we were in Montana, at The Little Big Horn State Park, site of the famous Custer versus a whole lot of pissed off Native Americans, I got one of the Sioux participants, Sitting Bull on my mind.

I have always loved history, and am primarily drawn to the history of what is called The Old West. Looking out over that battle-field, I thought of Sitting Bull, who was present in the Sioux camp, and then I thought of him being in the Wild West Show, and finally dying at the hands of Indian police. I thought about his grave. The story began to develop.

By the time I finally got to the story, about three years later, the gravesite had changed to Geronimo's grave, which meant part of the story had to take place in Oklahoma. I liked the sound of the title better with Geronimo in it, so the very thing that had originated the story fell by the wayside, and a different Native American and his grave took its place.

I sat down to write a story to fit the title, one that would some-how involve a car, and I decided I would place the tale during the Great Depression. As I have said, I felt comfortable writing about that era, and I loved writing about young people finding their way in the world, so I thought I would put it all in this story. Originally it was about a young man taking his hateful grandpa on a trip so he could see where he had been born and raised, and bonding was to ensue.

That didn't develop into a story I wanted to tell. After a page or so, I abandoned it, kept the basic idea, but thought, what if a relative you didn't know died, and there was no one to claim the body, and you were assigned the task? That sounded more interesting to me.

To add to the misery, the body was a long way off and you had to go there by car, even if you were a kid, and worse, you had to take your little sister on the mission, and she's a smart-ass and a rascal, which doesn't make the trip any easier.

What I thought was this is good story material. I still think it is. So, relax, fall back in time, and take a ride.

DRIVING TO
GERONIMO'S
GRAVE

We ought to never do wrong when people are looking.

—MARK TWAIN

I hadn't even been good and awake for five minutes when Mama came in and said, "Chauncey, you got to drive on up to Fort Sill Oklahoma and pick up your Uncle Smat."

I was still sitting on the bed, waking up, wearing my night-dress, trying to figure which foot went into what shoe, when she come in and said that. She had her dark hair pushed up on her head and held in place with a checkered scarf.

"Why would I drive to Oklahoma and pick up Uncle Smat?"

"Well, I got a letter from some folks got his body, and you need to bring it back so we can bury it. The Wentworths said they were gonna leave it in the chicken house if nobody comes for it. I wrote her back and posted the letter already telling her you're coming."

"Uncle Smat's dead?" I said.

"We wouldn't want to bury him otherwise," Mama said, "though it took a lot longer for him to get dead than I would have figured, way he honky-tonked and fooled around with disreputable folks. Someone knifed him. Stuck him like a pig at one of them drinking places, I figure."

"I ain't never driven nowhere except around town," I said. "I don't even know which way is Oklahoma."

"North," Mama said.

"Well, I knew that much," I said.

"Start in that direction and watch for signs," she said. "I'm sure there are some. I got your breakfast ready, and I'll pack you some lunch and give you their address, and you can be off."

Now this was all a fine good morning, and me hardly knowing who Uncle Smat was, Mama not really caring that much about him, Smat being my dead daddy's brother. She had cared about Daddy plenty, though, and she had what you could call family obligation toward Uncle Smat. As I got dressed she talked.

"It isn't right to leave a man, even a man you don't know so well, laying out in a chicken house with chickens to peck on him. And there's all that chicken mess too. I dreamed last night a chicken snake crawled over him."

I put on a clean work shirt and overalls and some socks that was sewed up in the heels and toes, put on and tied my shoes, slapped some hair oil on my head and combed my hair in a little piece of mirror I had on the dresser. I packed a tow sack with some clothes and a few odds and ends I might need. I had a toothbrush and a small jar of baking soda and salt for tooth wash. Mama was one of the few in our family who had all her teeth, and she claimed that was because she used a brush made from hair bristles and she used that soda and salt. I believed her, and both me and my sister followed her practice.

Mama had some sourdough bread, and she gave that to me, and she filled a couple of my dad's old canteens with water, put a blanket and some other goods together for me. I loaded them in a good sized tow sack and carried it out to the Ford and put the bag inside the turtle hull.

In the kitchen, I washed up in the dish pan, toweled off, and sat down to breakfast, a half a dozen fried eggs, biscuits, and a pitcher of buttermilk. I poured a glass of milk and drank it, and then I poured another, and ate along with drinking the milk.

Mama, who had already eaten, sat at the far end of the table and looked at me.

"You drive careful now, and you might want to stop somewhere and pick some flowers."

"I'm picking him up, not attending his funeral," I said.

"He might be a bit stinky, him lying in a chicken coop and being dead," Mama said. "So I'm thinking the flowers might contribute to a more pleasant trip. Oh, I tell you what. I got some cheap perfume I don't never use, so you can take that with you and pour it on him, you need to."

I was chewing on a biscuit when she said this.

I finished chewing fast as I could, said, "Now wait a minute. I just got to thinking on this good. I'm picking him up in the car, and that means he's going to go in the backseat, and I see how he could have grown a mite ripe, but Mama, are you telling me he ain't going to be in a coffin or nothing?"

"The letter said he was lying out in the chicken coop, where he was living with the chickens, having to only pay a quarter a week and feed the chickens to be there, and one morning they came out to see why he hadn't gathered the eggs and brought them up—that also being part of his job for staying in the coop—and they found him out there, colder than a wedge in winter. He'd been stabbed, and he had managed to get back to the coop where he bled out. Just died quietly out there with their chickens. They didn't know what to do with him at first, but they found a letter he had from his brother, that would be your father—" She added that like I couldn't figure it on my own. "—and there was an address on it, so they wrote us."

"They didn't move the body?"

"Didn't know what to do with it. They said in the letter they had sewed a burial shroud you can put him in; it's a kind of bag."

"I have to pour perfume on him, put him in a bag, and drive him home in the backseat of the car?"

"Reckon that's about the size of it. I don't know no one else would bother to go get him."

"Do I have to? Thinking on it more, I'm not sure it's such a good idea."

"Course you got to go. They're expecting you."

"Write them a letter and tell them I ain't coming. They can maybe bury him out by the chicken coop or something."

"That's a mean thing to say."

"I didn't hardly know him," I said, "certainly not enough to perfume him, bag him up, and drive him home."

"You don't have to have known him all that well, he's family."

My little sister, Terri, came in then. She's twelve and has her hair cut straight across in front and short in back. She had on overalls with a work shirt and work boots. She almost looked like a boy. She said, "I was thinking I ought to go with you."

"You was thinking that, huh," I said.

"It might not be such a bad idea," Mama said. "She can read the map."

"I can read a map," I said.

"Not while you're driving," Mama said.

"I can pull over."

"This way, though," Mama said, "you can save some serious time, just having her read it and point out things."

"He's been dead for near two weeks or so. I don't know how much pressure there is on me to get there."

"Longer you wait, the more he stinks," Terri said.

"She has a point," Mama said.

"Ain't they supposed to report a dead body? Them people found him, I mean? Ain't it against the law to just leave a dead fella lying around?"

"They done us a favor, Uncle Smat being family and all," Mama said. "They could have just left him, or buried him out there with the chickens."

"I wish they had," I said. "I made that suggestion, remember?"

"This way we can bury him in the cemetery where your daddy is buried," Mama said. "That's what your daddy would have wanted."

She knew I wasn't going to say anything bad that had to do with Daddy in any manner shape or form. I thought that was a low blow, but Mama, as they say, knew her chickens. She knew where I was the weakest.

"All right then," I said, "I'm going to get him. But that car of ours has been driven hard and might not be much for a long trip. The clutch hangs sometimes when you press on it."

"That's a chance you have to take for family," Mama said.

I grumbled something, but I knew by then I was going.

"I'm going, too," Terri said.

"Oh, hell, come on then," I said.

"Watch your cussing," Mama said. "Daddy wouldn't like that either."

"All he did was cuss," I said.

"Yeah, but he didn't want you to," she said.

"I think I'm gonna cuss," I said. "My figuring is Daddy would have wanted me to be good at it, and that takes practice."

"I ain't forgot how to whip your ass with a switch," Mama said.

—

Now it was figured by Mama that it would take us two days to get to the Wentworths' house and chicken coop if we drove fast and didn't stop to see the sights and such, and then two days back. As we got started out early morning, we had a pretty good jump on the first day.

The clutch hung a few times but seemed mostly to be cooperating, and I only ground the gears now and again, but that was my fault, not the car's, though in the five years we had owned it, it had been worked like a stolen mule. Daddy drove that car all over the place looking for spots of work. His last job had been for the WPA, and we seen men working those jobs as we drove along, digging out bar ditches and building walls for what I reckoned would be schools or some such. Daddy used to say it was mostly busywork, but it paid real money, and real money spent just fine.

Terri had the map in her lap, and from time to time she'd look at it, say, "You're doing all right."

"Of course I am," I said. "This is the only highway to Marvel Creek. When we need the map is when we get off the main road and onto them little routes back in there."

"It's good to make sure you don't get veered," Terri said.

"I ain't getting veered," I said.

"Way I figure it, it's gonna take three days to get there, or most near a full three days, not two like Mama said."

"You figured that, did you?"

"I reckoned in the miles and how fast the car is going, if that speedometer is right, and then I put some math to it, and I come up with three days. I got an A in Math."

"Since it's the summer, I reckon you've done forgot what math you learned," I said.

"I remember. Three days at this pace is right, and this is about as fast as you ought to go. Slowing wouldn't hurt a little. As it is, we blowed a tire, they wouldn't find nothing but our clothes in some bushes alongside the road, and they'd be full of shit."

End of that day we come near the Oklahoma border. It was starting to be night, so I pulled us over and down a little path, and we parked under a tree for the night. We had some egg sandwiches Mama had made, and we ate them. They had gotten kind of soggy, but it was that or wishful thinking, so we ate them and drank some water from the canteens.

We threw a blanket on the ground and laid down on that and looked up through the tree limbs at the stars.

"Ever wonder what's out there?" Terri said.

"I read this book once, about this fella went to Mars. And there was some green creatures there with four arms."

"No joke?"

"No joke."

"Must have been a good book."

"It was," I said. "And there was four-armed white apes, and regular-looking people too, only they were red-skinned."

"Did they have four arms too?"

"No. They were like us, except for the red skin."

"That's not as good," Terri said. "I'd like to have had me four arms, if I was one of them, and otherwise looked regular."

"You wouldn't look regular with four arms," I said.

"I could stand it," Terri said. "I could pick up a lot of things at once."

When we woke up the next morning, my back hurt considerable. I had stretched the blanket out on an acorn, and it had stuck me all night. I come awake a few times during the night and was going to pull back the blanket and move it, but I was too darn tired to move. In the morning, though, I wished I had. I felt like I had been shot with an arrow right above my belt line.

Terri, however, was as chipper as if she had good sense. She had some boiled eggs in the package Mama had ended up giving her after it was decided she was going, and we had one apiece for breakfast and some more canteen water.

After wrapping up the blanket, we climbed back in the car and started out again, drove on across the line and into Oklahoma, crossing the Red River, which wasn't really all that much of a river. At that time of the year, at least where we crossed, it wasn't hardly no more than a muddy trickle, though as we crossed the bridge, I could see down a distance to where it was wider and deeper looking.

We come to a little town called Hootie Hoot, which seemed to me to be a bad name for most anything, and there was one gas pump outside a little store there, and by the door going into the store was a sign that said they was looking for a tire-and-rim man. We could see the gas in the big jug on top of the pump, so we knew there was plenty, and we pulled up to it. Couple other stations we had passed were out of gas.

After we had sat there awhile, an old man with bushy white hair wearing overalls so faded they was near white as his hair came out of the station. He had a big red nose and looked like he had just got out of bed. We stood outside the car while he filled the tank.

"They say the Depression has done turned around," he said. "But if it did, it darn sure didn't turn in this direction."

"No, sir," I said.

"Ain't you a little young to be driving around?" he said.

"Not that young," I said.

He eyed me some. "I guess not. You children on an errand?"

"We are," I said. "We're going to pick up my uncle Smat."

"Family outing?"

"You could say that."

"So we will," he said.

"We might want something from the store too," I said.

"All right, then," he said.

Me and Terri went inside, and he hung up the gas nozzle and trailed after us.

I didn't have a lot of money, a few dollars Mama had given me for gas and such, but I didn't want another soggy egg sandwich or a boiled egg. I bought some Vienna sausages, some sardines and a box of crackers, and splurged on Coca-Colas for the two of us. I got some shelled and salted peanuts to pour into the Coca-Colas, bought four slices of bread, two cuts of bologna, and two fat cuts of rat cheese. The smell of that cheese made me seriously hungry; it was right smart in aroma and my nose hairs tingled.

We paid up, and I pulled the car away from the pump, on around beside the store. We sat on the bumper and made us a sandwich from the bread, bologna and cheese. It was a lot better than those soggy egg sandwiches Mama had made us, and though we had two more of them, they had reached a point where I considered them turned, and I planned on throwing them out on the road before we left.

That's when a ragged-looking fellow come up the road to the store and stopped when he seen us. He beat the dust off the shoulders and sides of his blue suit coat. His gray hat looked as if a goat had bitten a hunk out of the front of it. The suit he was wearing had been a nice at one time, but it was worn shiny in spots and hung on him like a circus tent. His shoe toes flapped when he walked like they were trying to talk. He said, "I hate to bother you children, but I ain't ate in a couple days, nothing solid anyway, and was wondering you got something to spare?"

"We got some egg sandwiches," Terri said. "You can have both of them."

"That would be right nice," said the ragged man.

He came over smiling. Up close, he looked as if he had been boiled in dirt, his skin was so dusty from walking along the road.

One of his nose holes was smaller than the other. I hadn't never seen nobody like that before. It wouldn't have been all that noticeable, but he had a way of tilting his head back when he talked.

Terri gave him the sandwiches. He opened up the paper they was in, laid them on the hood of our car, took hold of one, and started to wolf it down. When he had it about ate, he said, "That egg tastes a might rubbery. You ain't got nothing to wash it down?"

"We could run you a bath if you want, and maybe we could polish your shoes for you," Terri said. "But we ain't got nothing to wash down that free sandwich."

The dusty man narrowed his eyes at Terri, then gathered himself.

"I didn't mean to sound ungrateful," he said.

"I don't think you give a damn one way or the other," Terri said.

"Look here," I said. "I got the last of this Coca-Cola; you don't mind drinking after me, you can have that. It's got a few peanuts in it."

He took the Coca-Cola and swigged some. "Listen here, could you spare a few other things, some clothes, some more food? I could give you a check."

"A check?" Terri said. "What would it be good for?"

The man gave her a look that was considerably less pleasant than a moment ago.

"We don't want no check," Terri said. "We had something to sell, and we don't, we'd want cash money."

The man's eyes narrowed. "Well, I ain't got no cash money."

"There you are, then," Terri said. "A check ain't nothing but a piece of paper with your name on it."

"It represents money in the bank," said the man.

"It don't represent money we can see, though," Terri said.

"That's all right," I said. "Here, you take this dollar and go in there and buy you something with it. That's my last dollar."

It wasn't my last dollar, but when I pulled it out of my pocket, way he stared at it made me nervous.

"I'll take it," he said. He started walking toward the store. After a few steps, he paused and looked back at us. "You was right not to take no check from me, baby girl. It wouldn't have been worth the paper it was written on. And let me tell you something. You ought to save up and buy yourself a dress and some hair bows, a dab of makeup, maybe take a year or two of charm lessons."

He went on in the store, and I hustled us up, taking what was left of our sandwiches with us and getting into the car.

"Why you in such a hurry?" Terri said, as I drove away.

"Something about that fella bothers me," I said. "I think he's trouble."

"I don't know how much trouble he is," Terri said, "but I darn sure had him figured on that check. As for a dress and hair bows, he can kiss my ass. I wish him and all fools like him would die."

"You can't wish for all fools to die, Terri. That ain't right."

Terri pursed her lips. "I guess you're right. All them fools died, I'd be pretty lonely."

—

I guess we went about twenty miles before the motor steamed up and I had to pull the Ford over. I picked a spot where there was a wide place in the road, and stopped there and got out and put the hood up and looked under it like I knew what was going on. And I did, a little. I had developed an interest in cars, same as Daddy. He liked to work on them and said if he wasn't a farmer he'd like to fix engines. I used to go with him when he went outside to put water in the radiator and mess with the motor. Still, I wasn't what you'd call a mechanic.

"You done run it too long without checking the water," Terri said.

I gave her a hard look. "If you weren't here, I don't know what I'd think was wrong with it."

I got a rag out of the turtle hull, got some of our canteen water, and using the rag, unscrewed the radiator lid. I had Terri stand back, on account of when I poured the water in some hot, wet spray boiled up. Radiator was bone dry.

We got enough water in the car to keep going, but now we were out of water to drink. We poked along until I saw a creek running alongside the road and off into the woods. We pulled down a tight trail with trees on both sides, got out and refilled the canteens from a clear and fast-running part of the creek. The water tasted cold and clean. I used the canteens to finish filling the radiator, and then we filled them for us to drink. I decided to take notice of this spot, in case we needed it on the way back. While I was contemplating, Terri picked up a rock, and zinged it side-arm into a tree and a red bird fell out of it and hit the ground.

"You see that," she said. "Killed it with one shot."

"Damn it, Terri. Wasn't no cause for that."

"I just wanted to."

"You don't kill things you don't eat. Daddy taught you that."

"I guess we could eat it."

"No. We're not eating any red birds. And don't you never kill another."

"All right," she said. "I didn't really know I'd hit it. But I'm pretty good with rocks. You know Gyp Martin? Well, he called me a little bitch the other day, and I hit him with a rock so hard it knocked him cold out."

"No it didn't."

"Yes it did. Sharon Miller was with me and seen it."

"Terri. You got to quit with the rocks. I mean, well, I give you this. That was a good shot. I don't know if I can even throw that far."

"I'd be surprised if you could," she said. "It's a natural talent for a rare few, but then you got to develop it."

We got to where we were going about dark that day.

"I thought you said three days," I said. "We made it in two, way Mama said."

"Guess I figured in too many stops and maybe a cow crossing the road or something."

"You did that, did you?"

"I was thinking you'd want to stop and see the sights, even though you said you didn't."

"What sights?"

"That turned out to be the problem. No sights."

"Terri, you are full of it, and I don't just mean hot wind."

———

The property was off the road, up in the woods, and not quite on top of a hill. We could see the house as we drove up the dirt drive. It was big, but looked as if it might slip off the hill at any moment and tumble down on us. It was even more weathered than our home place. The outhouse out back was in better shape than where they lived.

As we come rest of the way up the hill, we saw there were hog pens out to the side with fat black-and-white hogs in them. Behind that we could see a sizable run of henhouses. I had expected just one little henhouse, but these houses were plentiful and had enough chicken wire around them you could have used it to fence in Rhode Island.

I parked the Ford and we went up and knocked on the door. A man came to the door and looked at us through the screen. Then he came out on the porch. He had the appearance of someone that had been thrown off a train. His clothes were dirty and his hat was mashed in front. His body seemed about forty, but his face looked about eighty. He was missing all his teeth, and had his jaw packed with tobacco. I figured he took that tobacco out, his face would collapse.

"Who are you?" he said, and spat tobacco juice into a dry flower bed.

"The usual greeting is hello," Terri said.

I said, "Watch this, sir." And I gave Terri a kick in the leg.

"She had that coming," he said.

Terri hopped off the porch and leapt around yipping while I said, "We got a letter from your missus, and if we got the right place, our uncle Smat is in your chicken house."

"You're in the right place. When she quits hopping, step around to the side, start up toward the chicken houses, and you'll smell him. He ain't actually up in a henhouse no more. A goddang old dog got in there and got to him, dragged him through a hole in the fence, on up over the hill there, into them trees. But you can smell him strong enough you'd think he was riding on your back. You'll find him."

"You didn't have to kick me," Terri said.

"I got a bit of thrill out of it," said Mr. Wentworth. "I thought maybe you was a kangaroo."

Terri glared at him.

A woman wiping her hands with a dish towel, and looking a lot neater, came to the door and stepped out on the porch.

"You take these kids to their uncle," she said to the man.

"They can smell him," he said.

"You take them out there. I'll go with you."

She threw the dish towel inside the door, said, "But I got something you'll need."

Mrs. Wentworth went in the house and came out with a jar of VapoRub and had us dab a good wad under our noses so as to limit the smell of Uncle Smat. I was beginning to get a bit weak on the whole idea of a Christian burial for a man I'd never seen, and by all accounts wasn't worth the water it'd take to put him out if he was on fire.

Dabbed up, we all started around the house and up the higher part of the hill. We passed the chicken coops, and as we did, this gave Mrs. Wentworth a moment for a bit of historical background concerning their time with Uncle Smat.

"He walked up one day and said he needed a job, most anything so he could eat. So we put him out there chopping firewood, which he did a fair job of. We let him sleep in one of the coops that didn't have a lot of chickens in. We couldn't have some unknown fella sleeping in the house. Next day he wanted more work, and so he ended up staying and taking care of the chickens, a job at which he was passable. Then one night he come up on the porch, a-banging on the door, drunk as Cooter Brown. We wouldn't let him in and told him to go on out to the coop and sleep it off."

Mr. Wentworth picked up the story there. "Next morning he didn't come down to the back porch for his biscuits, so I went up there and found him dead. He'd been knifed. I guess maybe he wasn't drunk after all."

"He was drunk all right," Mrs. Wentworth said. "That might have killed some of the pain for him. Fact was, I don't know I'd ever heard anyone drunk as he was that was able to stand. I went through his clothes, and he had some serious money on him, and I won't lie to you, we took that as his room and board money."

"You robbed a dead man for sleeping in your chicken coop?" Terri said. "Why didn't you just take his shoes too?"

Mr. Wentworth cleared his throat. "Well, they *was* the same size as mine, and he didn't need them."

Wentworth lifted a foot and showed us a brown brogan.

"Them toes was real scuffed up," Mrs. Wentworth said, "so I put some VapoRub on them, rubbed it in good, and put a solid shine on them, took out some of that roughness."

"Damn," Terri said, looking down at the shoes on Mr. Wentworth's feet. "You did take his shoes."

"You're talking like a gun moll," Mrs. Wentworth said to Terri.

"I'm talking like someone whose uncle was robbed of money and shoes, that's how I'm talking," Terri said.

"It's all right," I said. "Let's see him."

31

As we walked along, Mr. Wentworth said, "When I come to look in on his body yesterday, he wasn't in the coop, but the coop was broke open, and something had dragged him off. It was either a pack of dogs or coyotes. They dragged him up there a ways and chewed off one of his feet. They got a toe off the other foot."

Terri looked at me. I gently shook my head.

Top of the hill near a line of woods, we seen his body. The smell was so strong that VapoRub might as well have been water. I ain't never smelled nothing that bad in all my life. If at the bottom of the hill it had been strong as a bull, at the top it was a bull elephant.

Uncle Smat wasn't a sight for sore eyes, but he damn sure made the eyes sore. He was up next to a line of woods, half in a feed bag. It was over his head and tied around his waist with twine. His legs stuck out, and his pants legs was all ripped from animals dragging him out of the coop, on up where he lay. One foot, as Mr. Wentworth had said, was gnawed off, and Mr. Wentworth was right about that missing toe on the other foot; the big toe, if you're curious.

"So the man dies, you put a bag over his head and leave him with the chickens and write us a letter?" Terri said.

Mr. Wentworth nodded.

"Yeah," Terri said. "I guess there ain't no use denying any of that."

"It's been too hot for digging, and thing is we don't know him. We found he had his name and your address on a letter in his billfold, and we wrote your family. We figured we'd leave the rest to his kin."

I went over and untied the twine around his waist and pulled the bag off his head. Uncle Smat was not a pretty man, but I recognized the family nose. His eyes was full of ants and worms and such. His stomach was bloated up with gas.

"He's all yours," Mr. Wentworth said.

"Oh," said Mrs. Wentworth. "I guess you ought to have his hat. I put it on the back porch and put corn in it for the squirrels. I like squirrels. Oh, one more thing. He had a car, but the night he died, he didn't bring it back with him. He come on foot or someone dropped him off. Didn't want you to think we took his car."

"Just his billfold and what was in it," Terri said.

"Yeah," Mrs. Wentworth said, "just that."

———

In the car, Uncle Smat laying in the backseat, tucked completely inside a big burlap bag, we started out. I had paid a quarter for the used jar of VapoRub, which was far too much, but at the time seemed a necessity. I poured Mama's perfume over him, but if it knocked back the smell any, I couldn't tell it. We drove through the night with the windows down and the car overflowing with the aroma of Uncle Smat. Terri hung out of her window like a dog.

"Oh baby Jesus," she said. "This here is awful."

I was driving and leaning out my window as much as was reasonable and still be able to drive. The air was helping a little, but there wasn't nothing that could defeat that smell short of six feet of dirt or the bottom of the deep blue sea.

The Ford's headlights was cutting a path through the night, and I felt we were making pretty good time, and then I seen the smoke from under the hood. It was the radiator again.

I pulled over where the road widened against the trees, and parked. I got the hood up and looked at the radiator. It was really steaming. I knew then it had a hole in it. I decided it was a small hole, and if I could keep water in the radiator and not drive like John Dillinger in a getaway car, I might make it home

With the car not moving, Uncle Smat's stink had taken on a power that was beyond that of Hercules.

"Oh, hell." Terri was in the woods throwing up and calling out. "I holler calf rope. You win, Uncle Smat. Lord have mercy on all His children, especially me."

I used most of our water to fill the radiator, and was going to call Terri up from the woods, when the wind changed and the smell hit me tenfold. It was like I was in that bag with Uncle Smat.

Terri was coming up the hill. I said, "You're right. We can't keep going on like this. Uncle Smat deserves a burial."

"We ain't got no shovel," Terri said.

This was an accurate observation.

"Then he deserves a ditch and some Christian words said over him."

"I'm all for that ditch, but we ain't got no preacher neither."

"Damn it," I said.

"I say we just put him in a ditch and go on to the house," Terri said.

"That ain't right," I said.

"No, but it sure would be a mite less smelly."

———

We packed our noses with VapoRub, dragged Uncle Smat out of the car by the bag he was in, and pulled him down a hill that dropped off into the woods. The bag ripped on a stob. Uncle Smat came out of the bag and rolled down the hill, caught up on a fallen tree branch, and stopped rolling. I could see that Uncle Smat's coat had ripped open. The pale lining was fish-belly white in the pale moonlight.

"Ah, hell," Terri said. "Can't believe that bag was holding back the smell that much. Oh heavens, that is nastier than a family of skunks rolled up in cow shit."

I was yanking the branch away from under Uncle Smat so he could roll the rest of the way down, when Terri said, "Hey, Chauncey. Something fell out of his coat."

I looked at what she had picked up. It was a folded piece of paper.

Dark as it was, we went up to the car and I turned on the headlights, stood in front of them, and looked at the paper. It had some lines on it, a drawing of some tombstones, and the words *Fort Sill* and *Geronimo's grave* written on it. There was a dollar sign drawn on one of the tombstones.

"It was in his coat," Terri said.

"Probably stitched up in the lining."

"He must have had a reason for hiding it," Terri said.

"If he hadn't, Wentworths would have found it."

"What you think it is?"

"A map."

"To what?"

"You see what I see," I said. "Where do you think?"

"Geronimo's grave?"

"Domino," I said.

"I ain't going there," she said.

"Me neither. We're going home. Remember, Terri. The hogs ate him. Nobody is going to believe the chickens did it. It would take them too long."

———

Back with Uncle Smat, I finally managed to pull the branch aside that was holding him, and as there was a deep, damp sump hole at the bottom of the hill between two trees, I gave him a bit of a boost with my foot and he rolled down into it. One of his legs stuck out, and it was the one with the chewed-off foot. I scrambled down and bent his leg a little and got it into the sump, and then I tossed the ripped bag over him, kicked some dirt in on top of that, but it was like trying to fill in the ocean with a pile of dirt, a spoon, and good intentions.

"Hell with it," Terri said.

"Maybe we can come back for him later," I said.

"Ha," Terri said. "I say we stick to that story about how the Wentworths' hogs got to him and ate him."

"I can live with that," I said.

"Mostly I can live with him being out of the car," Terri said.

"It ain't much of a Christian burial," I said.

Terri inched closer to the sump hole, put her hand over her heart, said, "Jesus loves you... Let's go."

———

We drove with all the windows down, trying to drive out memories of Uncle Smat. When we got to the Red River, and was about to cross, the car got hot again and I had to pull over. We didn't have any more water, other than a bit for drinking, so I decided wasn't no choice but for me to take the canteens and go down the hill and under the bridge and dip some out of the river.

Terri stayed with the car. I took the canteens with me and dipped water out of the river, and when I came back up the hill, there, sitting on the hood with Terri, was the man we had seen the other day. He was sitting there casual-like with his hand clutched in the collar of Terri's shirt, and the moonlight gleamed on a knife blade he had in his hand, resting it on his thigh.

"There he is," the man said. "Good to see you and Miss Smart Ass again."

I placed the canteens gently on the ground and picked up a stick lying by the side of the road and started walking toward him. "Let go of her," I said, "or I'll smack you a good one."

He held up the hand with the knife in it.

"I wouldn't do that, boy. You do, I might have to cut her before you get to me. Cut her good and deep. You want that boy?"

I shook my head.

"Put down that limb then."

I dropped it.

"Come over here," the man said.

"Don't do it," Terri said.

"You shut up," the man said.

I came over. He got down off the car and dragged Terri off of it and flung her on the road.

"I'm gonna need this car," he said.

"All right," I said.

"First, you're gonna put water in it, and then you're going to drive me."

"You don't need me," I said. "I'll give you the keys."

"Now, this here is embarrassing, but I can't drive. Never learned."

"Just put your foot on the gas and turn the wheel a little and stomp on the brake when you want to stop."

"I tried to drive once and ran off in a creek. I ain't driving. You are. The girl can stay here."

"All right," I said.

"I ain't staying," she said. "He needs me to read the map and such."

"I ain't going the same place you was going," the man said.

"Where are you going?" I said.

"Back the way you come," he said.

He reached in his coat pocket and pulled out the folded sheet of paper I had left lying on the front seat. He pointed at the map.

"I'm going here, to see where my partner hid the bank money."

Damn you, Uncle Smat. I said, "You mean that dollar sign means real money."

"Real paper money," he said.

⸺

After I put water in the radiator, the man sent me back down to get more water, while he stayed with Terri. I didn't have no choice but to do what he wanted. Next thing I knew I was turning the car around and heading back the way we had come.

"It stinks in here," said the man.

I was at the wheel; he was beside me, his knife hand lying against his thigh. Terri was in the backseat.

37

"You ought to be back here," Terri said. "I think I'm going to be sick."

"Be sick out the window," said the man.

"So you and Uncle Smat were partners?" I said.

"Guess you could say that. Ain't this just the peachiest coincidence that ever happened? You coming along, him being your uncle, and me being his partner."

"I think you stabbed your partner," Terri said.

"There is that," said the man. "We had what you might call a falling-out on account we split up after we hit the bank and he didn't do like he said he would. Let me tell you, that was one sweet job. I had a gun then. I wish I had it now. We come out of the bank in Lawton with the cash, and the gun went off and I shot a lady. Not on purpose. Bullet ricocheted off a wall or something. Did a bounce and hit her right between the eyes. Went through a sack of groceries she was carrying and bounced off a can in the bag or something, hit right and betwixt."

I didn't believe his story, but I didn't bring this to his attention.

"So Smat, he decides we ought to split up, to divide the heat on us, so to speak, and he was going to give me a map to where he hid the money. He said he'd hid it in haste but had made a map, and when things cooled, we could go get our money."

Terri leaned over the seat.

"So he come and told you he had a map for you, and he was right with you, and he didn't give it to you?"

"Get your nose back, before I cut it off," the man said, and he showed her the knife. Terri sat back in the seat.

"All right, here it is," he said. "It wasn't no bank job at all. We robbed a big dice game in Lawton. One that was against the law, but the law was there playing dice. This was a big game and there were all these mighty players there from Texas and Oklahoma, Arkansas, Louisiana, I think Kansas. Hot arms, they were. Illegal money earned in ways that didn't get the taxes paid. This was a big gathering, and the money was going into a big dice game and there was going to be some big winners. We were just there as small potatoes, me and Smat. Kind of bodyguards for a couple of fellas. And then it come to me and Smat we ought to rob the dice game. It wasn't that smart an idea, them knowing us and all, but it was a lot of money. Right close to a million dollars. Can you imagine? You added up every dollar I've ever made sticking up banks and robbing from folks here and there, and what I might make robbing in the future, it ain't anywhere near that. Me and Smat decided right then and there we was going to take the piles of money heaped there on the floor, and head out. We pulled our guns and took it. That woman I shot, it wasn't no damn accident. She started yelling at us, and I can't stand screeching, so I shot her. It was a good shot."

"Yeah," Terri said. "How far away were you from her?"

"I don't know."

"I bet you was right up near her. I bet it wasn't no great shot at all."

"Terri," I said. "Quiet."

"Yeah, Terri," the man said. "Quiet."

"Well, we robbed them, made a run for it in Smat's car, and then we hid out. Smat, after a few days, he starts thinking he's done shit in the frying pan. Starts saying we got to give it back, like they were gonna forgive and forget, like we brung a lost cat home. We hid the money near Geronimo's grave one night, took some shovels up there in the dark and buried it by an oak tree. There ain't nobody guards that place. There ain't even a gate. It was a lot of money and in a big tin canister—and I mean big. A million dollars in bills is heavier than you'd think. We took about ten thousand and split that for living money, but the rest we left there, so if we got caught by cops for other things we'd done, we wouldn't have all that big loot on us. If we went to jail, when we got out, there'd be a lot of money waiting. Right then, though, we didn't plan on being caught. That was just a back up idea. We were going to wait until the heat died down, go back and get it. But Smat, he got to thinking, considering who we robbed, the heat wasn't going to die down. He reckoned they'd start coming after us, and keep coming, and that worried him sick. It didn't do me no good to think about it either, but I didn't like what he wanted to do. He was planning on making a map and mailing it to them so they could come get the money. He showed me the map. We had driven to Nebraska by then, where we was hiding out. He was gonna send them the map with an apology, just keep moving, hoping they'd say, 'Well, we got our money, so let's forget it.' He thought he could go on then and live his life, go back to small stick-ups or some such, and steal from people who would forget it. But them boys at that dice game, I tell you, they aren't forgetters. With a million dollars, I tell him, we can go off to Mexico and live clear and good the rest of our lives. You can buy a señorita down there cheaper than a chicken. Or so I'm told. Shit, them boys were gonna forget it like they would forget their mamas. Wasn't going to happen."

"Yeah," Terri said. "I'd be mad, I was them. I can hold a grudge."

"Damn right," the man said. "What I told Smat. Mama Johnson didn't raise no idiots."

"I guess that's a matter of opinion, Mr. Johnson," Terri said.

"I swear, girl, I'm gonna cut you from gut to gill if you don't hush up."

Terri went silent. I glanced at her in the mirror. She was smiling. Sometimes Terri worries me.

"Thing was, I couldn't let him mail that map, now could I? So we had this little scuffle and he got the better of me by means of some underhanded tricks and took off with the car, left me stranded but not outsmarted. You see, I knew he had a gal he had been seeing up around Lawton, and the money was around there, so I figured he'd go back. He might mail that map, and he might not. Finding the map in your car when I come up on missy here, that was real sweet. I knew then you knew Smat, and that he was the uncle you were going to see."

"Did Uncle Smat ever mention us?" I said.

"No," Johnson said. "I hitched my way back to Oklahoma, went up to where we buried the money one night, had me a shovel and all, but I didn't use it. Wasn't nothing but a big hole under that tree. Smat had the money. I thought, *damn him*. He pulled it out of that hole on account of me. I didn't know if he reckoned to give the bad boys a new map with the new location of the money, or if he took it with him, deciding he wasn't going to give it back at all. Now he could keep it and not have to split it, which might have been his plan all along. I was down in the dumps, I tell you."

Terri was leaning over the seat now, having forgotten all about Johnson's harsh warning and the knife.

"Sure you were," she said. "That's a bitter pill to swallow."

"Ain't it?" Johnson said.

"I'd have been really put out," Terri said.

"I was put out, all right. I was thinking I caught up with him, I'd yank all his teeth out with pliers. One by one, and slow."

"He wouldn't have liked that," she said.

"No he wouldn't," Johnson said. "But like I said, I knew he liked a gal in Oklahoma, and I'd met her, and he was as moony over her as a calf is over its mother, though it wasn't motherly designs he had."

"It wouldn't be that, no, not that," Terri said.

I thought, how does Terri know this stuff? Or does she just sound like she knows?

"I got me a tow sack of goods I bought with some of that money I had, and I made my way to her house, and hid out in the woods across the road from her place. I lived off canned beans and beer for two or three days, sleeping on the dirt like a damn dog, getting eat up by chiggers and ticks, but he didn't come by. I didn't know where he was staying, but it wasn't with her. I was out of beer and

Joe R. Lansdale

on my last can of beans, and was about to call in the dogs on my plans, when I seen him pull up in front of her house. He got out of his car, and let me tell you, he looked rough, like he'd been living under someone's porch. He went inside the house, and I hid in the back floorboard of his car. When he come out and drove off, I leaped up behind him, and put my knife to his throat, which was all I had, having lost my gun in a craps game on the way back to Oklahoma. I had some good adventures along the way. If you two are alive later, I'll tell you about them."

Considering Johnson was telling us everything but what kind of hair oil he used, I figured he wouldn't want us around later. We knew too much.

"So there I was with my knife to his throat, and you know what he did?"

"How would we?" Terri said.

"He drove that car into a tree. I mean hard. It knocked me winded, and the next thing I know I'm crawling out through the back where the rear windshield busted out, and then I'm falling out on the ground. I realize I'm still holding the knife. When I got up, there was Smat, just wandering around like a chicken with its head cut off. I yelled at him about the money, and he just looked at me, and seemed drunk as a skunk, which I know he ain't. I say, 'Smat. You tell me where that money is, or I'm going to cut you a place to leak out of.' He says to me, 'I ain't got no mice.'"

"Mice?" Terri said.

"I'm sure that's what he said. Anyway, I got mad and stabbed him. I'm what my mama used to call real goddamn impulsive. Next thing we're struggling around, and he falls, and I fall, and I bang my head on the side of the car, and when I wake up I'm on my back looking at stars. I got up and seen Smat had done took off. So I went looking for him, high and low, thinking I'd got a good knife thrust or two on him, and he'd be dead thereabouts. But he wasn't. So, I

42

went wandering about for a few days, thumbed a ride back to Texas, knowing Smat knew a fellow just over the river. But Smat wasn't there. I cut that guy good to find out if he knew anything about where he was, but I killed him for nothing. He didn't know shit. I went wandering for a couple days, and then I seen you two at that station. Ain't that something? Ain't life funny?"

"Makes me laugh," Terri said.

"I wandered a couple more days, finally caught a ride from a farmer and was dropped off at the Red River bridge, and when I got to the other side, what do I see but your car and this little fart outside of it, and I think, where's that boy? He's gonna drive me. Then I seen the map on the seat and knew you knew Smat and knew he hadn't mailed any map at all, 'cause there was the same one he'd drawn. I figured you knew where he was, that he'd been in your car, and then the rest of it you can put together."

Before Terri could say anything, I said, "He ain't alive no more, but before he died he said he done that map to trick you, so you'd think he was letting go of the loot, but he came back for it. He moved it all right, but it's still in the same graveyard, buried right behind Geronimo's grave. You missed it."

He studied me a moment, to see if there was truth in what I said, and he saw truth where there wasn't any, which goes to prove if I want to lie, I can do it. So we got our bearings and headed out in the direction of Geronimo's grave, after stopping at a station for gas, and at a General Store across the street from it to buy a shovel and some rope. Johnson gave me some money and I went in and bought the goods. Johnson sat in the backseat with Terri to make sure I didn't talk to anyone at the station or the store. He kept the knife close to her.

At the store I was supposed to ask how far it was to Fort Sill, where Geronimo was buried, and I did. When I told Johnson how far it was, he figured we could drive through the night and be there early morning before, or just about the time the sun came up.

It started raining that afternoon, and it was a steady rain, but we drove on, the wipers beating at the water on the windshield.

Johnson said, "Every time it rains, someone says 'The farmers need it.' I don't give a hang about the farmers. Papa raised hogs and chickens and grew corn and such, and he spent a lot of time beating my ass with a plow line. To hell with the farmers and their rain. I hope their lands blow away. I can eat pork or beef or chicken, or a squirrel. I don't care about the farmers. The farmers can go to hell."

"If I'm reading you right, you don't seem to like farmers," Terri said.

"That's funny," Johnson said. "You're gonna funny yourself to death."

Johnson sat quiet after that and didn't say another word until we came close to Fort Sill. Now, it's supposed to be a fort and all that, but the graveyard wasn't really protected at all. We parked up near it, Johnson grabbed the shovel and coiled the rope over his shoulder, and we all trudged into the graveyard, the rain beating down on us so hard we could barely see. We fumbled around in the dark a while, but Johnson, having been there before, found Geronimo's grave easy enough. A blind man could have found it. There was a monument there. It was made of cemented stones, and it was tall and thin at the top, wide at the bottom. There was a marker that said GERONIMO. On the grave itself were pieces of glass and bones and stones that folks had put there as some kind of tribute. The sun was rising and the rain had slackened, but we could see it had beat down the dirt at the back of the grave, behind the pile of rocks that served as Geronimo's marker, and damn if we couldn't see a tin box down in a hole there. The rain had opened the soft dirt up so you could see it clearly as the sun broke over the trees in the graveyard.

I thought, Uncle Smat, you ole dog you. He had done exactly what I was pretending he did. The box really was there. Uncle Smat figured hiding it right near where it had been before would fool Johnson, and it would have, had I not told a lie that turned out to be the truth.

Uncle Smat might actually have meant to mail that map, but then he got stabbed, went off his bean, and somehow ended back at the chicken coop where he'd been staying, and died of the stabbing.

Johnson handed me the shovel, said, "Dig it the rest of the way out."

"What happens to us then?"

"You drive me out of here. I can't carry that on my back, and I can't drive. Later, I tie you up with the rope somewhere where you can be found alongside the road."

"What if no one comes along?" Terri said.

"That's not my problem," Johnson said.

I scraped some dirt off the box with the shovel, and then I got down in the hole to dig. Water ran over the tops of my shoes and soaked my socks and feet. I widened the hole and worked with the shovel until I pried the box loose from the mud. I slipped the rope under the box, and fastened it around the top with a loop knot. I climbed out of the hole to help pull the box up. Me and Terri had to do the pulling. Johnson stood there with his big knife watching us.

When we got it up and out of the hole, he took the shovel from me, told us to stand back, and then he used the tip of the shovel to try and force open the lid. This took some considerable work, and while he was at it Terri stepped around beside Geronimo's grave.

Johnson stopped and said to Terri, "Don't think I ain't watching you, girly."

Terri stopped inching along.

Johnson got the box open and looked inside. I could see what the sunlight was shining on, same as him. A lot of greenbacks.

"Ain't that fine-looking," Johnson said.

"Hey, Johnson, you stack of shit," Terri said.

Johnson jerked his head in her direction, and it was then I realized Terri had stooped down and got a rock, and she threw it. It was like the day she killed that bird. Her aim was true. It smote Johnson on the forehead, knocking off his hat, and he sort of went up on his toes and fell back, flat as a board, right by that hole we had just dug.

I looked down at Johnson. He had a big red welt on his forehead, and it was already starting to swell into a good-sized knot.

"Girly, my ass," Terri said as she came up.

I bent down and took hold of his wrist, but didn't feel a pulse.

"Terri, I think you done killed him."

"I was trying to. Did you hear the way it sounded when it hit him?"

"Like a gunshot," I said.

"That's for sure," she said. "Let's get this money."

"What?"

"The money. Let's get it and put it in the car and drive it home with us."

"A million dollars? Show up at the house without Uncle Smat, and with a large tin box full of money?"

"Here's the way I see it," Terri said. "Uncle Smat has left enough of himself in the car it ought to satisfy Mama that it was best we didn't bring the rest of him home, his stink being more than enough. And this money might further soothe Mama's disappointment about us not hauling him back."

"We just pushed him in a sump hole and left him," I said.

"Really want to go pick him up on the way home?"

I shook my head, looked down at the box. It had handles on either side. I bent down and took one of them, and Terri took the other. We carried the money down to the car and put it in the back-seat floorboard.

It was good and light by then, and I figured it might be best to leave without drawing a lot of attention to ourselves, or the dead body up by Geronimo's grave. I let the car roll downhill before starting it, and when we were going pretty fast, Terri said, "Oh goddamn it."

She was looking over the seat, and I glanced in the mirror, and there was Johnson. He wasn't dead at all. He was running after us, nearly on us, his arms flapping like a scarecrow's coat in the wind. He grabbed onto the back door handle and got a foot on the running board. I could see his teeth were bared and he had the knife in his free hand and he was waving it about.

I jerked the car hard to the right and when I did the car slid on the gravel road, and Johnson went way out, his feet flying in the air, him having one hand on the door handle, and then I heard a screeching sound as that handle came loose of the car and Johnson was whipped out across the road and into some trees.

"Damn it to hell," Terri said. "He done bent up in a way you don't bend."

I glanced back. I could see he was hung up in a low growing tree with his back broken over a limb so far he looked like a wet blanket hanging over it. That rock might not have killed him, but I was certain being slung across the road and into a tree and having his back snapped, had certainly done it.

The motor hummed, and away we went.

It took us another two days to get home on account of having to stop more and more for the radiator, and by the time we pulled up in the yard, the car was steaming like a tea kettle.

We sat in the car for awhile, watching all that steam tumbling out from under the hood. I said, "I think the car is ruined."

"We can buy a bunch of cars with what's in that box."

"Terri, is taking that money the right thing to do?"

"You mean Sunday school right? Probably not. But that money is ill-gotten gains, as they say in the pulp magazines. It was Uncle Smat and Johnson stole it, not us. Took it from bigger crooks than they were. We didn't take any good people's money. We didn't rob no banks. We just carried home money bad people had and were using for bad reasons. We'll do better with it. Mama's always saying how she'd like to have a new car and a house, live somewhere out west, and have some clothes that wasn't patched. I think a rich widow and her two fine-looking children can make out quite well out west with that kind of money, don't you?"

"How do we explain the money?"

"Say Uncle Smat left us an inheritance that he earned by mining, or some such kind of thing. Oil is good. We can say it was oil."

"And if she doesn't believe that?"

"We just stay stuck to that lie until it sounds good."

I let that thought drift about. "You know what, Terri?"

"What's that?"

"I think a widow and her two fine-looking children could live well on that much money. I really think they could."

Introduction to

IN THE MAD MOUNTAINS

I find this is a moment when I will talk about something other than the story, but I will talk about it as well. First, let me confess something.

I've never really been a big fan of Lovecraft's writing, but his science-horror ideas have permeated not only popular fiction, but our culture. There is no denying that. I was watching a cop show not long ago and damned if Lovecraft wasn't mentioned in passing. Except for stone-cold science fiction, horror and fantasy fans, I remember a time when the general populace had no idea who Lovecraft was.

Now, people who have never read Lovecraft often know what Lovecraftian means. The Cthulhu Mythos is one of the most powerful story ideas ever invented. I can attest to that fact, because I wasn't sure how to spell Cthulhu, but the dictionary on my computer knew. That's impact my friends.

I always found Lovecraft's prose syrupy and overdone. I discovered him when I was in my late teens. I had actually read a couple of his stories and seen some adaptations of his work on TV and in film, but I wasn't really conscious of who he was until my late teens. Odd that it took me that long to know about him, as I was already well read in horror and fantasy and science fiction, but that was the case. But again, as powerful an influence as he had been on a number of writers I did read, his presence didn't quite register with me until that moment.

Though I can't paint myself as a rabid fan of his work, I have written several Lovecraftian stories. This is one, of course. Recently the World Fantasy folk decided that the award that had been given for fiction for years, the Howard, named after Howard Phillips Lovecraft, had to go. I guess it went. I haven't kept up.

I understand their sentiments. Lovecraft was a racist. He disliked Jews, negroes, and just about anyone that was dark skinned. He was a lot like everyone else around him during that time, sad to say. This is the reason the award was voted out to be replaced by another.

Nothing I despise more than racism. I have written about it and touched on it in many of my works. Yet, removing this award seems like an odd choice to make about a man long dead, since way last century. The award wasn't for his racism, which most people didn't know anything about, it was about his impact on fiction, which is considerable. He is probably the most influential writer of horror since Poe.

I don't really have a dog in this fight, because as I said, I'm not a great fan of his original work, but his work has vastly influenced ideas in the science fiction, fantasy and horror fields. I never think, wow, I need to be a racist too since I've been asked to write a Lovecraftian story.

I also read Edgar Rice Burroughs and Robert E. Howard, and they are without question racists, or, as is often said, men of their time. That does not excuse racism, but what it does do is put them in the same boat with a lot of other folks, famous, and not so famous. And while we're at it, Henry Ford, oh my god. When you learn more about him it makes you want to give up driving a Ford, if you do.

And for heaven sakes, don't turn on your lights, because Edison, woof, he was a real asshole and was known for some pretty uncomfortable beliefs. Walt Disney was said to be an anti-Semite, and one of Disney's classic films, *Song of the South*, would be hard to watch these days due to racism. But, when I was young he inflamed my imagination. He dipped into the science fiction and fantasy pool more than any other upscale film maker at that time. He, along with others, gave me access to something that wasn't generally available then.

In fact, a lot of things we use today that are more valuable to us than a Lovecraft award, were invented by some pretty despicable people. Nazi supporters, black haters, Jew haters, homophobes, you name it.

Does this suggest I think we should embrace their beliefs?

Of course not. It's not the same as removing Confederate statues. Those are there for one reason only. To be spiteful. Most of them were erected during the Civil Rights movement, not ages ago. These people being honored with statues in this case, embraced an archaic and miserable view, and they were erected by people who still shared that viewpoint. We need to hold the history dear, but we don't have to embrace negative attitudes.

Stop comparing them to George Washington and Thomas Jefferson. They had slaves and they were of their time, but unlike the Confederacy, they also built something that had a better future, and in the long run, ended slavery. They built a nation. The Confederacy wanted to tear it apart.

I grew up and live in the South, and I saw horrible things back then. No murders, but just a day to day grinding of the souls of black people, constant humiliations designed to make the humiliators feel important. Racists are social bullies. They are self-loathing.

But, understand too, that the North, during the Civil War, did not rise up in self-righteous indignation about slavery. A lot of the Union couldn't have cared less about slavery. They wanted to keep the union together for other reasons, financial for one, the labor supplied by slaves. The Union didn't want to have blacks fight on their side, as many viewed them as inferior. It wasn't until they felt desperate that they allowed them to fight. The black troops proved outstanding when given the chance, and fought bravely, and have fought bravely in every war America has ever fought since.

And in the South, not everyone was fighting for slavery, some were fighting for their chicken coop, the fact that them up there had come down here. Hey, they're going to be in my yard, and they got guns. Think of all the black soldiers who fought for the U.S. in World War Two because it was their home, but when they came back from wars, they couldn't even ride in the front of the bus or use a public restroom.

Now, this may seem a detour discussion, considering I am here to talk about this story, but this whole Lovecraft award business put it on my mind. I think we need to point out his personal weaknesses, and yet at the same time acknowledge the impact Lovecraft has had on popular culture. He influenced some of our greatest writers. Robert Bloch and Ray Bradbury come to mind. He wrote tons of supportive letters to a number of writers and set them on their careers. Stephen King, who came along some years after Lovecraft, has mentioned his debt to Lovecraft's work, and has certainly touched on Lovecraftian themes more than once.

Here's the thing. Lovecraft is dead. When we write stories inspired by his creations, he isn't making a dime from it. If Lovecraft were alive, I would say, ignore him, no matter what you think of the work. He's profiting from this.

Roman Polanski, for example. I can't separate him from his art. They go together, and *Chinatown*, which he directed, is one of my favorite films. But Polanski is a child rapist in hiding. As soon as that was revealed to me, I have never watched another of his films. I won't support him. A hundred years from now we can enjoy the work, perhaps, but I will never watch another of his movies as long as he can profit from it.

I can continue a list of who I won't watch, listen to, or read. But there's no point to it. I think you get the idea.

Lovecraft wasn't Hitler. He wasn't Roman Polanski. He was human and flawed. My father was the best man I ever knew. He had horrid racist rhetoric that could turn my stomach, and it led to a number of heated disagreements, but he treated people the same, black or white, and practiced kindnesses that I can't explain to people he professed to hate. Hell, Lovecraft married a Jewish lady, though the marriage didn't last. But it's hard to reconcile that with some of the things he expressed as personal beliefs.

Does that make it okay?

Nope. But it does make it complicated.

Am I saying reinstate the Howard award?

I leave that to the World Fantasy folk. Again, I don't have a dog in that fight. But I am saying, in spite of his personal views, he impacted the field many of us work in, or like me, dip into on occasion. This has to be acknowledged. There is a great legacy of popular fiction that came out of his creations, and sometimes, even some people writing horror fiction may not recognize that his particular kind of genius has influenced them. Certain ideas, like DNA, are in their work, and it would require a literary ancestor search for some to be aware of it.

My story, *In the Mad Mountains*, is loosely based on *In the Mountains of Madness*, which I read during my teens. I read it in a book of Lovecraftian inspired stories. It was a series of tales by Lovecraft and those influenced by him, like Robert Bloch, Ramsey Campbell, and so on. That one stuck out. That one and *The Call of Cthulhu.*

When I was asked to write a Lovecraftian story, *The Mountains of Madness* came to mind. This story was the result. It was inspired in equal parts by Lovecraft, books I read about explorers and ship wrecks, and Jack London, who, by the way, said some awful things about Jack Johnson, the great, black boxer, but wrote some powerful and amazing fiction, including quite a few stories about what was once referred to as the frozen north.

I wanted to write something that was an adventure, something that was strange, and capture that element of mystery that Lovecraft, at his best, could conjure.

The result is here. *In the Mad Mountains.*

IN THE MAD
MOUNTAINS

Slept, awoke, slept, awoke, miserable life.

FRANZ KAFKA

Reality is that which, when you stop believing in it, doesn't go away.

PHILIP K. DICK

The oldest and strongest emotion of mankind is fear, And the oldest and strongest kind of fear is fear of the unknown.

H. P. LOVECRAFT

The moon was bright. The sea was black. The waves rolled and the bodies rolled with it. The dead ones and the live ones, screaming and dying, begging and pleading, praying and crying to the unconcerned sea.

Behind them the great ship tipped up as if to give a final display of its former magnificence, its bow parting the night-waters like a knife through chocolate, pointing its stern to the sky, slipping slowly beneath the cold waves, breaking in half as it rode down into the bottomless sea. Boilers hissed, the steam coughed up a great white cloud. The cloud pinned itself against the moon-bright sky, then faded like a fleeting dream.

The lifeboats bobbed and the survivors in the water swam for them, called to them. One of the boats, Number Three, stuffed full of human misery and taking on water, tried to rescue more survivors, and when it did it tipped, ejected two of its riders, then righted itself again. A man in nightclothes, and a woman wearing a fur coat, fell out. The coat took on water, grew heavy, and dragged her down. A shark rose up close to the boat with its mouth wide open, its teeth gleaming as if polished by rags. Its eyes rolled back in ecstasy, and then the man was in its jaws. The shark's teeth snapped together and blood blew wide and into the boat, along with a soft bed slipper. The shark took half of the man down under, the other half of him bobbed, and then another shark drove up from below and bit the other half, carried it down and away into Davy Jones' Locker.

Those that had swam for it, those remaining near Lifeboat Number Three, were taken by the sharks. The water grew thick with fins and an oily film of blood, the sounds of cries cut short. Then a wave caught Lifeboat Number Three and those still in it, pushed it forward, leaving the other lifeboats and the struggling swimmers near them far behind, bobbing like fishing corks.

There was a great strike of lightning in the distance, splitting what had been a clear sky with an electric crack of fire. When it flashed, those in Lifeboat Number Three saw a great iceberg, a cold but beaconing mass; something solid, waiting in the distance, lying jagged and white against the tumbling sea. Far beyond was an irregular rise of what appeared to be mountains. Out of the formerly clear night sky came a dark cloud, wide and thick as all creation. It sacked the moon. For the occupants in Lifeboat Number Three there was a sensation of being wrapped in black cotton.

The lightning flashed again and everything was bright, and then it was gone, and all was dark and empty again. They rode like that on the waves in the darkness, lighted now and then by bolts of lightning, cold rain driving down from the churning sky. They cupped the water that collected in the bottom of the boat with their hands and drank from it, parched. There was water all about them, water full of salt that would make them choke, sicken, and die, but this water was fresh, and their bodies called out for it.

They went through an eternity of jumping sea, darkness, and lightning-torn sky, and then they bumped against the iceberg, and then the boat was pushed back out into the sea. Then eternity ended and there was light and the storm passed and the sun peaked shyly over the waters and showed the survivors that there were still fins visible in its wide expanse. The sharks were waiting.

An iceberg was in sight, perhaps the one they had glimpsed before and bounced off of, possibly another, perhaps even the one their great ship had struck. Certainly it was a different view of the ice, because to their surprise they could see great ships of times long past pushed onto and into the berg, sometimes completely housed by it, like flies trapped and visible in blue-white amber. Attached to the berg, and somewhat in the distance, they could again see a flat expanse of ice, and that became their destination.

There were six oars in the boat and twelve survivors, eight men and four women. One of the men, a young fellow named Gavin, took charge without asking, called out for rowers, and soon six men held the six oars and cranked them, shoving Lifeboat Number Three toward an icy shore. One of the men, an older gent, collapsed at the oar and a young woman took it and began to row.

A gap in the flat ice was their destination, and they were able to row the boat to that spot and land it as if it were a beach. They climbed out of the boat—except the man who had collapsed—and onto the ice, and with fingers and feet aching from the cold, were able to pull the lifeboat out of the water, at least far enough for everyone to disembark.

The man who remained in the boat couldn't be roused. By the time they were able to lift him out and onto the ice, he was dead. Ice had formed where his nose had ran, and around the corners of his mouth and eyes. They stretched him out and pulled his arms across his chest.

Gavin said, "We have to leave him here, for now."

Another man, English, about Gavin's age, said, "Seems less than appropriate."

"You can carry him on your back if you like," said another of the men, middle-aged, an American.

"I suppose not," said the Englishman. "The women must be our first concern."

"Looks to me like we've come to a state of every man and woman for himself," said a younger American.

The young woman who had rowed said, "Seems to me it would be wiser if we all stuck together, helped one another. I think, as a woman, I can help the others as much as you."

"All of you do what you like," said the younger American. "I'm not bound to anyone."

Gavin said, "Very well then. Let's see who wants to stick together."

A quick poll was taken. Only the young American was not in agreement. "Very well," the young man said. "I'll strike out on my own."

"To where?" said Gavin. "Seems to me that we'll all end up in the same places."

"Could be," said the young American, "but I prefer to bear responsibility for me and no one else."

"Good luck to you then," Gavin said. "What's your name in case we have to say a few words over you, lower you into the water and such?"

"If that's the case, leave me where I fall," said the man, "but just for the record, the name is Hardin."

"First or last?" the woman asked.

"It'll do for both," said Hardin, and he started out walking across the ice in the direction of one of the great, frozen ships not encased in an iceberg, but instead pushed up on the ice.

The others watched Hardin for a while. He passed the ship and kept walking. The Englishman who had spoken before, said, "He isn't much of a team player, is he. Very American."

"I'm American," Gavin said.

"So you are," the Englishman said. "No offense. James Carruthers is my name."

"I'm Amelia Brand," said the woman who had rowed and suggested they stay together. "Also American."

An older woman, English, said, "They call me Duchess, but we can introduce ourselves later. Seems to me it would be wise to search out some sort of shelter, and one of the ships appear to be our only possibilities."

No one else seemed even the least bit interested in talking, or giving their names. They looked defeated and ready to collapse.

"True enough," Gavin said, and looked out across the ice at the ice-captured ship. Hardin was still visible, but far away. Considering the ice, he was making good time.

Gavin started out across the ice. Amelia walked beside him. The others fell in line behind them. Glancing back, Gavin saw the wild water had lifted Lifeboat Number Three off the ice and carried it back out to sea.

They kept walking, and came to the first ship.

After a bit, Amelia said, pointing. "Right there. At the stern. I think we can board it the easiest. We'll just have to go easy."

It was a large and ancient ship of dark wood. It looked surprisingly sturdy, and the back end, with its rise of ice against it, appeared to be their way in.

"Might as well," said Duchess. "In an hour it's likely we'll all be dead, and if I can find a way to become only slightly warmer, I'd prefer to die that way."

———

The side of the ship was high and there were tatters of sails, partly encased in ice like damaged butterfly wings. They made their way up the slope of ice that led to the stern, but it was slick beyond the ability of all but Gavin, Amelia, and the Englishman, Carruthers.

The three of them worked up the slope, finding pocks in the ice they could use to climb. When they made the summit and boarded the ship, they cautiously made for the wheelhouse. The view glass in the wheelhouse was frosted over and the door was jammed with ice, but the three of them leaned up against it and nudged it loose, knocking it back with an explosion of shattering ice and a surprising feeling of warmth, if for no other reason than the wind was blocked by the walls and the glass.

It was short-lived comfort, for in the next moment they saw a body hung up in the wheel. It was a man in a thick coat. His face was not visible, and for a moment it appeared he had been hung there with his back against the wheel, but within an instant they saw that this was not the case. It was the face that was misplaced. His neck was long and twisted, and his head had been wrenched about to face the opposite direction. His legs had collapsed beneath him, but his arms, caught up in the wheel, held him in place. There was a large gap in the top of his head, crusted with frozen blood.

Gavin stood where he could see the man's face. His mouth was wide open and so were his eyes, and they were glazed with ice; the eyes looked like two marbles in the bottom of a glass of water, his top lip was curled back from his teeth, and the teeth looked like stalactites, cracked and broken as they were.

"My god," said Carruthers.

"How could this happen?" said Amelia. "What could have done this?"

"Lets consider later," said Gavin. "It might be best to see if we can get the others up."

Gavin unfastened the latches on the cabinets and looked inside. Eventually he found a thick coil of rope.

"This should do for starters," he said.

———

They pulled the others up. It took some time, and the old woman, Duchess, had the hardest bout with it, but they got her on board with only a slight sprain to her ankle and some problems with her breathing. She heaved the cold air in and out like a bellows. After everyone was on board they removed the dead body at the wheel, took it out on deck and slipped it over the far side. It was a sad thing to do to what had once been a living human being, but Gavin and the others could see nothing else for it. Leaving it there was demoralizing.

The body was stiff as a hammer and went sliding over the rise of ice like a kid on holiday, making a kind of scratching sound as it glided along. Finally it drifted off the rise and shot out onto the ice and lay there like a sunning seal. Gavin said that later he'd try to get the body out to sea, which seemed more fitting than just letting it lie on the cold ice, but he knew as the others did, that it was a lie. He figured, as they all did, that they would soon be dead. Already their wet clothing had turned icy.

In the galley section they found a door had been knocked down, and with enough force to shatter it into several pieces. Not far beyond that they found a man's body with a large hole in his head, the blood around the wound frozen over so that it looked like some-one had scooped a large chunk out of a ripe tomato with a spoon. The revolver that had killed him was still clutched in his right hand. Obviously the scoop in his head had been made after he had shot himself, but by whom and why?

His body had to go over the side too, but it was becoming so cold, one of their number, a little middle-aged man they later learned was named Cyril, tried to get the gun out of the man's hand to use on himself, but the weapon was frozen in the dead man's fist, firm as if it were part of his fingers.

Gavin and Carruthers wrestled Cyril away from the gun that he was trying frantically to tug from the dead man's hand. They wrestled him to the floor, pulling the dead man along with them, yanking on the gun and taking two of the dead man's fingers with it, snapping them free like frozen asparagus sprouts.

"Kill me, but get off of me," Cyril said. "The cold, it's too much."

That ended the fight, and when it was done, Gavin and Carruthers were too weak to care anymore. Together, all of the survivors wandered off across the galley and down steps and into the hold below the upper deck. They found blankets there, and clothes, jackets, gloves, scarves, and wool hats. A veritable stockpile of items. They each peeled off and redressed. The women rid themselves of their wet clothes and dried on the blankets and wrapped themselves in them so that they might dress beneath them, though anything to be seen had been seen. Amelia was the only one that didn't follow that path. She boldly removed her clothes and dried in full view, and then dressed, in full sight of the men who had thrown modestly completely out the window.

Gavin took note of Amelia. What he saw he liked, though beyond that note of admiration, he was too cold for biological consideration, too eager to dress in dry and warmer clothes.

A few minutes later, with all of them dressed in the dry clothes and wearing thick, hooded coats taken from the larder, fat gloves on their hands, blankets draped over their shoulders, the world seemed slightly brighter, even if lit up only by a crack of fading sunlight through a split in the roof of the ship. Cyril, who moments before had been ready to shoot himself in the head, seemed happier and more secure. A bit of warmth had lifted everyone's spirits.

When they were dressed, they went back up the steps and found a storage room off the main section of the galley, and in there they found a man hanging from one of the meat hooks on the wall. A short piece of rope was tied about his neck and he had his hands stuck down through his belt. His head had been broken open like the others, again, most likely after death. He hung like smoked meat. Actual smoked meat dangled on either side of him, and like the man with the gun in his hand, they left him there, but took one of the smoked hogs down and carried it back below where it was warmer. They made it warmer yet by tying ropes across the length of the hold, finding plenty of them about, and from the ropes they dangled thick blankets and made a series of crude tents.

It was much warmer that way, and when Amelia found a small grate stove, they moved it to the side of the ship where there was a crack in the wall, and busted up some odds and ends they found, crates and an old chair, and built a fire. There were plenty of working matches that had been wrapped securely in waxed paper and then stuffed into leather bags, and there was tinder to get a fire started. When it was lit and burning, the smoke rose up through the split in the ceiling, drifted out through the wheelhouse and away. They cut strips of the hanging meat with Gavin's pocket knife. It was as fresh as the day it had been frozen. They warmed it at the fire and ate like starving wolves. Even with all that had happened to them at sea, the sharks, the cold rain, the dark toss on the waves, the dead bodies, for a moment they were hopeful.

When they were strong enough, Gavin and Amelia and Carruthers went to and dropped the other bodies down the slide of ice, and out onto the flat of it. Finished with that disconcerting chore, they returned to the hold and ate more meat.

———

Amelia, after eating, said to Gavin, "How old do you think this ship is?"

"1800s, I guess. I don't really know, but that seems right. An old sailing ship that went latitude when it should have went longitude. That's me trying to be cute. I don't know one from the other."

"Nor do I."

"I suppose it tried to enter an opening in the ice, tried to survive here, but things went wrong."

"What do you think happened here, besides things went wrong?"

Gavin shook his head. "I don't know. Someone on board must have went crazy and killed the men we found. As for the other sailors, no idea."

Gavin and Amelia moved to the far side of the hold and gathered up between two barrels, sitting close together for warmth. They could see the others nearby, in the tents or just outside of them.

"What do you think of our chances?" she said.

"Grim."

"I think you're right, but believe it or not, I'm optimistic."

"Are you now?"

"I am now. We have warmth and food, and maybe we'll be found. And if not that, maybe we can find a way to leave."

"That would be a neat trick," he said. "I have no idea where we are, and I have a feeling that our ship didn't either. It all looks wrong out there."

"Wrong?" Amelia said.

"Yeah. I don't know exactly. Stars and moon, even the sea and the sky. Even in the daylight, it all looks odd."

"Have you been at sea in a lifeboat before?"

"No," Gavin said. "I admit I haven't, and could have gone my whole life without it."

"Maybe everything looks different when you're in a small boat at sea."

"I suppose," he said. "But it all seems so odd. The ship was lost before we hit the berg. I overheard a crew member say something about being lost, that the stars weren't right."

"You think he meant the constellations?"

"I guess."

"But what about the navigational equipment? You don't need stars to guide anymore."

"Sailors still depend on them, though. I think the equipment went south, and then they tried the stars, and the stars were wrong."

"Or the sailors were out of practice."

"Maybe. But even the air tastes funny."

"When it's cold, and you're in an old ship, I think the air would taste funny."

"You're right, of course, but it seems so odd."

Amelia was thinking the same, but unlike Gavin, she wasn't yet ready to admit it.

They watched as the crack of light in the ship grew darker, then was re-lighted as the moon rose.

"Sitting and waiting to run out of food doesn't appeal to me."

"There's a lot of food. I saw canned goods as well. The cold has probably preserved them. Water we can manage by melting ice."

"Still, there's an end to it. It's best to find a way to leave, a boat we can manage."

"It won't be this one. It's got splits in the sides. And it's too damn big."

"I don't know how we leave," Amelia said. "Only that in time, we have to, by boat or by discovery, or by death."

———

They slept, and when the morning light came, Amelia awoke. Gavin was gone. Bundled in her found navy coat and with a blanket draped over her shoulders, she went exploring and discovered upstairs that the others had heated up the galley stove. It was a big stove, and they were roasting the hanging meat in it. There was a tremendous amount of warmth from the stove. It felt good. The fuel for the fire had been made from coal in a bin in the galley. There was still quite a bit of coal left. That alone was reassuring.

Gavin was supervising the cooking. As it turned out he had been a chef in a large hotel in New York City. He told them about it while the meat cooked. He told them his mother was an heiress, his father was in oil and gas and loved airplanes. No one else volunteered their history, not even Amelia.

When the meat was done, they ate. There was a lot of meat, and it was determined then that they needed to stretch it out as far as possible until another plan could be hatched. Cyril suggested they eat as much as they wanted and then go out and lay down on the ice and wait for death, who would most likely show up wearing a heavy coat and carrying an ice cutter.

"Don't be silly," Amelia said. "We need to see if we can find fishing equipment for more food. The other ships can provide wood for fuel when the coal runs out."

"And when the wood runs out. What then?" Duchess said, her old skin having grown tight in the cool air.

"Perhaps we'll be rescued," Amelia said. "Perhaps we can rescue ourselves. Perhaps if this is the edge of a continent, or even some icy island, there will be someone living here. Somewhere."

"Like Eskimos?" Duchess said.

"Like anyone," Amelia said.

"Aren't you the hopeful one," Carruthers said.

"I am at that, and I'm more hopeful if we do what we can to survive for as long as we can, have a purpose. I saw lifeboats on the deck, and we might cast to sea in one of those."

"I've told you how I feel about that," Gavin said.

"We had a lifeboat," Cyril said. "We were glad to get out of it."

"If we provision, take warm clothes, and perhaps prepare a sail, we might have a chance," Amelia said.

"Are you a sailor?" Cyril said.

"No, but I prefer to try something other than giving up."

"Die here in this ship, out on the ice, or at sea, makes no difference," Cyril said. "We're going to die. Have you forgotten the dead sailors? Someone killed them."

Gavin laughed. "Yeah, but not yesterday, not fifty years ago, but well over a hundred years ago. I doubt the murderer is alive and waiting on the ice, ready to sneak back on the ship and chop holes in our heads."

"Maybe it was some kind of animal," Cyril said. "Could be that. Like a polar bear. Another one could be around."

"Bears bite and claw," Duchess said. "They don't hit you in the head with some kind of weapon, an axe perhaps."

"One thing that would be helpful in your case, Cyril," Gavin said, "is if you're going to die, and constantly talk about it, go ahead and get it over with. That leaves more food for us. That gun probably wouldn't have worked anyway. Who knows? But you can always strip and lie on the ice like you suggested. That was your idea, wasn't it? Die on the ice? I've come to think that's not a bad idea for you at all. Anything to shut your negativity up. I mean, hell, I know things are bad, and I may not want to go to sea, but I'm not ready to throw in the towel just yet, even if I'm not sure we have a towel to toss."

The others, none of which had much to say before, and hadn't even given their names, chimed in with agreement. "Yeah, shut up about dying all the time," one of the older men said. "Go out and die, but shut up."

Cyril, now that he was warm, and in spite of his words, seemed a little less inclined to follow his own suggestion. He said, "Well, I'm just saying, things aren't looking too good."

"You think you're the only one that's made that observation?" Amelia said. "What we need to do is first decide how much food is to be provided to each of us, how far we can stretch it. No midnight snacks."

She looked around at the others. They nodded in agreement.

"Then," she said, "we need to find fishing equipment and put some sort of fishing crew together. After that, we can think about the boat, the sail, and for those who want to stay, they can. For those who would like to leave, we can try. The boats, I saw two. That way we can have two crews."

"Some crews we'll be," Carruthers said.

"I saw nautical books on board," Gavin said. "I'm good at learning things from books, maybe I can figure something out."

"Somehow," Cyril said, "I doubt there will be among those nautical books one about basic sailing."

"We can find out," Gavin said.

———

Amelia and Gavin discovered the sick bay on a search of the ship, and found that the table used for patients was folded out from the wall and covered in blood. Something had happened on board besides being marooned. The dead sailors were proof of that. Their wounds didn't seem to fit any type of available weapon. Duchess was right. Bears and other animals seemed unlikely. Did they turn on one another in claustrophobic fury? Cannibalism? There was food, so why resort to such? And here in the sick bay, had someone been wounded due to fighting? Had someone tried to help them, and if so, where were the rest of the bodies? Why weren't they frozen on board?

The general consensus among the group was that there had been some kind of mutiny, perhaps after the ship was marooned, and a blood bath incurred. Where the survivors, if any, had ended up was unknown, but certainly the ship had sailed a crew larger than the dead men they found. Perhaps they had struck out to find what they could discover, or escape whoever, or whatever, was killing them in that head-smashing fashion.

In another part of the ship, fishing tackle was located and fishing expeditions were sent out to cast heavy lines in the cold water, using small pieces of meat for bait, and in time, the intestines from landed fish, or smaller fish, were hooked and put back in the water as bait. Fish near the ice seemed ravenous, and they successful pulled large catches from the icy waters, cut them up, and cooked them in the great galley stove. With a reasonable supply of renewable food somewhat assured, the spirits of all involved increased.

This went on for a few days, the meals alternating between the meat in the galley and the fish from the sea, and then Amelia said she wanted to explore, see if there were other things they could use from the ice-locked ships, and so after a night of high wind and blowing snow, she and Gavin started out on an expedition. The daylight sky seemed as odd as the night sky had been, though the storm had long blown out. The sunlight was somewhat green on the horizon and cool yellow above them, like a light doughy crust on the sky.

Another point of contention, which had first been addressed by Carruthers, was the fact that there was day and night. It seemed logical, considering the ice, that they might well be at a point on the globe where night reigned for long periods before giving way to daylight for equally long stretches. But that wasn't the case here. Day came with its strange green and yellow tints and an anemic red-hazed sun that soon turned egg-yolk yellow. Day gave it up within hours to thick, blue-black darkness with a greasy moon that appeared to wobble when not being observed directly. The stars moved in great swirls, as if the earth and all the darkness and pulsing orbs were slowly traveling toward an exit by cosmic drain. None of this fit the fact that they had been crossing a calm and warm ocean the night before, but another weird factor was no one could remember ever having boarded the ship, and they could only remember vagaries of the trip, some events on board, drinks and dancing. Trying to discuss this led to a lot of quiet moments. No one remembered where they were going, or why they had chosen to be at sea, or for that matter, none could even remember if they were crossing the Atlantic or the Pacific. Atlantic seemed more likely to lead them to ice, still no one knew for sure. It was a distressing fact that could only be discussed briefly. It was like trying to remember what had happened in the womb.

—

Gavin carried the pistol with him, though he wasn't sure it worked. He didn't see any reason to need it, but it made him feel better somehow. They looked where they had dropped the body of their comrade over the side of the ship with the long dead sailors, but no bodies were there. Something had taken them away. Polar bears? So far nothing of the sort had been seen. There were no tracks and no drag marks, but considering the constantly blowing wind and renewing ice, as well as blankets of snow, there was nothing unusual about that.

After walking for a time, they began to feel certain they were not on an iceberg at all, but a large mass of ice that stretched far to the horizon. There were ships locked into it here and there, and some of the ships were more modern. Dog sleds were found, buried in the ice, and finally they came upon a prop airplane, blood-red in color. It seemed to have landed smoothly and sat there as if ready for take off. The exception being the wheels, which were sunk into the ice. Its nose was lifted upward, the tail was resting on the ice. In the far background, mountains, tinged puke-green by the light, rose up high and misty. As they stared at them, they seemed to move, every so slightly.

"How can that be?" Amelia said. "Moving mountains?"

"A mirage," Gavin said. "The movement part, anyway."

"Sure looked like it moved. It was subtle, but I saw it."

"Me too, but mountains don't move. Has to be a trick of the light... But the plane, it's here. It's an Electra. Late thirties or forties, I'm reasonable sure. My father owned one. Or one very similar. No expert, but I'm a little knowledgeable on recognizing a few of them. My dad also had models of a lot of other kinds of planes. So I was aware of certain things about them without really being highly knowledgeable."

"Can you fly?"

"I only have a general idea how it's done. You know, from listening to my dad. Besides, the plane would only comfortably carry a couple. Of course, that couple could be us. But then there's that whole almost knowing how, and if this plane has sat here for very long, the engine is certainly ruined by the weather. If it flew, I'd probably manage, at best, to run it into the sea, or take it up and have it come down too fast and on the nose."

Amelia let the thought of flying away with Gavin run around in her head. She owed the others nothing. Still, it seemed like a rotten thing to contemplate.

She examined the plane, saw that the hatch door was flung open. It had steps leading from the door to the ground. She walked up the steps and stuck her head inside.

"Jesus," she said. "It's warm in here. How could that be?"

Gavin climbed the steps and looked in. He stepped inside beside her. "It's more than warm, it's been flown. The motor has only been off a short time, that's why it's warm in here, even with the door open. Engine heat."

"That means someone just left it," Amelia said.

They went outside and looked around. No sign of anyone. They prowled the outside of the plane, gently touched its underbelly. No doubt. Gavin was right. The engine was warm.

"How can that be?" Amelia said, moving her hand away from the plane.

"Just because it's from another era doesn't mean it hasn't been kept in good condition, even flown recently by some plane enthusiast. But how anyone would end up way out here in a small plane like that is hard to guess."

"Where's the pilot?" Amelia said.

"They may have force landed here, fuel or weather reasons. A number of possibilities. Engine trouble, perhaps. They went outside to look about, trying to figure things out, same as us, or deciding to pee, the storm hit. Remember how fast that storm came? I was looking at that crack in the ship. The sky was clear. I could see the moon. And then there was a moan of storm and a blow of snow, and the sky went white. It happened in the time it takes to blinks. The pilot could have been trapped outside and unable to make it back to the plane. They might have been covered by snow, iced over. Hell, we could be standing on them. Or they stumbled off blind, walked into a snow bank or the sea. It would be easy to become lost in a storm like that."

"Could be," Amelia said. "Think about how we ended up here. We were fine on our ship one minute, and the next, we weren't."

"Warm, clear seas, and then some place full of ice," Gavin said.

"Exactly. And we don't even know why we were on the ship, how we got there."

"I thought it would come back to me. Thought we were all in shock. Now, I'm not so sure. What I am sure of is things aren't right here, Amelia. All these ships and planes. It's as if they all went through some hole and ended up here. Maybe a hundred years ago, maybe five minutes ago."

The wind swirled particles of snow. It seemed chill enough to freeze an open flame.

Amelia tugged her scarf tight over her mouth and the tip of her nose. "Why are we standing here? Let's get inside the plane for awhile."

They stepped inside, closed the door against the wind and the cold. Already the warmth was dying.

Prowling the front of the plane, in a pocket by the controls, Amelia found a small revolver. It was loaded with five rounds.

"Now we're both armed, in case we're attacked by a sea bird," Amelia said.

"I think there's a lot more than sea birds to fear out here," Gavin said. "At first I didn't think so, but now I wonder. More I think about it, the more worried I am. Maybe those ships haven't been here as long as it seems."

"The hole in time idea?"

"Something like that."

"Right now I'm not ruling anything out," Amelia said.

They looked about. There were a few clothes in the plane and a small mattress. They looked for anything usable, but found nothing other than the gun, and a sweater that Amelia took with her as they left, slipping it on and then putting her coat back on over it. It gave her a bulky appearance, but the sweater was flexible beneath the coat, and she was warmer. They found a flight manual, a couple of hardback books, but nothing else. They left it all.

At the view glass, they looked out at the sky. It had turned azure and there were strange strips of yellow and gold leaking into it, and even as they watched those gave way to blue then black. Amelia said, "The sky's colors are always changing."

"Nothing seems right here," Gavin said.

The moon appeared like a blister, high and full, ready to pop. The stars were plentiful, but it was as if a hand had stirred them into new formations. They were of varying sizes, like coins and pinheads tacked to the heavens. There were large numbers of jetting streaks, shooting stars, red, blue, and green, and variations of those colors. Amelia was reminded of schools of bright darting fish in an inky pond.

They decided it was best to return. The night was bright, and in time the plane would grow cold. So out they went, carefully stepping onto the moon-glared ice.

Using ships and sleds they had passed before as their guides, they made their way back to the ship where their companions waited. The wind kicked up, and the already intense cold became nearly unbearable. Tugging the collars of their coats tight around their necks, wrapping their scarves around their heads like bandages, leaving only their eyes visible, they continued. Snow was as thick as exploded goose down blown loose from a pillow.

They stumbled forward, trying their best to keep an eye-line, back to their ship. Now and then there was a gap in the snow, and it gave them an occasional glimpse of a recognizable ice formation, but those kinds of things could change quickly, reshaped by snow and wind.

Amelia tripped over one of the dog sleds they had encountered earlier. As she was rising, the wind and blowing snow shifted, and she saw moving in the brief gap of white, a naked man wearing a strange and oversized head dress. The head gear was flapping and blowing in the wind with the frantic movements of a bird with its feet tied to the ground. It was visible for an instant, then gone.

"Did you see that?" Amelia said.

"Hardin," Gavin said. "It was Hardin."

"Naked? Wandering through snow? How could that be?"

"How could it be anyone?"

They tried to see Hardin again, but the snow had wrapped him up and hidden him away.

"What was he wearing on his head?" she asked.

"No idea."

"Should we try and find him?"

Gavin shook his head. "We are lost ourselves. And remember, he didn't want to be found. Maybe he stripped down to die quicker."

"But he's been out here for days now."

"Perhaps he holed up somewhere for awhile before he made his final move."

"So he hung out, then today stripped naked, put on a weird head-dress, and wandered out in the snow?"

"Hell. I don't know, Amelia. I know what you know."

They found themselves, without discussing it, moving away from where Hardin had been seen, heading away from the direction he had taken. Trudging on for some distance, they ran up against the wall of a ship. They immediately knew it was not their ship. Its wood was black and tarred where there had been repairs. They found it too high to access by normal means, but near the bow they discovered there was a crude ladder, and though it was slippery, they managed it, and climbed on board.

The interior of the ship was a brief respite from the blowing wind and snow.

———

They combed the ship. No food supplies or frozen bodies were found. The crew had obviously abandoned the sailing rig, taking whatever was edible with them, as well as stripping it of furniture and the like. Most likely to make sleds to drag their goods, or to provide firewood. The vessel seemed to be from a similar era as the ship where their group had ended up. The lifeboats had been removed, and Amelia wondered if they had made it to somewhere safe by sea, or were they dead on the ice, preserved like frozen sardines with the tops of their heads torn open? And how long ago did this ship arrive here?

"You know what's odd," Amelia said. "In the back of my mind I feel like I know the answer to this, or a piece of it, but I just can't get that answer to surface."

"I know exactly what you mean," Gavin said.

In the back of the ship's hold they found a mass of blankets, and they covered themselves in them, pulling them over their heads, and then they lay on others, and listened to the snow blast about outside. Cold air came through cracks in the ship and licked at them, but the stack of blankets warmed them, and they lay there reveling in the warmth.

They were snuggled close together, and without suggestion, they touched noses. They lay in silence for awhile, and then Amelia reached out and touched Gavin, and then Gavin touched her, and then their lips pressed together. They pulled at one another's clothes, and for a time they were all right beneath the mass of blankets, wriggling into each other, as if trying to be absorbed by the other's warmth.

When they were finished they lay panting beneath the blankets, snug and comfortable as they had been since landing in the wet ocean, and then on the ice.

"Guess we needed that," Amelia said.

"Needed and wanted," Gavin said.

Amelia lay in Gavin's arms. He was strong. She could feel the muscles in his arm beneath her neck.

"The wind has stopped," Amelia said.

"Now we're back to living in the real world. Or the unreal world. Whatever the hell kind of world we are in. Look. I think the smartest thing would be, when the storm calms, we go back to our ship, bring rope, use one of the dog sleds to drag lumber back for fire wood. You know, chop it out of this one with the axe. We can mount expeditions that can take us farther, the way you suggested. Figure out some way to make tents, devise heating vessels to take with us. Go as far as we can, using our ship as base."

"We will need to make snowshoes to travel long distances," Amelia said. "I think we can figure out how to do that. There's a lot of odds and ends on board our ship. And to go back to my theme, seeing what's out there is better than waiting to freeze, or eventually starving."

"I've come to agree," Gavin said. "Especially now that I have another reason to live."

Amelia touched his face and kissed him. "You mean me, right?"

Gavin laughed. "Of course. But listen, girl. I'm willing to try and see what we can find, but to be honest, I don't expect that within a few miles we will come to green grass and cows grazing in a pasture."

"We could try my other plan, use one of the lifeboats, rig a sail of some sort. Try and find land. Land that isn't freezing. Land where someone lives and things make sense. I know. I've suggested it before, and no one has been keen on the idea, but it's still something to consider."

"I'd rather die on the ice than in some boat on a black-ass sea."

"I'd rather not die," Amelia said. "Period."

"A fine sentiment," Gavin said. "But for the time being we have food at the ship, and we can carry some of these blankets with us to add to our store there. Later we can come back for more, bring some of the others so we can tote more supplies."

"Provided we can get them to leave the ship to do anything but fish."

"Food from the sea has proven reasonably certain," Gavin said. "What's out here beyond the ships, toward the mountains, there's nothing certain about that."

The snow quit swirling and the wind ceased to howl. Moonlight speared through the cracks in the ship. They dressed and climbed off the ship and started walking again. The night was clear and bright, so bright it was as if they were walking under a giant street lamp. The wind had left snow piled on the ice. As they walked, they came across footprints—bare footprints.

Amelia said, "Hardin?"

"Possibly."

They went surely in the direction of their ship, able to see landmarks now—ships and sleds and juts of ice they recognized that were close to their destination. Before long they came to a broad snow bank, and lying in it was Hardin.

He was face down and there was blood on the snow, it had crystallized like ruby jewels and smears of strawberry jam.

Amelia bent down and looked close at Hardin. Finally, with help from Gavin, she rolled him over. It was difficult, and Hardin made a ripping sound as the ice tore away from his flesh. His mouth was open, his eyes were wide as well. He had died with his nostrils flared, like a horse blowing air. High on his forehead was a tear in his skull, wide and deep.

"He looks terrified," Gavin said.

"Yes, and look here."

There were drag marks in the blood. There were places in the snow that gave the impression of an octopus wriggling, and then the places grew larger, and finally there was a great shape in the snow. It was a cylindrical shape with a large star-shape at the top. There were thrash marks in the snow all around it. They could see marks where it had crawled off across the snow, its size swelling.

"Whatever it was," Amelia said. "It grows rapidly."

"And it came out of Hardin's head."

"Or attached itself to him. What in hell does that?"

"I don't know, but here's another thing," Gavin said. "He walked."

"Perhaps not on his own power," she said.

"That's insane."

"You saw what was on his head. Some kind of parasite. He may have been dead for days, moving around, but not truly alive, being fed on and articulated like a puppet by that monster."

"All right, but the question has to be, what does this parasite feed on normally if humans aren't in supply?"

"Seals. Sea life. Maybe it's sea life itself, comes on shore from time to time, but exists in the waters as well. Maybe it eats what it eats because it's there to eat, not because it needs it for sustenance. Something left that imprint, and whatever it is, is certainly not human."

They traveled on, tingling with unease. They felt as if they were being watched, but when they looked, nothing was there. Just mounds of snow, a few juts of ice in the peculiar moon and star light. Still, the persistent feeling of being observed moved with them, and with it came a strange feeling of nausea, as if they were breathing air that had been disgorged by something foul, a primitive perception that something primal and dangerous was nearby.

"Suddenly I'm hoping this pistol works," Gavin said, pulled it from his pocket and held it in his gloved hand.

Amelia followed suit with the pistol she had found in the plane.

——

They trudged along with their pistols, and walking near the water line, they saw a lifeboat banging up against the ice.

"It's Lifeboat Number Three," Amelia said. "It washed up here."

"Well, I never want to be in it again," Gavin said. "I hate water."

"And you took a trip on a ship?"

"Thought I might meet women."

Amelia laughed. "That part worked."

As they watched, the dark waters caught up the boat and moved it out into the night. The moonlight coated the lifeboat in silver paint, and they watched until it bobbed up and down and out of sight, as if hiding behind the waves.

They continued until their ship was in sight, then tucked their guns away. When they climbed the ice at the stern and stepped on board, they found a sheet of dark ice running from the bridge to the stairs that led to the hold. The ship was as quiet as a snail's progress.

"That looks like blood," Amelia said, pushing back her jacket hood, unwinding the scarf over her face. Gavin pushed his own hood back, pulled down his scarf.

They pulled their pistols again, followed the dark trail, crept down the stairs, trying not to slip on the ice. At the bottom of the stairs they encountered cold, though not freezing cold. There were remnants of warmth from human bodies and a near dead fire in the small stove below. The coals glowed weakly through ash and semi-devoured chunks of wood formerly belonging to what might have been a chifferobe.

There was a clank toward the back of the hold, in the shadows, and Amelia and Gavin hesitated, then eased in that direction, pistols at the ready.

Movement.

Something running in the dark.

Gavin said, "Hey folks. It's us."

A flash of shadows, something whirling in the dark, catching moonbeams from a crack in the hold. A flutter of rubbery movement atop something, and then it was gone.

Amelia turned to the right where she heard a faint sound, saw nothing, then turned completely around.

That's when a shadow broke loose and darted into the moonlight, came for Amelia with a shriek and a flash of tentacles.

———

It was Duchess, or what she had been. Her head was broken open and a great mass of writhing tentacles flapped from her skull. A bladder shape dangled out of a wide crack in her forehead, and the bladder almost covered her eyes. She was stripped of clothing. Her saggy breasts flapped like something skinned. Her hands were reaching, her mouth was screeching.

Just as Duchess reached her, Amelia lifted the pistol and shot her in the face, right above the bridge of the nose, right below the wide crack in her skull. Duchess's hands brushed Amelia's shoulders and a black mess came from the bladder inside her skull, squished out and into the moonlight in one long squirt. The beast in Duchess's head tore loose from its cranial house, flipped through the air, smashed against the deck, began to puff and swell like a bagpipe. Duchess's lifeless body collapsed in a heap at Amelia's feet. The thing on the floor hissed, then squeaked, and then revealed an extended torso that slid slickly out of the bladder like a fat rat from a greased pipe. Its body was tubular and long with a starfish head. It swelled as it slithered. Sucker-covered tentacles extended from the cylindrical portion of its body, slapped at the floor and waved in the fat slit of moonlight as if trying to grab the moon's attention.

Amelia stepped close and shot the star-head. Tentacles snapped out, smacked the top of her hand, nearly knocking the gun loose, leaving a circular welt, red and inflamed, just above her thumb. It made a gaseous sound and slid greasily across the flood as if pulled on a rope, collapsed, tentacles falling and flailing like electrified noodles.

Amelia heard Gavin's gun snap without firing, snap again. Amelia turned and shot at what was charging across the floor at them, Cyril, his head broken open, giving ride to one of the tentacle-bearing bladders. She shot directly for the bladder this time, and when she did, the black goo went up and out, darker than the shadows around it. Cyril stumbled as if he had stepped into a hole, fell face down, his naked ass humping up in the air once, then collapsing, his pelvis slamming against the floor. The creature detached from Cyril, scuttled away. Amelia was about to shoot again, but Gavin stopped her.

"Save the shot," he said. He tossed his useless pistol aside. There was an axe near the stove, one they had used to shatter wood for burning. Gavin grabbed it, swung it into the creature, chopping the star-head loose, causing a dark mess to gush across the floor.

"Jesus," Amelia said. "What are those things?"

Gavin trembled. "I'm going to guess nothing known to science."

Gavin made his way to the stove, picked up the matches that lay on the floor nearby, scooped out a partly lit stick of wood from the stove, waved it about in the cold air until it flamed slightly. Amelia, all the while, was turning with her pistol, watching. She had one shell left, as the revolver had only housed five loads. Gavin's gun was useless, packed as it was with ineffectual loads.

Gavin wagged the small torch about. In the shadows they saw a heap of nude bodies. The remains of their lifeboat companions. Cautiously, Amelia and Gavin moved nearer. All of the heads were broken open, but none contained their former passengers. Carruthers lay on top. All of them were nude. Either their clothes had been ripped from them by the creatures, or they had torn them loose themselves, as if the things made their bodies boil.

Something clattered in the dark.

They turned. Gavin lifted the small torch. Creatures fluttered in the light and hustled away. Nothing was seen distinctly.

"They're all over the place," Gavin said.

"We have to go," Amelia said. "Right now."

———

Gavin dropped the torch, and carrying the axe at a battle ready position, he and Amelia rushed up the steps, onto the deck, and over the side where the ice was high. They scrambled so quickly they fell into one another and slid down the ice in a tumble. At the bottom of their fall, they looked up. There, on the deck, were the things, tentacles waving about like drunks saying howdy. The creatures pushed together. At first Amelia thought it was for warmth, and then she thought: No, they live here. They endure here.

As they watched, the things came together, tighter. There was a great slurping sound, and then they hooked together and twisted and writhed and became one large, bulbous shape with a multitude of heads and an array of tentacles. It started to edge over the side of the ship.

Amelia and Gavin began to run.

They ran along the snow-flecked ice, falling from time to time, and when they looked back, they saw the thing dropping off the side of the ship, falling a goodly distance, striking the ice heavily, and then rolling and gliding after them.

The snow began to flurry again. It blew down from the sky in a white funnel. It spread wide and wet against them, pushed them like a cold, damp hand. They wound their scarves around their mouths as they ran, pulled their hoods down tight, only looked back when they feared it might be at their very heels, but soon it was lost to them, disappearing within a swirling surge of blinding snow.

Winded, they began to trudge, having no idea where they were heading. Without snowshoes, it was a hard trek. Eventually they came to the plane, its bright red skin flaring up between the swirling flakes of snow. They stood and stared at it.

"I'm so cold I don't care if that thing catches up with me," Gavin said. "I've got to get warm. If only for a little while."

Amelia nodded. "Yeah. That thing can have me, but only if I get a bit warm first."

They slipped inside, having to really tug the door free this time, the whole machine having been touched with frost. They closed the door and locked it. They moved to the cockpit and looked out. There was nothing to see. Just snow. It had ceased to flurry as violently as before, but it was still blowing. After a brief rest, Amelia looked around the plane, more carefully this time, found a few more rounds of over-looked ammunition, enough to fill her pistol. There was a flare gun they had not found in their initial search, and there were four flares in a box beneath the cockpit. Gavin took the flare gun and loaded a flare in it. It wasn't a perfect weapon, but it was something. Gavin stuck the remaining flares in his coat pocket. Finally, exhausted, they laid down on the mattress together, and without meaning to, fell asleep.

At some point, much later, Amelia thought she heard a kind of coughing, and then a loud growl. She tried to wake up, but exhaustion held her. If the things were on her, then they could have her. She was warm and exhausted by fear. She couldn't move a muscle. Shortly, the growling ceased, and Amelia drifted back down into deep sleep. Down in that dark well of exhaustion she sensed a darkness even more complete. Things moved in the dark, bounded about inside her head. Images struck her like bullets, but then they were gone, unidentified. It was a sensation of some terrible intelligence, a feeling of having a hole in the fabric of reality through which all manner of things could slip. She slept deep down in that crawling dark, but yet, it was still a deep sleep and in time even the horrors down there in her dreams let her be.

———

When Amelia awoke, Gavin was missing.

Or so she thought. She sat up. He was sitting in the pilot chair in the cockpit. It was daylight. She went to join him, sat in the co-pilot chair. Gavin had a manual in his lap and was reading it.

"No monsters yet?" she said.

"I think we lost them, confused them, or they're taking a nap. I don't know. You know what? I can fly this. Theoretically, anyway."

"Will it fly?"

"The engine was warm not that long ago. It hasn't been ruined by the cold yet. While you slept, I tried it. After a few false starts it fired."

Amelia realized this was what she had heard while sleeping. Not the roar of some monster, but the roar of a machine.

"I think it hasn't been in the cold so long the engine is ruined, frozen up. It's cold, though. I think the pilot was driven down by a sudden storm. Nothing in the sky one moment, the next a storm. They probably flew here through some dimensional gap, the way we sailed here in the ship. Slipped right through, like a child's toy through a crack in the floor."

"Then why haven't you flown us out, you're sure you can do it."

"I'm not all that sure, actually. Like I said, theoretically, I can fly us out. I cut the engine because I could tell it was stuttering. I wanted it to warm a bit more, or rather I have plans to warm it, and running it before its warmer would just use up gas, and I couldn't see to fly anyway. I couldn't see six inches in front of me. I got started, though. While you slept I used a board and dug around the wheels, freed them. Wore me out. I'm going to build a fire out front of the plane to warm it more. It might ruin things, catch the damn plane on fire, or it might improve things. I don't know. But if the storm passes, as the daylight comes, the sun will warm the engine and then I'll warm it with a bit of fire."

"A bit of fire might be too much fire. Why not just let the sun warm it?"

"It will be warmer, but it won't be warm," Gavin said. "The sun will need some help."

"That would be the fire," Amelia said.

Gavin nodded. "It's warm, then, we might fly out. For all I know I won't be able to fly it at all. Or I'll manage to get it up, only to have it come right back down. Or say I get it up and we fly away. Where are we flying to? How much fuel do we have? Still, what else is there. You with me?"

"Get us up, and fly us out," Amelia said. "You can do it. Any place is better than here."

———

It seemed like a long time, sitting in the cockpit waiting for daylight. Sitting there expecting the monsters to arrive and break through the plane and knock holes in their heads, cause them to tear off their clothes and turn them into naked staggering corpses. They sat back and waited for light, but it was a nervous wait.

The wind died down, the snow blew out, and the daylight finally came. The sun looked at first like a gooey hot-pink lozenge. It turned slowly from pink to orange, spread light like a hot infection across the horizon.

Amelia and Gavin dragged the mattress outside, under the front of the plane, cut it open with the axe. The cotton stuffing inside sprang up through the splits. They piled debris from inside the plane on top of that. They tore pages from the books they had discovered inside, and used them for tinder. Gavin used the matches he had taken from the ship to light the pages. Gradually the flames caught, sputtered, began to eat the tinder and the pages. They watched the pile burn, and watched for any tentacle-bearing visitors that might show.

When the fire was licking at the bottom of the plane, they went inside and waited. Gavin said, "Here's to no unfortunate explosions."

"I agree," Amelia said.

They touched their fists as if they held drinks in their hands.

They watched as the flames grew and licked up around the nose, saw the paint start to bubble and flake.

"I think it's time," Gavin said.

Gavin tried turning the engine over.

———

It did nothing at first. And then it coughed, and then it died, and then Gavin tried again. It coughed again, started to die, but clung to life, blurted and chugged, and then began to roar. Eventually, it began to hum.

Gavin took another look at the manual, which he had again placed in his lap, said, "Let me see now."

"That does not inspire confidence," Amelia said.

"All right. I got this. Mostly."

Gavin touched the controls, managed to move the plane, rock it along on its wheels, veer it to the right, away from the direction of the fire and the sea. Then he gunned it. It rolled and slid on the ice. As they rattled forward on the icy surface, it seemed as if the plane might come apart.

But there were worse things happening. They saw it coming across the ice, the star-heads united into one fat star-head, a hunk of dark meat coated in sun-glimmered slime with pulsing bladders and thrashing tentacles. Somehow it had found them, heard them perhaps, seen the fire. It was directly in their path.

"Ah hell," Gavin said.

He worked the controls, turned the plane a little, moving to the left of the creature.

Now Gavin turned again, placing the creature at the rear of the plane. The plane slipped and wobbled, but continued to rush over the ice.

"I forget how to lift," Gavin said.

"What?"

"I forget how to lift off. Damn. I just read it."

Amelia grabbed the manual. "All right, let me see... No that's how to land."

"The ice ends."

"What?"

Amelia looked up. The ice sheet had a drop off, and the drop off was jagged and deep.

"Turn," she said. "Turn the goddamn plane."

Gavin turned to his left, the wheels managing to stay on the ice, but not without sliding. They could see the creature again from this position, out the side window. It was rising up and smashing down on the ice, throwing up crushed sparkles like fragments of shattered glass, then it inched forward with the flexibility of a caterpillar, rising up again, smashing down, repeating the method, traveling at surprising speed. The plane was moving away from it, though, gaining speed and gaining space.

"Okay. The throttle," Amelia said. "Listen to me, now. Do what I say."

Slowly and loudly she read out the instruction booklet. Gavin following them as well as he understood them, the machine lifting up, then coming down on the wheels, bouncing, slipping, yet moving forward. Not too distantly in front of them were large snow banks.

"It's now or never," Gavin said.

Amelia read from the manual, and Gavin, listening intently, did as he was told, trying to be careful about it, trying to cause the plane to rise.

The plane jumped up into the frosty air like a flame-red moth, into the richly dripping sunlight. Below the white face of the earth shimmered and the montage monster hastened across it, lifted its great starred head toward the vanishing plane, its shadow falling down behind it to lie dark on the ice. It cried out loud enough to be heard even inside the speeding plane, then the beast fell apart. The creatures from which it had been constructed came unstuck and collapsed against the ice, their multitude of shadows falling with them.

The plane sailed on.

———

For a time, Amelia and Gavin coasted in the sun-rich sky, over the ice, toward a green haze drifting above jagged mountain peaks.

Gavin tipped the wheel, the nose lifted, and the plane sailed up. When he was as high as he felt he could comfortably go, he leveled out. The mist, white and foamy as mad-dog froth, parted gently. Below them were wet mountain tops, and straight before them were higher mountains tipped by clouds. To the right of those peaks, was a V shaped gap.

"There," Amelia said, pointing at the gap. "Go there."

"You know I don't really know how to fly, right?"

"You know enough," Amelia said. "You learned more from your dad than you thought, and that manual. We're up here, aren't we? Go there."

Gavin tilted the plane to the right, then settled it, set a nose-aligned course for the gap in the mountains. Shortly, they were in the center of the gap, mountains on either side of them. When they came to the other side of the gap there was a valley of ice and snow, and far to the left there was the darkness of the great waters. Directly before them were more mountains, and above those a green mist shimmered with sunlight. They saw something on the ice directly below them that took their breath away.

———

There were spires, golden and silver, and what could have been thick glass or ice, great structural rises of wicked geometry. Littered before the structures, in a kind of avenue, were what looked to be white humps of stones.

"My god," Gavin said. "A city. The place is enormous."

"How could those things build this?"

"Most likely they didn't," Gavin said. "But whoever built it, built it while drunk."

And on and on the city stretched, toward the blue-black mountains tipped by what looked like a green fungus.

As they neared them, Amelia felt as if a great presence was moving behind the sky and sliding down and into her thoughts. It was the same as during her sleep in the plane, but more intense. In fact, it was painful, even nauseating. She felt stuffed with thought and information she couldn't define.

They flew above the irregular city, watching with awe. When they finally passed over it and the rocky avenue, Gavin turned the plane for a return pass, and when he did, the plane coughed, sputtered, and started going down.

"Out of fuel," Gavin said.

"Priceless," Amelia said.

"I'll try and glide it."

There was a stretch of ice beyond the avenue, and as the plane began to spit and sputter and hurry down, Gavin leveled it, cruised over the avenue toward the ice. It was not a perfect plan, but they were less likely to catch the wheels in the rocks and flip.

Gavin said, "I'm pretty sure I can land it." His hands trembled at the controls.

"No doubt, one way or another you will," Amelia said.

The plane's engines sputtered and died.

Gavin did his best to glide it down and smooth it out for a landing, but the plane was moving fast and he was uncertain what to do. Amelia read frantically aloud from the instruction manual. She was reading it when they came within twenty feet of the ice. She stopped reading then. There was nothing else left to say, and no time to say it.

The plane came down on the ice and the wheels touched. The plane bounced, way up, then back down, went into a sideways skid, and then Gavin lost control and the nose dipped and hit the ice, and the plane spun and started coming apart.

—

The cold brought Amelia around. She could see the sky. It was odd, that sky. She thought she was seeing reflections off the ice, but instead she was looking as through a transparent wall. She could see people walking, riding horses, clattering about in wagons, cars of all eras driving, boats sailing and planes flying. There was depth to her view. People stacked on top of one another as they walked, drove, flew, or sailed. People floated by, sleeping in their beds, and there were the star-head things, and monstrous, unidentifiable visions, and all the images collided and passed through one another like ghosts. She was flooded with the soul-crushing realization that she was less than a speck of dust in the cosmos. The knowledge of her insignificance in the chaotic universe overwhelmed her with sadness and self-pity. Whatever was out there not only had a physical presence, it had a powerful presence in her unconscious, a place where it revealed itself more and more.

She awoke with something warm and wet running down her face. She lifted her hand and opened her eyes. She saw blood was on her gloved fingers. There were tears in her eyes. She touched the wound on her head. Not bad she determined, a scrape.

The sensation passed. She tried to sit up, only to realize she was in the plane seat, and it was lying with its back on the ice, and she was lying in it. It had come free of the plane and she was sliding along the ice with it.

She rolled out of the chair, put her gloved hands on the ice, got her knees under her and stood up. She wobbled. There was wreckage strewn across the ice. There was a vast churn of black smoke on the ice. Gavin came walking out of the black smoke and into the clear carrying the axe he had taken from the ship, and now recovered from the wreckage of the plane. His face was bloody and blackened from smoke, he had a limp, but he was alive.

As they came together and embraced, Gavin said, "Told you I could land it."

They both laughed. It was a hearty laugh, a bit insane really.

"What now?" Amelia said.

"I think we have no other choice than the city. Out here we'll freeze. The wind is picking up, and it's damp, so if nothing else we have to get out of the wind."

"It's chancy."

"So is being out here. No shelter. No food. No plane."

They looked toward one of the buildings, a scrambled design of spires and humps, silver and gold, or so it had seemed from the sky. Now they could see that the light had played on it in a peculiar way, giving it a sheen of colors it did not entirely possess.

"Very well, then," Amelia said, and holding hands they started toward the structures.

They came to the rocky, white road, discovered the lumps were not stones, but skulls and bones, all of the skeletal parts pushed into the ice by time. There were animal skulls and bones amidst human bones and skulls, long and narrow skulls, wide and flat skulls, vertebrae of all manner were in the bone piles, many impossible to identify, some huge and dinosaur-like.

Amelia glanced at the city buildings, which stretched to one side as far as the eye could see, and to the other until they reached the sea. She stared at the building before them, saw it was connected to others by random design. It was hard to figure a pattern.

The wind whistled and hit them like a scythe of ice.

"You're right," she said. "We have to go inside."

They made their way inside the city.

It was warmer inside. No wind, and there seemed to be a source of heat. They didn't notice that until they were well inside and found the path beneath the structure divided and twisted into a multitude of narrow avenues, like a maze. The floor was smooth, but not slick, and the walls were the same.

Gavin marked the walls with the axe as they went, forming a Hansel and Gretel escape path. Soon they unwound their scarves and let them hang, they removed their gloves and stuffed them in coat pockets and loosed the top buttons on their shirts. It was comfortably warm.

They were eventually overtaken by exhaustion. Amelia said, "We should rest while we have the opportunity. I think I may be more banged-up than I first realized."

"We don't know what's inside this place," Gavin said.

"We know that right this minute we are okay. There is nothing more we can know in this place, and I don't know about you, but being in the cold, flying in an airplane with an untrained pilot, crash landing on the ice, has tuckered me a little."

Gavin chuckled. "Yeah. I'm pretty worn."

The stopped and leaned against the wall, stuck their feet out. The warmth inside the structure was pleasurable. It was like a nice down blanket, though there was a faint foul smell.

"I had this vision, of sorts," Amelia said. "Or maybe I actually saw something."

"Vision? Worlds and animals and people and things stacked on one another, flowing through one another. A feeling of...miasma."

"You too?"

"Yeah. I don't know what I was seeing exactly, but when I awoke it was in my head. I feel better awake than asleep, like out here I can see what is happening, but inside of my dreams I can feel what is happening, and it's worse."

"Like a truth was trying to be revealed?"

"Yeah," Gavin said. "Like that, and it was like my primitive brain understood it, but my logical brain couldn't wrap itself around it. Like the answer was in sight, but on a shelf too high for my mind to reach."

"Oh, I think I know. I think you know. Our minds know what's there on that shelf now, they just don't want to reach up and take hold of it. Don't want to know that truth. You see, Gavin, I think we saw a glimpse of the in-betweens."

"In-betweens?" he said, but she could tell it was mostly a rhetorical question. He knew exactly what she was talking about. She could see it in his eyes.

"Talking out loud," she said, "it's like finding a footstool and being able to reaching that high shelf. What if there's a crack in our subconscious that allows us, from time to time, to slip from what we perceive as our own life, into a nightmare of sorts. One that's real. Not dream logic altogether, but a real place that we perceive as nightmare, but sometimes it's more than that. A dimensional hole, like you suggested. We sometimes pass through it, like the people and things you saw in your dream. Not by choice, but by chance.

The hole is there, and the right dream and the right time, well, we fall through. Or we're pulled through."

"Yeah," Gavin said, picking up where she left off, really feeling it now. "We get pulled in. Our world, the one where we're lying in bed, is now the dream, and we can't get back. The hole closes, or we just can't find it. Maybe on our old world, we're one of those who unexpectedly dies in their sleep. But what is us now, the us in this dimension, we stay here, and we experience whatever it is we find here, and our other self truly dies. We have left the building back home, so to speak."

"Exactly," Amelia said. "The things that people see in nightmares, monsters. Perhaps they really see them. At a distance sometimes. See them, and then the dreamer slides back to where they belong. Sometimes they don't. And perhaps, sometimes it works the other way. What's on the other side seeps into our world like a kind of cosmic sewage."

Gavin interrupted her before she could speak another word.

"And us, and all the people on the ship, the others who came here, the pilot of the plane, we all fell through the same hole. We were having different dreams, but we all fell through, and then we were all having a similar dream. Some of us dreamed of a ship, and we all were on board, and the dream ship slipped through. Same for the plane, the other ships and dog sleds. Say someone was traveling over the ice, an explorer for example, pulled by sled dogs, and that night he makes his tent and he dreams. Dreams himself into another dimension, this dimension, and the dogs go with him. Imagination becomes flesh and blood because he and his dream have passed through that dimensional hole. We've collectively dreamed ourselves into another reality. We've fallen into our subconscious and we can't get out. We have all found the same pit on the other side of the hole."

Amelia was silent for a long time before she spoke.

"As much as it can be explained, that's it. I feel it in my bones. Whatever is here in this horrid world is not just those star-heads, but something else of greater intelligence. Something that stands here waiting at the hole in our dreams, waiting for something or someone to slip through."

"To what purpose?"

Amelia reflected a moment, then, "It's like we're experiencing some eternal truth, and the horrid thing about it is, it's nothing wonderful. It's merely a place where we go and suffer. A sort of hell inside the mind that becomes solid. The Christian hell may not be Christian, but it may not be myth. And in our case, it's not fire on the other side, but ice."

"Maybe we can dream ourselves out," Gavin said.

"Do you feel that you can?"

Gavin shook his head. "No. I feel the gap to the other side has winked closed, and dreaming doesn't open it. Dreaming just makes you susceptible when the gap is open is my guess. Dreaming here you just get tapped into by this intelligence, as you called it. It wants us, for whatever reason, but the reason isn't reasonable."

Amelia laughed. "That makes no sense."

"Because it isn't within our concept of logic. It wants what we can't understand. Things that would make no sense whatsoever to us. It feels hopeless."

"It's giving us the knowledge it wants us to have," Amelia said. "And only because it's a knowledge that fills us with defeat. And here's another thing, who says that knowledge is real? That may be part of its powers. It affects the mind, lets you imagine what it wants you to imagine. You can control it to a certain extent, but the closer you are to it, and we must be right on top of it, the stronger that power is. We have to decide not to let it defeat us with negative thoughts and uncomfortable revelations, because they may all be projection, and not reality."

"All right," Gavin said. "All right. We won't let it win."

They rested awhile, and without meaning to, they slept. It came over them as if they had been drugged. They fought it but it won, and they dreamed. A dream of great darkness rising up to overwhelm them, swallow them down and take them away, chewing up flesh and sucking out souls, their little sparks of life force being sucked away into some horrid eternity even worse than where they were.

———

When they awoke, they saw no remedy to their problem other than to explore, plotting together to see if they could find and kill this thing that was wiggling in their brains. That was the plan. They would kill it. They had a gun and an axe, and Gavin still had the flare gun and flares in his coat pocket. They had something to fight with, and that meant they had a chance.

There was an array of irregular pathways that twisted and turned, and there were spears of light coming in through gaps in the structure, and the sunlight lit the halls and walls with enough intermittent illumination they could see clearly. They chose one of the pathways and followed it. It became narrow and low, and to exit it, they had to crawl on their hands and knees for some distance before it opened into a larger chamber. A smell like all the death and rot that had ever occurred wafted toward them in a hot, sticky stench. Gavin was overwhelmed by it, and threw up against the wall.

"Might want to step around that," he said, wiping his mouth.

"May have some to add to it," Amelia said.

They pulled their scarves around their noses and mouths and kept going. The chamber went wide, and then it went small. The stink intensified. They came to narrow halls again, and they kept going, not searching for anything in particular, but searching.

They arrived at a great drop off, wide and deep and full of stink, lit by cracks of light from above. Hanging over the pit, fastened there by a scarf to what looked like a dry hose running above her, was a woman. She was wearing khaki pants and a leather jacket. She wore pilot gear, goggles pushed up on her head, and tight on her skull was a leather cap with ear flaps. Her skin was yellow, and her neck was long. The meat was beginning to rot, speeded up by the hot stink rising from the pit beneath her. Her feet dangled over the great and stinking pit, and one boot was slipping free of her rotting flesh, soon to fall into the pit below.

"The pilot," Gavin said. "Has to be. She ended up here somehow, and it must have been too much for her. The things we felt she must have felt, that damn presence, force, whatever. She didn't have anyone to bolster her and give her strength. She was on her own, so she just quit."

Amelia nodded, looked down into the pit.

"What is that?"

There was very little light now, just a split of gold through a crack here and there, so Gavin put a flare in his gun, fired it downwards. It glowed bright, and then it hit something below and sputtered with red light. The pit was full of blackened meat and rotting guts and all manner of offal.

Slowly Amelia's face paled.

"What?" Gavin said, staring at her face in the rising glow of the flare.

"I've got it figured, Gavin, and it's worse than we thought. This isn't a building. This place isn't a city. Above, those aren't hoses. They're veins, or arteries. Down below, that's afterbirth. We're inside a corpse, a drying one. Like a huge mollusk. Don't you see, Gavin? Down below, that's a womb. The star-shaped things. They were born here. Look around. There aren't any corridors. Those are artery paths that we've walked through, chambers for organs. Not humanlike organs, but organ housings just the same. And this is the birth canal, and down below, the womb. The bones we saw outside, they're from this thing's digestive system, crapped out and onto the ground where they were dried by time and cold wind.

Bones of humans and all manner of creatures that have ended up here. Those star-heads, they link up and grow, become solid at some part, don't separate anymore, and then they give birth and die, leaving these shells."

"You're sensing this?" Gavin asked.

"No. I'm speculating this, or you'd feel the same thing. Perhaps they're hermaphrodite. Once birth is completed, the host for the children dies. The replacements feed on what they can find. Maybe their mother, or whatever this thing can be called. And then they feed on whatever comes through the dream hole. These aren't buildings in a city. These are the remains of dead creatures, and they have given birth and left their remains, and the cycle continues."

Gavin looked about. "Maybe," he said.

"I can't be absolutely sure I'm right, but close enough, I think. What I am certain of, is I don't think being here is a good idea. We are too close to whatever that primal power is, the thing we sense, the thing that pulls us in from our dreams, it's nearby. And that can't be good. We have to find food, drinkable water. And most important, I can't stand this stink anymore."

They went back the way they had come, following the axe scratches, seeking the exit, fearing the arrival of the star-heads.

—

The cold was almost welcome.

They moved along the bone walk, toward the mountains, choosing a central range that looked dark with dirt and green with foliage, but no sooner had they started out, then the central mountain range trembled. The stretch of the horizon trembled. The green mist that floated above the mountains was sucked back toward the peaks, as if inhaled, and then the mist was blown back out in a great whirling wad, as if by a sleeping drunk.

And then they understood.

There were no cities, and there were no mountains. Only giant, irregular-shaped shells of creatures. Old ones that had given birth. Some larger than others.

Some as big as mountain ranges that still lived and were most likely stuffed tight with new life being baked inside a womb, and in this case, a womb much larger than any of those that had made up the false city. For before them was a beast. Not a mountain, but an impossible slug. The flesh had yet to harden. It trembled like jello and it was vast.

The mountain trembled again, and then moved. Ever so slowly, but it moved. It was easy to outrun, of course. It inched its way. It would take days for it reach where they now ran. But they soon came up against the coal-black sea, stood on the shore with nowhere to go. Waves crashed in against the ice, flowing up to the toes of their boots. Gavin began to cry.

"It's all insane," he said. "That pilot was right after all."

Amelia touched his shoulder.

There was a banging to their left. It made them both jump. It was their old friend, Lifeboat Number Three. It had drifted away and back again, sailing crewless along the stretch of icy shore.

"Fate doesn't hate us after all," Amelia said.

Gavin laughed. He turned and looked back toward the mountain. It was difficult to tell it had moved. It seemed in the same place, but he knew it had. Tentacles, the size and length of four lane highways, lifted off of the beast and snapped at the sky. They had appeared like rows of rock and dirt, but now they were revealed for what they were. The ice screeched with the monster's glacial progress.

Amelia ran to the boat, slipped on the ice, struggled to her feet and grabbed at it. The back end of it swung around, banging against the hard ice. Another few minutes and they would never have known it was there. It would have washed out to sea again.

Amelia held the boat and looked at Gavin.

"The oars are still in it."

Gavin hurried to join her. He smiled at her. She smiled back. And then the smile dropped off her face.

Coming much closer than the mountain were the star-heads that they had outdistanced. They were as one again, larger than before, but smaller by far than the mountainous monster. They moved much faster than their creator, slurping over the ice, tentacles flaring, mouths open, showing multitudinous teeth, licking at the air with a plethora of what might have been tongues.

"This can't be real," Gavin said. "It's a mad house. One mad thing and then another. I have to wake up."

"I'd rather not stay here and find out if it's a dream, Gavin. Come on. We have to go. Now."

They pushed the boat into the water and climbed aboard, pushed at the ice with the oars, shoved out into the dark and raging waters. They began to row savagely.

—

The star-head thing moved to the edge of the water and broke apart and its many bodies spilled into the waves.

Amelia and Gavin rowed wildly. The star-heads swam fast, cruising through the water, tentacles tucked. On they came, and soon Amelia and Gavin knew there was no chance of outdistancing them. They clutched their oars ready to fight. The star-heads loomed out of the sea, tentacles flashing, attempting to clutch.

Amelia and Gavin were sitting at different ends of the boat, and they positioned themselves on their knees, swinging the oars, batting back tentacles, slamming down on star-heads as they peeked up over the rim of the boat. Tentacles slapped about like limbs whipped by a violent storm. Amelia felt them brush her, burning her with their sucker mouths, but they failed to manage a solid grip. She frantically wiggled free and swung the oar, knocking them aside.

"Oh god," she heard Gavin say. She glanced back. One of the star-heads had risen up beside the boat and whip-snapped its tentacles around Gavin and his oar, causing it to lie against his chest; the paddle part of the oar pointed up as if in sword-like salute. The star-head dropped completely back into the water, its tentacles stretched out and lifted Gavin up like a mother holding a young child on display.

Gavin stared down at Amelia as he was hoisted out of the boat and dangled above the water. Amelia leaned out and swung the oar, struck the tentacles with it, but they were too strong, their grip too tight.

Gavin's face was as bland and white as the ice. He ceased to struggle, dangled in the monster's grip. The tentacles coiled him close and pulled him away, took him down under with little more than a delicate splash.

Amelia began to scream at the beasts, as if bad language might frighten them. She continued to struggle, whipping the oar through the air, contacting other star-heads. They came in a horde now. Tentacles flashed everywhere, popped at her legs, snapped against her arms. The black water turned greasy with blood. Star-heads were grabbing at the boat from all sides, shaking it with their tentacles, as if they might tear it apart or pull it down under. Gavin's head, minus his body, surfaced, rolled, and then was taken by a star-head's wide open mouth. As it started to jerk Gavin's head below, fins broke the surface of the water.

Sharks. A mass of them.

A great white leapt out of the water, rolled its black eyes up inside its head as it snapped at the star-head's tentacle, pulled it and the remains of Gavin down with it. Sharks began to jump from the waves as easy as flying fish. They grabbed the star-heads in their toothy mouths, crunched them like dry toast, then pulled the remains of their squirming meals into the deeps.

More sharks came and went, like a pack of wolves, cutting through the blood-slick waters, snapping at the star-heads quickly, darting away and under, only to rise and circle back and strike again.

And then the battle ceased. The sharks had won. Both sharks and star-heads were gone. One to eat, one to be eaten.

The night rolled in and a ragged moon floated up out of the sea, found a place to hang against the night. The waters churned and the boat jumped. Exhausted, Amelia lay down in the boat and was eased into sleep by exhaustion. The dark things moved inside her head.

———

When Amelia awoke the next morning it was still dark, but light was bleeding in with squirts of red, and in short time the sun trembled up and turned bright gold. She thought of Gavin, almost expecting to see him when she had the strength to rise from the bottom of the boat, but his fate was soon sharp in her memory. All she could think about was how he had been taken away by different monsters of the sea. Yet, the sharks had been her saviors, and after a long time with the sun warming the boat and the sea, she found a dead shark floating on its back in the water, the bottom half of its tail eaten off in what had probably been a continued and cannibalistic shark frenzy from the night before. She paddled up beside it and saw that its belly was ripped open, and strings of innards hung out of it. A meal abandoned for whatever reason. She reached down and pulled the creature's insides loose, tugged them into the boat, snapping them off, tossing them on the floor of the craft like enormous tomato-sauced noodles. The guts were filled with offal. She shook that out as best she could, washed it clean with the waters of the sea, then ate it raw. It tasted good at first, but then when she was past her savage hunger, it made her stomach churn. Still, she scooped more out of the shark and tossed it in the bottom of the boat for later.

She had no idea what to do. Perhaps the only choice was to try and see if she could find a place farther down on the slate of ice where the mountainous monster and the star-heads didn't dwell. If such a place existed.

It was surprisingly warm, considering the ice. From way out she could see the mountainous creature. It took up all her eye line when she looked to the shore. It had moved ever closer, changing the landscape in an amazing way, slipping along on a monstrous trail of slime that oozed out from under it and greased its way toward the sea.

It was massive. She would have to sail for days to get around it, if that was even possible.

Amelia ate some more of the shark, but the guts had gone bad in the sunlight. She vomited over the side.

———

Amelia counted four days at sea, and then she lost count. She had been lucky. A fairly large fish had leaped into the boat, and she had bashed its head with an oar. She ate its brains where the oar had broken its skull, ripped it open with her bare hands and used her teeth on the soft belly, biting off chunks, wolfing it down. It was far more palatable than the shark had been, and when she finished, she was refreshed. It was all she would have that day, and by next day she was hungry again, but no prize fish presented itself. She did manage to nab a few floating chunks of ice and suck on those for water.

She sailed hungry through a day and night. She wasn't sleeping. It was too dark down there in her dreams, so she tried to stay awake. Inside her thoughts the creature continued to come to her. It didn't speak to her, but it communicated with her nonetheless. It was a terrible communication that made her dreams scream and her skin crawl.

Her hunger helped keep her awake.

Another fish might present itself, and that was something to think about instead of the monster that stretched for as far as she could see. Earlier in the day she had seen a seal, or something quite like one, swimming near the boat, not too far under water, quite visible when the sun hit the waves just right. She hoped she might come across another, one more foolish, willing to rise up and present its head to be banged with an oar. It amazed her that animals she knew existed here amongst things her world had no idea existed.

By mid-day the boat had actually caught an underwater current of some sort, and it drifted out and away from the shoreline. But then an odd thing happened. It was discernable, but only a little, and near impossible to assimilate mentally. The mountain had reached beyond the shoreline. It was about to enter the water. And that's what happened. The entire icy shoreline cracked with an ear-piercing sound, and the great mountain dropped straight into the water, part of it disappearing like the fabled continent of Atlantis. Monstrous tentacles writhed from it.

It was so insane Amelia began to gulp air, like a fish that had been docked.

As the mountain slipped into the water, the sea rose up and the boat rose with it. The weight of the mountainous monster, a small continent of sorts, swelled the sea level. The impossible creature kept drifting down into the waters, and then abruptly it ceased to drift. It had hit bottom, but still the peaks of it rose out of the sea and the tentacles, as big as redwood trees, thrashed at the air and smacked the water like an angry child. The broken ice popped up before it and along its impossible length in iceberg chunks, bobbing like ice cubes in a glass.

The boat was borne toward the shore line, which was entirely taken up by the behemoth. And then, all along the visible part of the beast, there was a horizontal fissure. The fissure spread wide with a cracking sound so loud Amelia covered her ears. The fissure spread for miles. There were jagged rows of teeth inside of it, each the size of mountain tops, and there was spittle on the teeth, running in great wet beads, as if it was tumbling snow from an avalanche, and rising out of the great mouth was a sudsy foam, like white lava from a volcano. The teeth snapped together with an explosion so loud it deafened Amelia. When the impossible mouth opened again, it became wider yet; the bottom of it touched the sea. The water flowed into it with the briskness of a tsunami, and in the drag of it, the lifeboat jetted toward the mouth.

Amelia grabbed the oars and tried to use them, but it was useless. The rush of the water toward the open mouth of the creature was too strong and too swift; it could not be denied.

She saw the great fissure of a mouth tremble, and then the boat came closer, flowing now with even greater speed.

"Why?" she yelled to the wind and water. "I am nothing. I'm not even an appetizer."

Amelia began to laugh, loud and hysterical. She could hear herself, and it frightened her to hear it, but she couldn't stop.

And then the little fly-speck of a boat, with its smaller laughing speck inside, entered into the trembling, foam-flecked mouth that was a length beyond full view of the eye, and tumbled as if over a vast waterfall. The boat banged against one of the jagged teeth like a gnat hitting a skyscraper, came apart, and it and Amelia, who gave one last great laugh, were churned beneath the water and carried into the monster's gullet, along with creatures of the sea.

Introduction to

WRESTLING JESUS

This is a favorite story of mine. I would put it in my top twenty, if anyone cared to know, and they might not. I wrote it for Gardner Dozois and George R. R. Martin for an anthology titled *Dangerous Women*.

There were some who felt every story had to be about female empowerment, but that isn't what mine is about. I assumed there would be plenty of that in the book, and I had a story I wanted to tell, and in this one, the woman may or may not be a femme fatale, and in its own way, it may in fact be about female empowerment. But many readers wanted all the women in the stories to be the heroes. I was thinking a different way.

I have written a number of novels and stories with women as the leads and heroes, but I don't feel obligated to make anyone good or bad due to gender, sex, or race or political correctness. The story dictates who does what, not fashion. Good and bad come in all colors and denominations. Life is mixed, and so are people. Life is muddy and complex a lot of the time and frequently fails to fulfill our wishful thinking, our hopes and dreams. People disappoint us, and people inspire us. Sometimes the same people do both.

This story is really about a father and son relationship, even though the main characters are not related. It is also a story about a young boy learning about bullies, learning certain skills that give him confidence. Confidence itself is sometimes the best weapon against bullies. A positive sense of self makes a person less of a target for bullies. But I like to think it's about more than that, but

I don't want to reveal too much. I'll let you discover the things you think it is about.

A side note is the character of X-Man has much in common with my father. He was an unusually strong man. He could not read or write. He was a mechanic. He was a man of his time, but he was a decent man who worked hard for his family and always inspired me to do my best.

He also was my first martial arts instructor. He taught me boxing and wrestling techniques. He learned them here and there as a young man, and during the Great Depression caught hobo rides on trains and stopped off in towns where there were fairs. There was nearly always a wrestling or boxing show, and he would volunteer to be part of it, the winner receiving money. This was the beginning of professional wrestling, but it was before the matches were all decided beforehand. Anyway, he did that and learned a lot and he taught me a lot of it at my request.

I wasn't very good then, but it gave me an interest in martial arts, and I began to study numerous systems. I became skilled over time. I have now been in martial arts fifty-five years. I have achieved some recognition as a student and practitioner. I still practice. I still teach. And will as long as I am able to do it convincingly.

One of the greatest gifts my father gave me was confidence and a love for martial arts. In a roundabout way, he gave me this story, and now I give it to you.

WRESTLING JESUS

First they took Marvin's sack lunch, then his money, and then they kicked his ass. In fact, he felt the ass whipping, had it been put on a scale of one to ten, was probably about a fourteen. However, Marvin factored in that some of the beating had been inconsistent, as one of his attackers had paused to light a cigarette, and afterwards, two of them had appeared tired and out of breath.

Lying there, tasting blood, he liked to think that, taking in the pause for a smoke and the obvious exhaustion of a couple of his assailants, points could be taken away from their overall performance, and their rating would merely have been nine or ten instead of the full fourteen.

This, however, didn't help his ribs one little bit, and it didn't take away the spots swimming before his eyes just before he passed out from the pain. When he awoke, he was being slapped awake by one of the bullies, who wanted to know if he had any gold teeth. He said he didn't, and the thug insisted on seeing, and Marvin opened his mouth, and the mugger took a look.

Disappointed, the thug threatened to piss in his mouth or fuck him, but the thug and his gang were either too tired from beating him to fuck him, or weren't ready to make water, because they started walking away, splitting up his money in fourths as they walked. They had each made about three dollars and twenty cents, and from his backpack they had taken a pretty good ham sandwich and a little container of Jell-O. There was, however, only one plastic spoon.

Marvin was beginning to feel one with the concrete, when a voice said, "You little shits think you're something, don't ya?"

Blinking, Marvin saw that the speaker was an old man, slightly stooped, bowlegged, with white hair and a face that looked as if it had once come apart and been puzzled back together by a drunk in a dark room with cheap glue. His ear—Marvin could see the right one—contained enough hair to knit a small dog sweater. It was the only visible hair the man had that was black. The hair on his head was the color of a fish belly. He was holding up his loose pants with one hand. His skin was dark as a walnut and his mouth was a bit overfull with dentures. One of his pants pockets was swollen with something. Marvin thought it might be his balls; a rupture.

The gang stopped in their tracks and turned. They were nasty looking fellows with broad shoulders and muscles. One of them had a large belly, but it was hard, and Marvin knew for a fact that all of them had hard fists and harder shoes. The old man was about to wake up dead.

The one who had asked Marvin if he had any gold teeth, the hard belly, looked at the old man and said, as he put down Marvin's stolen backpack, "You talking to us, you old geezer?"

"You're the only shit I see," said the old man. "You think you're a real bad man, don't you? Anyone can beat up some pussy like this kid. My crippled grandma could, and she's been dead some twenty years. Kid's maybe sixteen; what are you fucks—twenty? You're a bunch of cunts without any hair on your slit."

Marvin tried to crawl backwards until he was out of sight, not wanting to revive their interest in him, and thinking he might get away while they were killing the old man. But he was too weak to crawl. Hard Belly started strutting toward the old man, grinning, preening.

When he was about six feet away, the old man said, "You gonna fight me by yourself, Little Shit? You don't need your gang to maybe hold me?"

"I'm gonna kick out any real teeth you got, you old spic," said Hard Belly.

"Ain't got no real ones, so have at it."

The boy stepped in and kicked at the old man, who slapped his leg aside with his left hand, never taking the right away from holding up his pants, and hit him with a hard left jab to the mouth that knocked him down and made his lips bleed. When Hard Belly tried to get up, the old man made with a sharp kick to the windpipe. Hard Belly dropped, gagging, clutching at his throat.

"How's about you girls? You up for it, you little cunts?"

The little cunts shook their heads.

"That's good," said the old man, and pulled a chain out of his pocket. That had been the bulk in his pocket, not a ruptured nut. He was still holding his pants with his other hand.

"I got me an equalizer here. I'll wrap this motherfucker around your head like an anchor chain. Come over here and get Mr. Butt Hole, and take him away from me, and fast."

The three boys pulled Mr. Butt Hole, a.k.a. Hard Belly, to his feet, and when they did, the old man pushed his face close to Hard Belly's and said, "Don't come back around here. I don't want to see you no more."

"You'll be sorry, spic," said Hard Belly, bubbling blood over his lips and down his chin.

The old man dropped the chain on the ground and popped Hard Belly with a left jab again, breaking Hard Belly's nose, spewing blood all over his face.

"What the fuck you got in your ears?" the old man said. "Mud? Huh? You got mud? You hear me talkin' to you? Adiós, asshole."

The three boys, and Hard Belly, who was wobbling, made their way down the street and were gone.

The old man looked down at Marvin who was still lying on the ground.

"I've had worse beatings than that from my old mother, and she was missing an arm. Get the hell up."

Marvin managed to get his feet under him, thinking it a feat equal with building one of the Great Pyramids—alone.

"What you come around here for?" the old man said. "Ain't nobody around here but shits. You look like a kid might come from someplace better."

Marvin shook his head. "No," he said. "I'm from around here."

"Since when?"

"Since a week ago."

"Yeah? You moved here on purpose, or you just lose your map?"

"On purpose."

"Well, kid, you maybe better think about moving away."

There was nothing Marvin wanted to do more than move. But his mother said no dice. They didn't have the money. Not since his father died. That had nipped them in the bud, and quite severely, that dying business. Marvin's dad had been doing all right at the factory, but then he died and since then their lives had gone downhill faster than a little red wagon stuffed full of bricks. He and his mom had to be where they were, and there was nothing else to be said about it. A downgrade for them would be a cardboard box with a view. An upgrade would be lifts in their shoes.

"I can't move. Mama doesn't have the money for it. She does laundry."

"Yeah, well, you better learn to stand up for yourself then," said the old man. "You don't, you might just wake up with your pants down and your asshole big as a dinner plate."

"They'd really do that?"

"Wouldn't put it past them," said the old man. "You better learn to fight back."

"Can you teach me?"

"Teach you what?"

"To fight."

"I can't do it. I have to hold my pants up. Get yourself a stick."

"You could teach me, though."

"I don't want to, kid. I got a full-time job just trying to stay breathing. I'm nearly eighty fucking years old. I ought to been feeding the worms five years ago. Listen up. You stay away from here, and if you can't...well, good luck, boy."

Holding his pants with one hand, the old man shuffled away. Marvin watched him go for a moment, and then fled. It was his plan to make it through the week, when school would turn out for the summer, and then he'd just stay in the apartment and never leave until school started up in the fall. By then, maybe he could formulate a new plan.

He hoped that in that time the boys would have lost interest in punching him, or perhaps been killed in some dreadful manner, or moved off themselves. Started a career, though he had a pretty good idea they had already started one—professional thugs.

He told his mother he fell down. She believed him. She was too preoccupied with trying to keep food on the table to think otherwise, and he didn't want her to know anyway. Didn't want her to know he couldn't take care of himself, and that he was a walking punching bag. Thing was, she wasn't too alert to his problems. She had the job, and now she had a boyfriend, a housepainter. The painter was a tall, gangly guy that came over and watched TV and drank beer, then went to bed with his mother. Sometimes, when he was sleeping on the couch, he could hear them back there. He didn't remember ever hearing that kind of thing when his dad was alive, and he didn't know what to think about it. When it got really loud, he'd wrap his pillow around his ears and try to sleep.

———

During the summer he saw some ads on TV about how you could build your body, and he sent off for a VHS tape. He started doing push-ups and sit-ups and a number of other exercises. He didn't have money for the weights the tape suggested. The tape cost him what little money he had saved, mostly a nickel here, a quarter there. Change his mother gave him. But he figured if his savings kept him from an ass whipping, it was worth every penny.

Marvin was consistent in his workouts. He gave them everything he had, and pretty soon his mother mentioned that he seemed to be looking stronger. Marvin thought so too. In fact, he actually had muscles. His arms were knotted and his stomach was pretty flat, and his thighs and calves had grown. He could throw a jab and a cross now. He found a guide online for how to do it. He was planning on working on the uppercut next, maybe the hook, but right now he had the jab and the cross down.

"All right," he said to the mirror. "Let them come. I'm ready."

———

After the first day of school in the fall, Marvin went home the same way he had that fateful day he had taken a beating. He didn't know exactly how he felt about what he was doing. He hoped he would never see them again on one hand, and on the other, he felt strong now, felt he could handle himself.

Marvin stuck his hand in his pocket and felt for the money he had there. Not much. A dollar or so in change. More money saved up from what his mother gave him. And he had his pack on his back. They might want that. He had to remember to come out of it, put it aside if he had to fight. No hindrances.

When he was where it happened before, there was no one. He went home feeling a bit disappointed. He would have enjoyed banging their heads together.

—

On his third day after school, he got his chance.

There were only two of them this time. Hard Belly, and one of the weasels that had been with him before. When they spotted him, Hard Belly smiled and moved toward Marvin quickly, the weasel trailing behind as if looking for scraps.

"Well, now," Hard Belly said as he got closer. "You remember me?"

"Yes," Marvin said.

"You ain't too smart, are you, kid? Thought you had done moved off. Thought I'd never get a chance to hit you again. That old man, I want you to know, he caught me by surprise. I could have kicked his ass from Monday to next Sunday."

"You can't whip me, let alone him."

"Oh, so, during the summer, you grew a pair of balls."

"Big pair."

"Big pair, huh. I bet you I can take that pack away from you and make you kiss my shoes. I can make you kiss my ass."

"I'm going to whip your ass," Marvin said.

The bully's expression changed, and Marvin didn't remember much after that.

He didn't come awake until Hard Belly was bent over, saying, "Now, kiss it. And pucker good. A little tongue would be nice. You don't, Pogo here, he's gonna take out his knife and cut your dick off. You hear?"

Marvin looked at Hard Belly. Hard Belly dropped his pants and bent over with his hands on his knees, his asshole winking at Marvin. The weasel was riffling through Marvin's backpack, strewing things left and right.

"Lick or get cut," Hard Belly said.

Marvin coughed out some blood and started to try and crawl away.

"Lick it," Hard Belly said. "Lick it till I feel good. Come on, boy. Taste some shit."

A foot flew out and went between Hard Belly's legs, caught his nuts with a sound like a beaver's tail slapping on water. Hard Belly screamed, went forward on his head, as if he were trying to do a headstand.

"Don't never do it, kid," a voice said. "It's better to get your throat cut."

It was the old man. He was standing close by. He wasn't holding his pants this time. He had on a belt.

Pogo came at the old man and swung a wild right at him. The old man didn't seem to move much but somehow he went under the punch, and when he came up, the uppercut that Marvin had not practiced was on exhibition. It hit Pogo under the chin and there was a snapping sound, and Pogo, the weasel, seemed to lose his head for a moment. It stretched his neck like it was made of rubber. Spittle flew out of Pogo's mouth and Pogo collapsed on the cement in a wad.

The old man wobbled over to Hard Belly, who was on his hands and knees, trying to get up, his pants around his ankles. The old man kicked him between the legs a couple of times. The kicks weren't pretty, but they were solid. Hard Belly spewed a turd and fell on his face.

"You need to wipe up," the old man said. But Hard Belly wasn't listening. He was lying on the cement making a sound like a truck trying to start.

The old man turned and looked at Marvin.

"I thought I was ready," Marvin said.

"You ain't even close, kid. If you can walk, come with me."

Marvin could walk, barely.

"You got some confidence somewhere," the old man said. "I seen that right off. But you didn't have no reason for it."

"I did some training."

"Yeah, well, swimming on dry land ain't the same as getting into it. There's things you can do that's just in the air, or with a partner that can make a real difference, but you don't get no feel for nothing. I hadn't come along you'd have been licking some ass crack and calling it a snow cone. Let me tell you, son. Don't never do that. Not unless it's a lady's ass and you've been invited. Someone wants to make you do something like that, you die first. You do that kind of thing once, you'll have the taste of shit in your mouth for the rest of your life."

"I guess it's better than being dead," Marvin said.

"Naw, it ain't neither. Let me tell you. Once I had me a little dog. He wasn't no bigger than a minute, but he had heart big as all the outdoors. Me and him took walks. One day, we was walking along, not far from here actually, and there was this German shepherd out nosing in some garbage cans. Rough-looking old dog, and it took in after my little dog. Mike was his name. And it was a hell of a fight. Mike wouldn't give. He fought to the death."

"He got killed?"

"Naw. The shepherd got killed."

"Mike killed the shepherd?"

"Naw. 'Course not. I'm jerking you. I hit the shepherd with a board I picked up. But the lesson here is you got to do your best, and sometimes you got to hope there's someone around on your side with a board."

"You saying I'm Mike and you're the guy with the board?"

"I'm saying you can't fight for shit. That's what I'm saying."

"What happened to Mike?"

"Got hit by a truck he was chasing. He was tough and willing, but he didn't have no sense. Kind of like you. Except you ain't tough. And another drawback you got is you ain't a dog. Another thing, that's twice I saved you, so you owe me something."

"What's that?"

"Well, you want to learn to fight, right?"

Marvin nodded.

"And I need a workout partner."

The old man's place wasn't far from the fight scene. It was a big, two-story concrete building. The windows were boarded over. When they got to the front door, the old man pulled out a series of keys and went to work on several locks.

While he did that, he said, "You keep a lookout. I got to really be careful when I do this, 'cause there's always some asshole wanting to break in. I've had to hurt some jackasses more than once. Why I keep that two-by-four there in the can."

Marvin looked. There was indeed a two-by-four stuffed down inside a big trash can. The two-by-four was all that was in it.

The old man unlocked the door and they went inside. The old man flicked some lights and everything went bright. He then went to work on the locks, clicked them into place. They went along a narrow hall into a wide space—a very wide space.

What was there was a bed and a toilet out in the open on the far wall, and on the other wall was a long plank table and some chairs. There was a hot plate on the table, and above and behind it were some shelves stuffed with canned goods. There was an old refrigerator, one of those bullet-shaped things. It moaned loudly, like a child with a head injury. Next to the table was a sink, and not far from that was a shower, with a once-green curtain pulled around a metal scaffold. There was a TV under some posters on the wall and a few thick chairs with the stuffing leaking out.

There was a boxing ring in the middle of the room. In the ring was a thick mat, taped all over with duct tape. The sun-faded posters were of men in tights, crouched in boxing or wrestling positions. One of them said, "Danny Bacca, X-Man."

Marvin studied the poster. It was a little wrinkled at the corners, badly framed, and the glass was specked with dust.

"That's me," the old man said.

Marvin turned and looked at the old man, looked back at the poster.

"It's me before wrinkles and bad knees."

"You were a professional wrestler?" Marvin said.

"Naw, I was selling shoes. You're slow on the upbeat, kid. Good thing I was out taking my walk again or flies would be having you for lunch."

"Why were you called X-Man?"

"'Cause you got in the ring with me, they could cross you off the list. Put an X through your name. Shit, I think that was it. It's been so long ago, I ain't sure no more. What's your name, by the way?"

"Marvin."

"All right, Marvin, let's you and me go over to the ring."

———

The old man dodged through the ropes easily. Marvin found the ropes were pulled taut, and he had more trouble sliding between them than he thought. Once in the ring, the old man said, "Here's the thing. What I'm gonna do is I'm gonna give you a first lesson, and you're gonna listen to me."

"Okay."

"What I want—and I ain't fucking with you here—is I want you to come at me hard as you can. Try and hit me, take me down, bite my ear off. Whatever."

"I can't hurt you."

"I know that."

"I'm not saying I'm not willing," Marvin said. "I'm saying I know I can't. You've beat a guy twice I've had trouble with, and his friends, and I couldn't do nothing, so I know I can't hurt you."

"You got a point, kid. But I'm wantin' you to try. It's a lesson."

"You'll teach me how to defend myself?"

"Sure."

Marvin charged, ducking low, planning to try and take the old man's feet. The old man squatted, almost sitting on his ass, and threw a quick uppercut.

Marvin dreamed he was flying. Then falling. The lights in the place were spotted suddenly. Then the spots went away and there was only brightness. Marvin rolled over on the mat and tried to get up. His eye hurt something awful.

"You hit me," he said when he made a sitting position.

The old man was in a corner of the ring, leaning on the ropes.

"Don't listen to shit like someone saying 'Come and get me.' That's foolish. That's leading you into something you might not like. Play your game."

"You told me to."

"That's right, kid, I did. That's your first lesson. Think for yourself, and don't listen to some fool giving you advice, and like I said, play your own game."

"I don't have a game," Marvin said.

"We both know that, kid. But we can fix it."

Marvin gingerly touched his eye. "So, you're going to teach me?"

"Yeah, but the second lesson is this. Now, you got to listen to every goddamn word I say."

"But you said…"

"I know what I said, but part of lesson two is this: Life is full of all kinds of contradictions."

———

It was easy to get loose to go to practice, but it wasn't easy getting there. Marvin still had the bullies to worry about. He got up early and went, telling his mother he was exercising at the school track.

The old man's home turned out to be what was left of an old TB hospital, which was why the old man bought it cheap, sometime at the far end of the Jurassic, Marvin figured.

The old man taught him how to move, how to punch, how to wrestle, how to throw. When Marvin threw the X-Man, the old guy would land lightly and get up quickly, and complain about how it was done. When the workout was done, Marvin showered in the big room behind the faded curtain and went home the long way, watching for bullies.

After a while, he began to feel safe, having figured out that whatever time schedule the delinquents kept, it wasn't early morning, and it didn't seem to be early evening.

When summer ended and school started up, Marvin went before and after school to train, told his mother he was studying boxing with some kids at the Y. She was all right with that. She had work and the housepainter on her mind. The guy would be sitting there when Marvin came home evenings. Sitting there looking at the TV, not even nodding when Marvin came in, sometimes sitting in the padded TV chair with Marvin's mother on his knee, his arm around her waist, her giggling like a schoolgirl. It was enough to gag a maggot.

It got so home was not a place Marvin wanted to be. He liked the old man's place. He liked the training. He threw lefts and rights, hooks and uppercuts, into a bag the old man hung up. He sparred with the old man, who once he got tired—and considering his age, it seemed a long time—would just knock him down and go lean on the ropes and breathe heavily for a while.

One day, after they had finished, sitting in chairs near the ring, Marvin said, "So, how am I helping you train?"

"You're a warm body, for one thing. And I got this fight coming up."

"A fight?"

"What are you, an echo? Yeah. I got a fight coming up. Every five years me and Jesus the Bomb go at it. On Christmas Eve."

Marvin just looked at him. The old man looked back, said, "Think I'm too old? How old are you?"

"Seventeen."

"Can I whip your ass, kid?"

"Everyone can whip my ass."

"All right, that's a point you got there," the old man said.

"Why every five years?" Marvin asked. "Why this Jesus guy?"

"Maybe I'll tell you later," the old man said.

———

Things got bad at home.

Marvin hated the painter and the painter hated him. His mother loved the painter, and stood by him. Everything Marvin tried to do was tainted by the painter. He couldn't take the trash out fast enough. He wasn't doing good enough in school for the painter, like the painter had ever graduated so much as kindergarten. Nothing satisfied the painter, and when Marvin complained to his mother, it was the painter she stood behind.

The painter was nothing like his dad, nothing, and he hated him. One day he told his mother he'd had enough. It was him or the painter.

She chose the painter.

"Well, I hope the crooked painting son-of-a-bitch makes you happy," he said.

"Where did you learn such language?" she asked.

He had learned a lot of it from the old man, but he said, "The painter."

"Did not," his mother said.

"Did too."

Marvin put his stuff in a suitcase that belonged to the painter and left. He waited for his mother to come chasing after him, but she didn't. She called out as he went up the street, "You're old enough. You'll be all right."

He found himself at the old man's place.

Inside the doorway, suitcase in hand, the old man looked at him, nodded at the suitcase, said, "What you doing with that shit?"

"I got thrown out," Marvin said. Not quite the truth, but he felt it was close enough.

"You mean to stay here? That what you're after?"

"Just till I get on my feet."

"On your feet?" the X-Man said. "You ain't got no job. You ain't got dick. You're like a fucking vagabond."

"Yeah," Marvin said. "Well, all right."

Marvin turned around, thinking maybe he could go home and kiss some ass, maybe tell the painter he was a good guy or something. He got to the door and the old man said, "Where the fuck you going?"

"Leaving. You wanted me to, didn't you?"

"Did I say that? Did I say anything like that? I said you were a vagabond. I didn't say something about leaving. Here. Give me the goddamn suitcase."

Before Marvin could do anything, X-Man took it and started down the hall toward the great room. Marvin watched him go; a wiry, balding, white-haired old man with a slight bowlegged limp to his walk.

One night, watching wrestling on TV, the old man, having sucked down a six-pack, said, "This is shit. Bunch a fucking tough acrobats. This ain't wrestling. It ain't boxing, and it sure ain't fighting. It's like a movie show or something. When we wrestled in fairs, we really wrestled. These big-ass fuckers wouldn't know a wrist lock from a dick jerk. Look at that shit. Guy waits for the fucker to climb on the ropes and jump on him. And what kind of hit is that? That was a real hit, motherfucker would be dead, hitting him in the throat like that. He's slapping the guy's chest high up, that's all. Cocksuckers."

"When you wrestled, where did you do it?" Marvin asked.

The old man clicked off the TV. "I can't take no more of that shit... Where did I wrestle? I rode the rails during the Great Depression. I was ten years old on them rails, and I'd go from town to town and watch guys wrestle at fairs, and I began to pick it up. When I was fifteen, I said I was eighteen, and they believed me, ugly as I was. I mean, who wants to think a kid can be so goddamn ugly, you know. So by the end of the Great Depression I'm wrestling all over the place. Let me see, it's 1992, so I been doing it awhile. Come the war, they wouldn't let me go because of a rupture. I used to wrap that sucker up with a bunch of sheet strips and go and wrestle. I could have fought Japs bundled up like that if they'd let me. Did have to stop now and then when my nuts stuck out of the rip in my balls. I'd cross my legs, suck it up and push them back in, cinch up those strips of sheet, and keep on keeping on. I could have done that in the war, but they was all prissy about it. Said it'd be a problem. So I didn't kill no Japs. I could have, though. Germans. Hungarians. Martians. I could kill anybody they put me in front of. 'Course, glad I didn't in one way. Ain't good to kill a man. But them son-of-a-bitches were asking for it. Well, I don't know about the Hungarians or the Martians, but the rest of them bastards were.

"I learned fighting by hard knocks. Now and then I met some guys knew a thing or two, and I picked it up. Some of them Jap tricks and the like. I had folks down in Mexico. So when I was in my twenties, I went there and became a wrestler for money."

"Wasn't that fake?"

The old man gave Marvin a look that made the water inside Marvin's body boil.

"There was them that put on shows, but then there was us. Me and Jesus, and ones like us. We did the real thing. We was hitting and kicking and locking and throwing. Look at this."

The old man jerked up a sleeve on his sweatshirt. There was a mark there like a tire track. "See that. Jesus bit me. I had him in a clench, and he bit me. Motherfucker. 'Course, that's what I'd have done. Anyway, he got loose on account of it. He had this technique—the

Bomb, he called it, how he got his nickname. He'd grab you in a bear hug, front or back, lift you up and fall back and drive your head into the mat. You got that done to you once or twice, you felt like your ears were wiggling around your asshole. It was something. Me, I had me the step-over-toe-hold. That was my move, and still is."

"Did you use it on Jesus?"

"Nope. He got the Bomb on me. After the Bomb I thought I was in Africa fucking a gorilla. I didn't know my dick from a candlewick."

"But you're still wrestling him?"

"Haven't beat him yet. I've tried every hold there is, every move, every kind of psychology I know, and nothing. It's the woman. Felina Valdez. She's got the mojo on me, the juju, the black doo-doo, and the silent dog whistle. Whatever there is that makes you stupid, she's got it on me."

Marvin didn't follow any of that, but he didn't say anything. He drank his glass of tea while X-Man drank another beer. He knew he would come back to the subject eventually. That's how he worked.

"Let me tell you about Felina. She was a black-eyed maiden, had smooth, dark skin. A priest saw her walking down the street, he'd go home and cut his throat. First time I seen her, that stack of dynamite was in a blue dress so tight you could count the hairs on her thingamajig.

"She was there in the crowd to watch the wrestling. She's in the front row with her legs crossed, and her dress is slithering up to her knee like a snake creeping, and I'm getting a pretty good look, you see. Not seeing the vine-covered canyon, but I'm in the neighborhood. And looking at that broad, I'm almost killed by this wrestler named Joey the Yank. Guy from Maine who takes my legs out from under me and butts me and gets me in an arm bar. I barely manage to work out of it, get him and throw him and latch on my step-over-toe-hold. I put that on you, you pass through time, baby.

Past and future, and finally you're looking at your own goddamn grave. He tapped out.

"Next thing I know this blue-dress doll is sliding up next to me taking my arm, and, well, kid, from that point on I was a doomed man. She could do more tricks with a dick than a magician could with a deck of cards. I thought she was going to kill me, but I thought too it was one hell of a good way to go. Hear what I'm saying?"

"Yes, sir," Marvin said.

"This is all kind of nasty talk for a kid, ain't it?"

"No, sir," Marvin said.

"Fuck it. You're damn near eighteen. By now you got to know about pussy."

"I know what it is," Marvin said.

"No, kid. You talk like you know where it is, not what it is. Me, I was lost in that stuff. I might as well have let her put my nuts in a vise and crank it. She started going to all my fights. And I noticed something pretty quick. I gave a great performance, won by a big margin, the loving was great. It was a mediocre fight, so was the bedding. I had it figured. She wasn't so much in love with me as she was a good fight and my finishing move, the step-over-toe-hold. She had me teach it to her. I let her put it on me one time, and kid, I tell you, way she latched it, I suddenly had some mercy for all them I'd used it on. I actually had to work my way out of it, like I was in a match, 'cause she wasn't giving me no quarter. That was a cheap price to pay though, all that savage monkey love I was getting, and then it all come apart.

"Jesus beat me. Put the Bomb on me. When I woke up I was out back of the carnival lying on the grass with ants biting me. When I came to myself, Felina was gone. She went with Jesus. Took my money, left me with nothing but ant bites on my nuts."

"She sounds shallow."

"As a saucer, kid. But once she slapped that hoodoo on me, I couldn't cut myself loose. Let me tell you, it was like standing on the railroad tracks in the dark of night, and you can see a train coming, the light sweeping the tracks, and you can't step off. All you can do is stand there and wait for it to hit you. One time when we were together, we're walking in Mexico City, where I had some bouts, and she sees a guy with a wooden cage full of pigeons, six or seven of them. She has me buy all of them, like we're gonna take them back to the States. But what she does is she takes them back to our hotel room. We had to sneak them in. She puts the cage on an end table and just looks at the birds. I give them some bread, you know, 'cause they got to eat, and I clean out their cage, and I think: this girl is one crazed bird lover. I go and take a shower, tell her to order up some dinner.

"I take my time in there. Shit and shave, good hot shower. When I come out, there she is, sitting at one of those little push tables room service brings up, and she's eating fried chicken. Didn't wait on me, didn't say boo. She was like that. Everything was about her. But right then I learned something else. I saw that cage of birds, and they were all dead. I asked her what happened to the birds, and she says, 'I got tired of them.'

"I went and looked, and their necks was wrung."

"But why?" Marvin asked.

The old man leaned back and sucked his beer, took his time before he spoke. "I don't know, kid. Right then I should have thrown my shit in a bag and got the hell out of there. But I didn't. It's like I told you about those train tracks. Christ, kid. You should have seen her. There wasn't never nothing like her, and I couldn't let her go. It's like you catch the finest fish in the world, and someone's telling you to throw it back, and all you can think about is that thing fried up and laid out on a bed of rice. Only it ain't really nothing like that. There ain't no describing it. And then, like I said, she went off with Jesus, and everyday I get up my heart burns for her. My mind says I'm lucky to be shed of her, but my heart, it don't listen. I don't even blame

Jesus for what he done. How could he not want her? She belonged to whoever could pin the other guy to the mat. Me and him, we don't fight nobody else anymore, just each other. Ever five years. If I win, I get her back. I know that. He knows that. And Felina knows that. He wins, he keeps her. So far, he keeps her. It's best he does. I ought to let it go, kid, but I can't."

"She really that bad?"

"She's the best bad girl ever. She's a bright red apple with a worm in the center. Since that woman's been with Jesus, he left a wife, had two of his children die, one in a house fire that happened while he was out, and Felina gave birth to two babies that both died within a week. Some kind of thing happens now and then. Cradle death, something like that. On top of that she's screwed just about everyone short of a couple of eunuchs, but she stays with Jesus, and he keeps her. He keeps her because she has a power, kid. She can hold you to her tight as liver cancer. Ain't no getting away from that bitch. She lets you go, you still want her like you want a drink when you're a drunk."

"The way you mentioned the fire and Jesus's kids, the two babies that died...you sounded like—"

"Like I didn't believe the fire was no accident? That the babies didn't die naturally? Yeah, kid. I was thinking about that cage full of pigeons. I was thinking about how she used to cut my hair, and how she had this little box she had with her, kept it in the purse she carried. I seen her wrap some hair into the knot of a couple twisted pipe cleaners. Oh, hell. You already think I'm nuts."

Marvin shook his head. "No. No, I don't."

"All right, then. I think she really did have the hoodoo on me. I read somewhere that people who know spells can get a piece of your hair and they can use that as part of that spell, and it can tie you to them. I read that."

"That doesn't mean it's true," Marvin said.

"I know that, kid. I know how I sound. And when it's midday I think thinking like that is so much dog shit, but it gets night, or it's early morning and the light's just starting to creep in, I believe it. And I guess I always believed it. I think she's got me in a spell. Ain't nothing else would explain why I would want that cheating, conniving, pigeon-killing, house-burning, baby-murdering bitch back. It don't make no sense, does it?"

"No, sir," Marvin said, and then after a moment he added, "She's pretty old now, isn't she?"

"'Course she is. You think time stood still? She ain't the same. But, neither am I. Neither is Jesus. But it's me and him, and one of us gets the girl, and so far he always gets her. What I want is to have her back, die quick, and have one of those Greek funerals. That way I get the prize, but I don't have to put up with it."

"What's a Greek funeral?"

"Heroes like Hercules had them. When he died they put him on a pile of sticks and such and burned up the body, let his smoke rise to the heavens. Beats being buried in the ground or cooked up in some oven, your ashes scraped into a sack. Or having to spend your last days out with that woman, though that's exactly what I'm trying to do."

"Do Jesus and Felina live here in the city?" Marvin asked.

"They don't live nowhere. They got a motor trailer. And they got some retirement money. Like me. Jesus and me worked other jobs as well as wrestled. You couldn't make it just on the wrestling circuit, especially the underground circuit, so we got some of that social security money coming, thank goodness. They drive around to different places. He trains, and he comes back every five years. Each time I see him, it's like there's this look in his eyes that says 'Beat me this time and take this bitch off my hands.' Only he always fights like a bear and I can't beat him."

"You win, sure she'll go with you?"

"It's me or him, and that's all there is to it. Ain't nobody else now. Me or him. It's us she's decided to suck dry and make miserable."

"Can't you let it go?" Marvin asked.

X-Man laughed. It was a dark laugh, like a dying man that suddenly understands an old joke. "Wish I could, kid, 'cause if I could, I would."

———

They trained for the fight.

X-Man would say: "This is what Jesus the Bomb does. He comes at you, and next thing you know you're on your ass, 'cause he grabs you like this, or like this. And he can switch from this to this." And so on.

Marvin did what he was told. He tried Jesus's moves. Every time he did, he'd lose. The old man would twist him, throw him, lock him, punch him (lightly) and even when Marvin felt he was getting good at it, X-Man would outsmart him in the end and come out of something Marvin thought an oiled weasel couldn't slither out of. When it was over, it was Marvin panting in the corner, X-Man wiping sweat off his face with a towel.

"That how Jesus does it?" Marvin asked, after trying all of the moves he had been taught.

"Yeah," said the old man, "except he does it better."

———

This went on for months, getting closer and closer to the day when the X-Man and Jesus the Bomb were to go at it. Got so Marvin was so focused on the training, he forgot all about the bullies.

Until one day Marvin was by himself, coming out of the store two blocks from the old man's place, carrying a sack with milk and vanilla cookies in it, and there's Hard Belly. He spotted Marvin and started across the street, pulling his hands out of his pockets, smiling.

"Well, now," Hard Belly said when he was near Marvin. "I bet you forgot about me, didn't you? Like I wasn't gonna get even. This time you ain't got your fossil to protect you."

Marvin put the sack on the sidewalk. "I'm not asking for trouble."

"That don't mean you ain't gonna get some," Hard Belly said, standing right in front of Marvin. Marvin didn't really plan on anything—he wasn't thinking about it—but when Hard Belly moved closer, his left jab popped out and hit him in the nose. Down went Hard Belly like he had been hit with a baseball bat. Marvin couldn't believe it, couldn't believe how hard his punch was, how good it was. He knew right then and there it was over between him and Hard Belly, because he wasn't scared anymore. He picked up the sack and walked back to the old man's place, left Hard Belly napping.

One night, during the time school was out for the Thanksgiving holiday, Marvin woke up. He was sleeping in the boxing ring, a blanket over him, and he saw there was a light on by the old man's bed. The old man was sitting on the edge of it, bent over, pulling boxes out from beneath. He reached in one and pulled out a magazine, then another. He spread the magazines on the bed and looked at them.

Marvin got up and climbed out of the ring and went over to him. The old man looked up. "Damn, kid. I wake you?"

"Woke up on my own. What you doing?"

"Looking at these old magazines. They're underground fight magazines. Had to order them through the mail. Couldn't buy them off the stands."

Marvin looked at the open magazines on the bed. They had a lot of photographs in them. From the poster on the wall, he recognized photographs of X-Man.

"You were famous," Marvin said.

"In a way, I suppose," X-Man said. "I look at these, I got to hate getting old. I wasn't no peach to look at, but I was strong then, looked better than now. Ain't much of the young me left."

"Is Jesus in them?"

X-Man flipped a page on one of the open magazines, and there was a photograph of a squatty man with a black mop of hair. The man's chest was almost as hairy. He had legs like tree trunks.

X-Man grinned. "I know what you're thinking. Couple mugs like me and Jesus, what kind of love magnets are we? Maybe Felina ain't the prime beaver I say she is?"

The old man went around to the head of the bed and dragged a small cardboard box out from under it. He sat it on the bed between them, popped the lid, and scrounged around in a pile of yellowed photographs. He pulled one out. It was slightly faded, but it was clear enough. The woman in it looked maybe mid-twenties. It was a full shot, and she was indeed a knockout. Black hair, high cheek-bones, full lips, and black as the Pit eyes that jumped out of the photo and landed somewhere in the back of Marvin's head.

There were other photos of her, and he showed Marvin all of them. There were close shots and far shots, and sneaky camera shots that rested on her ass. She was indeed fabulous to look at.

"She ain't that way now, but she's still got it somehow. What I was gonna do, kid, was gather up all these photos and pile them and burn them, then I was gonna send word to Jesus he could forget the match. That Felina was his until the end of time. But I think that every few years or so, and then I don't do it. You know what Jesus told me once? He said she liked to catch flies. Use a drinking glass and trap them, then stick a needle through them, string them on thread. Bunches of them. She'd knot one end, fasten the other to a wall with a thumbtack, watch them try to fly. Swat a fly, that's one thing. But something like that, I don't get it, kid. And knowing that, I ought to not get her. But it don't work that way... Tell you what, you go on to bed. Me, I'm gonna turn off the light and turn in."

Marvin went and crawled under his blanket, adjusted the pillow under his head. When he looked at the old man, he still had the light on and had the cardboard box with the pictures in his lap. He was holding up a photograph, looking at it like it was a hand-engraved invitation to the Second Coming.

As Marvin drifted off, all he could think about were those flies on the thread.

———

Next day the old man didn't wake him for the morning work-out, and when Marvin finally opened his eyes it was nearly noon. The old man was nowhere to be seen. He got up and went to the refrigerator to have some milk. There was a note on the door.

DON'T EAT HEAVY. I'M BRINGING THANKSGIVING.

Marvin hadn't wanted to spend Thanksgiving with his mother and the painter, so he hadn't really thought about it at all. Once his mother dropped him out of her mind, he had dropped the holidays out of his. But right then he thought about them, and hoped the painter would choke on a turkey bone.

He poured a glass of milk and sat in a chair by the ring and sipped it.

Not long after, the old man came back with a sack of groceries. Marvin got up and went over to him. "I'm sorry. I missed the workout."

"You didn't miss nothing. It's a fucking holiday. Even someone needs as much training as you ought to have a day off."

The old man pulled things out of the sack. Turkey lunch meat, some cheese slices, and a loaf of good bread, the kind you had to cut with a knife. And there was a can of cranberry sauce.

"It ain't exactly a big carving turkey, but it'll be all right," the old man said.

They made sandwiches and sat in the TV chairs with a little table between them. They placed their plates there, the old man put a video in his aging machine, and they watched a movie. An old black-and-white one. Marvin liked color, and he was sure he would hate it. It was called *NIGHT AND THE CITY*. It was about wrestling. Marvin didn't hate it. He loved it. He ate his sandwich. He looked at the old man, chewing without his dentures. Right then he knew he loved him as dearly as if he were his father.

———

Next day they trained hard. Marvin had gotten so he was more of a challenge for the old man, but he still couldn't beat him.

On the morning of the bout with Jesus, Marvin got up and went out to the store. He had some money X-Man gave him now and then for being a training partner, and he bought a few items and took them home. One of them was a bottle of liniment, and when he got back he used it to give the old man a rubdown.

When that was done, the old man stretched out on the floor on an old mattress, and fell asleep as easily as a kitten. While he slept, Marvin took the rest of the stuff he had bought into the bathroom and made a few arrangements. He brought the bag out and wadded it up and shoved it in the trash.

Then he did what the old man had instructed him to do. He got folding chairs out of the closet, twenty-five of them, and set them up near the ring. He put one of them in front of the others, close to the ring.

At four-fifteen, he gently spoke to the old man, called him awake.

The old man got up and showered and put on red tights and a T-shirt with a photograph of his younger self on it. The words under the photograph read: X-MAN.

It was Christmas Eve.

About seven that evening they began to arrive. On sticks, in wheelchairs and on walkers, supported by each other and, in a couple of cases, walking unassisted. They came to the place in dribbles, and Marvin helped them locate a chair. The old man had stored away some cheap wine and beer, and had even gone all out for a few boxes of crackers and a suspicious-looking cheese ball. These he arranged on a long foldout table to the left of the chairs. The old people, mostly men, descended on it like vultures alighting on fresh roadkill. Marvin had to help some of them who were so old and decrepit they couldn't hold a paper plate and walk at the same time.

Marvin didn't see anyone that he thought looked like Jesus and Felina. If one of the four women was Felina, she was certainly way past any sex appeal, and if any one of them was Jesus, X-Man had it in the bag. But, of course, none of them were either.

About eight o'clock Marvin answered a hard knocking on the door. When he opened it, there was Jesus. He was wearing a dark robe with red trim. It was open in front, and Marvin could see he had on black tights and no shirt. He was gray-haired where he had hair left on his head, and there was a thick thatch of gray hair on his chest, nestled there like a carefully constructed bird's nest. He had the same simian build as in the photograph. The Bomb looked easily ten years younger than his age; he moved easily, and well.

With him was a tall woman and it was easy to recognize her, even from ancient photos. Her hair was still black, though certainly it came out of a bottle now, and she had aged well, looked firm of face and high of bone. Marvin thought maybe she'd had some work. She looked like a movie star in her fifties that still gets work for her beauty. Her eyes were like wells, and Marvin had to be careful not to fall into them. She had on a long black dress with a black coat hanging off her shoulders in a sophisticated way. It had a fur collar that at first glance looked pretty good and at second glance showed signs of decay, like a sleeping animal with mange.

"I'm here to wrestle," Jesus said.

"Yes, sir," Marvin said.

The woman smiled at Marvin, and her teeth were white and magnificent, and looked as real as his own. Nothing was said, but in some way or another he knew he was to take her coat, and he did. He followed after her and Jesus, and, watching Felina walk, Marvin realized he was sexually aroused. She was pretty damn amazing, considering her age, and he was reminded of an old story he had read about a succubus; a female spirit that preyed on men, sexually depleted them, and took their souls.

When Felina sashayed in and the old man saw her, there was a change in his appearance. His face flushed and he stood erect. She owned him.

Marvin put Felina's coat away, and when he hung it in the closet, a smell came off it that was sweet and tantalizing. He thought some of it was perfume, but knew most of it was her.

Jesus and X-Man shook hands and smiled at each other, but X-Man couldn't take his eyes off of Felina. She moved past them both, as if unaware of their presence, and without being told took the chair that had been placed in front of the others.

The old man called Marvin over and introduced him to Jesus. "This kid is my protégé, Jesus. He's pretty good. Like me, maybe, when I started out, if I'd had a broke leg."

They both laughed. Marvin even laughed. He had begun to understand this was wrestling humor and that he had in fact been given a great compliment.

"You think you're gonna beat me this year?" Jesus said. "I sometimes don't think you're really trying."

"Oh, I'm trying all right," X-Man said.

Jesus was still smiling, but now the smile look pinned there when he spoke. "You win, you know she'll go with you?"

The old man nodded.

"Why do we keep doing this?" Jesus said.

X-Man shook his head.

"Well," Jesus said. "Good luck. And I mean it. But you're in for a fight."

"I know that," X-Man said.

—

It was nine o'clock when X-Man and Jesus took out their teeth and climbed into the ring, took some time to stretch. The chairs in the audience were near half empty and those that were seated were spread apart like Dalmatian spots. Marvin stood on the outside of the ropes at the old man's corner.

The old man came and leaned on the ropes. One of the elders in the audience, wearing red pants pulled up near to his armpits, dragged his chair next to the side of the ring, scraping it across the floor as he went. He had a cowbell in his free hand. He wheezed himself into the seat, placed the bell on his knee. He produced a large watch from his pants pocket and placed it on his other knee. He looked sleepy.

"We do this five years from now," X-Man said to Marvin, "it'll be in hell somewhere, and the devil will be our timekeeper."

"All right," said the timekeeper. "Geezer rules. Two minutes rounds. Three minutes rests. Goes until it's best two out of three or someone quits. Everybody ready?"

Both parties said they were.

Marvin looked at Felina. She was sitting with her hands in her lap. She appeared confident and smug, like a spider waiting patiently on a fly.

The timekeeper hit the watch with his left thumb and rang the bell with his right hand. X-Man and Jesus came together with a smacking sound, grabbing at each other's knees for a throw, bobbing and weaving. And then X-Man came up from a bob and threw a quick left. To Marvin's amazement, Jesus slipped it over his shoulder and hooked X-Man in the ribs. It was a solid shot, and Marvin could tell X-Man felt it. X-Man danced back, and one elderly man in the small crowd booed.

"Go fuck yourself," X-Man yelled out.

X-Man and the Bomb came together again. There was a clenching of hands on shoulders, and Jesus attempted to knee X-Man in the balls. X-Man was able to turn enough to take it on the side of the leg, but not in the charlie horse point. They whirled around and around, like angry lovers at a dance.

Finally X-Man faked, dove for Jesus' knee, got hold of it, but Jesus twisted on him, brought one leg over X-Man's head, hooked the leg under his neck and rolled, grabbed X-Man's arm, stretched it out, and lifted his pelvis against it. There was a sound like someone snapping a stick over their knee, and X-Man tapped out. That ended the round. It had gone less than forty-five seconds.

X-Man waddled over to his corner, nursing his arm a little. He leaned on the ropes. Marvin brought out the stool.

"Put it back," the old man said. "I don't want them to think I'm hurt."

Marvin put it back, said, "Are you hurt?"

"Yeah, but that cracking you heard was just air bubbles in my arm. I'm fine. Fuck it. Put the stool back."

Marvin put the stool back. X-Man sat down. Across the way Jesus was seated on his stool, his head hung. He and X-Man looked like two men who wouldn't have minded being shot.

"I know this," X-Man said. "This is my last match. After this, I ain't got no more in me. I can feel what's left of me running out of my feet."

Marvin glanced at Felina. One of the lights overhead was wearing out. It popped and went from light to dark and back to light again. Marvin thought for a moment, there in the shadow,

Felina had looked older, and fouler, and her thick hair had resembled a bundle of snakes. But as he looked more closely, it was just the light.

The cowbell clattered. They had gotten some of their juice back. They moved around each other, hands outstretched. They finally clinched their fingers together, both hands. X-Man suddenly jutted his fingers forward in a way that allowed him to clench down on the back of Jesus' fingers, snap him to the floor in pain. It was a simple move, but it put the Bomb's face in front of X-Man's knee. X-Man kneed him in the face so hard, blood spewed all over the matting, all over X-Man.

Still clutching Jesus' fingers, X-Man stepped back and squatted, pulled Jesus to his face. X-Man pulled free of the fingers, and as Jesus tried to rise, X-Man kicked him in the face. It was a hard kick. Jesus went unconscious.

The cowbell clattered. The timekeeper put the cowbell down and made his way to the ring. He climbed through and hitch-legged it over to Jesus. It took almost as much time as it would take for a blind man to find a needle in a haystack.

The timekeeper got down on one knee. Jesus groaned and sat up slowly.

His face was a bloody mess.

The timekeeper looked him over. "You up for it?" he said.

"Hell, yeah," Jesus said.

"One to one!" yelled the timekeeper, and he made his slow pilgrimage back to his chair.

Jesus got up slowly, went back to his corner, trying to hold his head up high. X-Man was sitting on his stool, breathing heavily. "I hope I didn't break something inside the old cocksucker," he said.

X-Man closed his eyes and sat resting on his stool. Marvin was quiet. He thought the old man was asleep. Three minutes later, the cowbell clattered.

Jesus huffed loudly, creaked bones off the stool, stuttered-stepped to the center of the ring. X-Man came out in a slow shuffle.

They exchanged a few punches, none of which landed particularly well. Surprisingly, both seemed to have gotten a second wind. They tossed one another, and rolled, and jabbed, and gouged, and the bell rang again.

When X-Man was on his stool, he said, "My heart feels like a bird fluttering."

"You ought to quit," Marvin said. "It's not worth a heart attack."

"It ain't fluttering from the fight, but from seeing Felina."

Marvin looked. Felina was looking at X-Man the way a puppy looks at a dog treat.

"Don't fall for it," Marvin said. "She's evil. Goddamn evil."

"So you believe me?"

"I do. You think maybe she has those pipe cleaners with your hair with her?"

"How would I know?"

"In her coat, maybe?"

"Again, how would I know." And then it hit the old man. He knew what Marvin was getting at. "You mean if she did have, and you got them…"

"Yeah," Marvin said.

Marvin left X-Man sitting there, made a bee-line for the closet. He opened the door and moved his hands around in there, trying to look like he was about natural business. He glanced back at X-Man, who had turned on his stool to look.

The cowbell rang. The two old gentlemen went at it again.

———

It was furious. Slamming punches to the head and ribs, the breadbasket. Clutching one another, kneeing in the balls. Jesus even bit the lobe off X-Man's ear. Blood was everywhere. It was a fight that would have been amazing if the two men in the ring were in their twenties, in top shape. At their age it was phenomenal.

Marvin was standing in the old man's corner now, trying to catch X-Man's eye, but not in a real obvious way. He didn't want him to lose focus, didn't want Jesus to come under him and lift him up and drive the old man's head into the ground like a lawn dart.

Finally the two clenched. They went around and around like that, breathing heavy as steam engines. Marvin caught X-Man's eye. Marvin lifted up two knotted pipe cleaners, dark hair in the middle of the knot. Marvin untwisted the pipe cleaners and the hair floated out like a puff of dark dandruff, drifted to the floor.

X-Man let out his breath, seemed to relax.

Jesus dove for him. It was like a hawk swooping down on a mouse. Next thing Marvin knew, Jesus had X-Man low on the hips in a two-arm clench, and was lifting him up, bending back at the same time so he could drive X-Man over his head, straight into the mat.

But as X-Man went over, he ducked his head under Jesus' buttocks, grasped the inside of Jesus' legs. Jesus flipped backwards, but X-Man landed on his back, not his head. Instead, his head was poking between Jesus' legs, and his toothless gums were buried in Jesus' tights, clamping down on his balls like a clutched fist. A cry went up from the crowd.

Jesus screamed. It was the kind of scream that went down your back and got hold of your tailbone and pulled at it. X-Man maintained the clamp. Jesus writhed and twisted and kicked and punched. The punches hit X-Man in the top of the head, but still he clung. When Jesus tried to roll out, X-Man rolled with him, his gums still buried deep in Jesus' balls.

Some of the oldsters were standing up from their seats, yelling with excitement. Felina hadn't moved or changed her expression.

Then it happened.

Jesus slapped out both hands on the mat, called "Time." And it was over.

———

The elders left. Except Jesus and Felina.

Jesus stayed in the bathroom for a long time. When he came out, he was limping. The front of his tights were plumped out and dark with blood.

X-Man was standing, one hand on the back of a chair, breathing heavy.

Jesus said, "You about took my nuts, X-Man. I took one of your towels, shoved it down my pants to stop the blood. Them's some gums you got, X-Man. Gums like that, you don't need teeth."

"All's fair in love and war," X-Man said. "Besides, old as you are, what you using your nuts for?"

"I hear that," Jesus said, and his whole demeanor was different. He was like a bird in a cage with the door left open. He was ready to fly out.

"She's all yours," Jesus said.

We all looked at Felina. She smiled slightly. She took X-Man's hand.

X-man turned and looked at her. He said, "I don't want her," and let go of her hand. "Hell, I done outlived my dick anyhow."

The look on Felina's face was one of amazement.

"You won her," Jesus said. "That's the rule."

"Naw," X-Man said. "Ain't no rule."

"No?" Jesus said, and you could almost see that cage door slam and lock.

"No," said X-Man, looking at Felina. "That hoodoo you done with the pipe cleaners. My boy here undid it."

"What the fuck are you talking about?" Felina said.

They just stared at each other for a long moment.

"Get out," X-Man said. "And Jesus. We ain't doing this no more."

"You don't want her?" Jesus said.

"No. Get out. Take the bitch with you. Get on out."

Out they went. When Felina turned the corner into the hallway, she paused and looked back. It was a look that said: You had me, and you let me go, and you'll have regrets.

X-Man just grinned at her. "Hit the road, you old bitch."

When they were gone, the old man stretched out on his bed, breathing heavily. Marvin pulled a chair nearby and sat. The old man looked at him and laughed.

"That pipe cleaner and hair wasn't in her coat, was it?"

"What do you mean?" Marvin said.

"That look on her face when I mentioned it. She didn't know what I was talking about. Look at me, boy. Tell me true."

Marvin took a moment, said, "I bought the pipe cleaners and some shoe polish. I cut a piece of my hair, made it dark with the shoe polish, twisted it up in the pipe cleaners."

X-Man let out a hoot. "You sneaky son-of-a-bitch."

"I'm sorry," Marvin said.

"I'm not."

"You're not?"

"Nope. I learned something important. I'm a fucking dope. She didn't never have no power over me I didn't give her. Them pipe cleaners and the hair, hell, she forgot about that fast as she did it. Just some way to pass time for her, and I made it something special. It was just me giving myself an excuse to be in love with someone wasn't worth the gunpowder it would take to blow her ass up. She just liked having power over the both of us. Maybe Jesus will figure that out too. Maybe me and him figured a lot of things out today. It's all right, kid. You done good. Hell, it wasn't nothing I didn't know deep down, and now I'm out of excuses, and I'm done with her. It's like someone just let go of my throat and I can breathe again. All these years, and this thing with Felina, it wasn't nothing but me and my own bullshit."

———

About seven in the morning X-Man woke up Marvin.

"What's the matter?" Marvin asked.

X-Man was standing over him. Giving him a dentureless grin. "Nothing. It's Christmas. Merry Christmas."

"You too," Marvin said.

The old man had a T-shirt. He held it out with both hands. It said "X-Man" and had his photograph on it, just like the one he was wearing. "I want you to have it. I want you to be X-Man."

"I can't be X-Man. No one can."

"I know that. But I want you to try."

Marvin was sitting up now. He took the shirt.

"Put it on," said X-Man.

Marvin slipped off his shirt and, still sitting on the floor, pulled the X-Man shirt over his head. It fit good. He stood up. "But I didn't get you nothing."

"Yeah you did. You got me free."

Marvin nodded. "How do I look?"

"Like X-Man. You know, if I had had a son, I'd have been damn lucky if he'd been like you. Hell, if he'd *been* you. 'Course, that gets into me fucking your mother, and we don't want to talk about that. Now, I'm going back to sleep. Maybe later we'll have something for Christmas dinner."

———

Later in the day Marvin got up, fixed coffee, made a couple of sandwiches, went to wake X-Man.

He didn't wake up. He was cold. He was gone. There were wrestling magazines lying on the bed with him.

"Damn," Marvin said, and sat down in the chair by the bed. He took the old man's hand to hold. There was something in it. A wadded-up photo of Felina. Marvin took it and tossed it on the floor and held the old man's hand for a long time.

After awhile Marvin tore a page out of one of the wrestling magazines, got up and put it to the hot plate. It blazed. He went over and held it burning in one hand while he used the other to pull out one of the boxes of magazines. He set fire to it and pushed it back under the bed. Flames licked around the edges of the bed. Other boxes beneath the bed caught fire. The bedclothes caught. After a moment, the old man caught too. He smelled like pork cooking.

Like Hercules, Marvin thought. He's rising up to the gods.

Marvin, still wearing his X-Man shirt, got his coat out of the closet. The room was filling with smoke and the smell of burning flesh. He put his coat on and strolled around the corner, into the hallway. Just before he went outside, he could feel the heat of the fire warming his back.

Introduction to
ROBO RAPID

The title was the catalyst. I don't know where it came from, but it had been working itself around in my head for at least twenty years, maybe more.

I didn't know what it meant. I had an idea it was a science fiction sort of story, but beyond that was a void.

So, the title was there, nudging me, but I needed a reason to find out what it meant, what the story was about. Bill Schafer gave that to me. He was doing an anthology based on art by David McKean. There were a series of wonderful pieces to pick from. I picked one where a young girl with exotic looks is standing in a desert, looking wistful. I felt I could go a lot of directions with that.

As I started writing, the story popped into place immediately, and instantly I knew what *Robo Rapid* was about. I couldn't wait to get up each morning and work on the story. I'm one of those who averages about three hours in the morning, three to five pages most days, sometimes a lot more, then I'm done. The rest of the story crawls into bed with me when bedtime comes, and in the morning when I put my fingers on the keyboard, it crawls out of me and crawls onto the screen, and finally the page, unless, of course, you read it on an electronic device of some sort.

When I talk about electronic devices, I sound like those folks who refer to the internet as the interweb. I'm a very unlikely writer of science fiction. The reason is, though I love science, and do read articles and books about it, I can't lay claim to much expertise in the matter. I was one of those whose greatest accomplishment with a home chemistry set was turning water blue, outside of the time I mixed outside ingredients, and somehow caused an explosion that blew up one of my test tubes and set a roll of toilet paper on fire.

Yep. Toilet paper.

Trust me, it's a story not worth telling.

In writing *Robo Rapid*, I had in mind the sort of science fiction tales I read as a kid, many of which had younger protagonists. Stories like the kind Andre Norton or Robert Heinlein wrote. Those stories were not always strong on science, but they had the feeling of something real at work. And since the science fiction I liked was primarily adventure, anthropological, and less about nuts and bolts science, I thought this was a great time to take a crack at it. It wasn't the first time I had written stories that fell into the science fiction file drawer, but it was an uncommon enough experience for me career-wise.

As for the story, I decided I wanted to keep it simple, focus on the female narrator and her world. I liked the idea that she has a noble cause in mind, but is about as prepared for adventure as I would be if I was told I was to go to Mars in the morning. I would seriously worry about which books to pack, other than the usual survival guides, though a usual survival guide might not do me much good on Mars.

I wanted my heroine to attempt to solve her problem with wits and spunk. I wanted her to venture into unknown lands. I wanted her to discover alien technology that defied gravity, and I wanted her to come in close and dangerous contact with the source of the story's title, *Robo Rapid*. I was very happy I finally knew what that title was about. A title is lonely without a story.

I wanted the story to have that old-fashioned sense of wonder I got from science fiction early on. This sense of wonder business may be more about being ten or so than it was about true wonders. A lot seemed wondrous then.

But, I like to think I do in fact have inside of me a sense of wonder, and sometimes when I hold my mouth right, I accomplish something that feels like the sort of stories I read way back then.

Truth is, I write a lot of different sorts of stories, and not many are science fiction in nature. But as I said, science fiction was my first passionate love, and I still remember our long nights together. I certainly read a lot of it.

Turned out my mind went other directions when I wrote. I did in fact date science fiction's cousins, fantasy and horror, but science fiction did something to me that still remains. Even though I am drawn more to different types of fiction much of the time, I have a science fiction writer's heart. That heart beats at the core of a lot of stories I write. It gives me a desire to make all of my work engaging, colorful, and from time to time, I can even litter them with decent ideas.

Science fiction taught me that. Its lessons have stayed with me, no matter what I write.

This story, at least in my mind, does fit the science fiction mode, and I like to think it manages to be a pretty cool coming of age story as well.

I'm so happy to finally find out what *Robo Rapid* means. It's as if my future self paid a visit to my younger self, and as a joke, whispered the title in my ear, and said, "Now, figure it out. You have a story to write."

I figured it out. I'm here now, in the present from which I came to suggest the title to my younger self. Thanks, older self, which is me, and thanks younger self who listened. Wow. Time travel can certainly be confusing.

ROBO
RAPID

When I unwound the cloak it was heavy and wide, having belonged to my father and being made to accommodate his size. I laid on half of it and folded the other half over me, covering my head against the blowing sand. If I was lucky, the sand wouldn't cover me so deep I would smother. Even though the night air was chill, I was warm beneath the fold of the cloak. My smaller bag of items rested beneath my head for a pillow. I watched the stars until I fell asleep.

I was two days out, and so far I had only found more sand, and as morning came and the sun shone bright, I could see the air was decorated with thin lines of sand that seemed to hang in the air like a beaded curtain.

I thought of the bad things that had brought me here, and for a moment I wished I hadn't come, that I had stayed with Grandfather back on the Flatlands. But that thought passed. Somewhere out there were my brother and sister, and I planned to find them.

So far, I hadn't found squat and I had sand in my teeth.

—

The night it all started, I had gone out behind one of the small sand dunes to answer the call of nature, and was just wrapping that up when I heard the machines. Peeking around the edge of the dune I saw them coming, slipping out from the shadows between high, drifting dunes, the moonlight bouncing off of their blue and white bodies. They came on tall and wide, strutting, hissing, clanging and clattering like large, metallic men, which was exactly what they were, toward those of our tribe who had gathered around the roaring fire. You could clearly see written across the machines' sides in bold black letters: robo rapid. There were three of them.

My parents, my brother and sister, like all the others, tried to run, but it was too late because the machines were swift and the camels were hobbled too far away for my people to free them and make an escape. I wanted to do something, but I didn't because I knew there was nothing I could do. I squatted where I was, sneaked a look around the side of that small dune, and watched as the machines charged, waving their metal arms about. The machines held in one metal hand a net, and in the other a large wrench that could have turned a bolt the size of my head.

These were different and smaller machines than I had seen before, but they were large enough, over twelve feet tall and eight feet wide, and their purpose was the same. Behind the face plates of the machines I could see dead riders, blackened by time, springs of hair like burnt twigs sticking up on mostly slick skulls. They bobbed in their seats, heads swinging right and left, held in place by shoulder straps and waist belts and probably by their flesh, most likely glued by time to the ancient seat leather. They had died so long ago it was amazing they still had form. The desert air, perhaps something inside the machines, had mummified them.

The machines rushed over the sand, stepping wide. Their nets soared out, and I saw my family, father and mother, brother and sister, fall down beneath a heavy net, and then the net scooped tight, and the monster machine hoisted them up and held them in front of its face as if the dead rider inside might examine the prize. A little red light blinked inside the machine, and then the other metal arm swung and the wrench smashed against my mother and father. There was a dark, wet blossom in the night air, and the net disgorged my mother and father, but maintained my brother and sister.

I let out a little scream, fell back behind the dune and began to cry, holding it in as best I could, feeling about as necessary as one more sand dune, a girl who moments before had only been interested in clearing her bowels, and now my parents were smashed and the machines were taking all the young ones away, including my brother and sister.

Not that I'm proud of it, but I stayed where I was, hoping no machine would find me, and in short time the Robo Rapids were gone. Easing out from behind the dune, I saw that some of the tribe had returned. I saw too my ancient grandfather, ninety-eight years old he claimed, and all that was left of my family. He came hobbling out from the shadows on his crutch, his tattered, dark rags dangling off of him like shredded flesh. He saw me and let out a bellow. I ran to him and we hugged. I almost knocked him off his crutch.

"They are dead, Sheann, all dead," he said, and he wept loudly. He wasn't the only one. The air was filled with crying and wailing and the gnashing of teeth, the tearing of garments, a habit that always seemed wasteful to me, no matter what the circumstances.

"They took Jacob and Della," I said. "They didn't kill them. They're alive."

"It's the same," he said. "They're dead, or soon will be. No one they take comes back."

We have a kind of fatalism, my tribe, and I decided not to share in it.

"No. They're still alive."

"The same as dead," Grandfather said. "The same."

We butchered the camels that had been killed and salted the meat, and then we gathered up the dead and piled them on old camel skins and dragged them away in the dark of the night. We came to the Flatlands by morning, though they weren't all that flat. Flatter than the desert with its rising and shifting dunes, but there was rubble there, pieces of metal, pieces of glass, pieces of stone, a piling and a rotting of ancient bones.

Once the Robo Rapids didn't come as far as the Flatlands, but now they did, so being in the Flatlands we were no more safe than the night before, but we were farther away from the home of the machines, and without all the dunes we could see them coming.

There were animals that lived in the dunes that provided meat, so it was part of our routine to wander out there. Load up the camels, make the great circle, which included the Flatlands, and when that was done, we did it again. In the last few years the sand rabbits and so many other beasts that had lived in the desert and provided meat and clothing were disappearing, as were the water holes, but still, there was more food in the harsh desert than in the calmer Flatlands. But Robo Rapids or no Robo Rapids, in time we would venture back to the desert, looking for small animals to eat, and then we would rotate back to here to rest.

We didn't go to the Green Place. That's where the Robo Rapids came from.

The next morning the breeze, as if helping with the planned cremation, blew a lot of tumble weeds into our campsite, and we piled those up and heaped dried camel dung from previous visits with them. We placed all the bodies on the weed and dung pile and set it afire.

The old folks, and I guess most of the young folks, believe as the bodies burn their smoke goes up to join the gods, but me, I think the smoke just goes up and turns thin and disappears. People only seem to believe in the gods when they need something that they usually don't get, or when they are grieving and like to think their loved ones have found a better place to be. Since most of us are in no hurry to depart for those finer shores, I have a feeling that deep down we know the truth that this is it, and beyond is nothing.

Watching the rise of that nauseating smoke, the burning of my mother and father's bodies, didn't make me feel good at all. All I could think about were my brother and sister. Everyone else had spent time praying on their loss, crying, and preparing to move on, but I just got madder.

That night our tent was roomier than before, due to the absence of our loved ones. Me and Grandfather tried to rest. The tent was patched in many places, and in some places not too well, because a needle of bone has never fit my hands well, and the stitching I had done during the day to patch the rips the Robo Rapids had made by walking over it, left gaps. The cold night wind whistled through those holes like throwing knives.

We spent considerable time crying over our family, but in time I couldn't cry anymore. All I could do was think about my brother and sister, carried away to the Green Place where the Robo Rapids ruled.

"You can sew again tomorrow," Grandfather said, looking up at the rips in the tent, pulling his heavy cloak tighter around his body. "I'd do it, but I don't want to, and you're younger and it's your job."

"I can't wait," I said.

Grandfather was trying to generate a bit of humor in our tent, but by this point I was too absorbed with thinking about Jacob and Della.

"You lived before things were like this," I said. "Why do the machines kill us? What do they want with the younger ones?"

"They kill us because they can, and what they want with the younger ones I don't know, but certainly young ones give the machines less trouble than the older ones would. Well, if you're as old as me I wouldn't give them much trouble. There's not enough left of me to give much trouble."

"That's not a very good answer."

Grandfather shrugged. "We live the way we live now because the weather changed and there were wars. I only know that at some point the war machines began to think, and their thoughts were not good."

"So, the machines get up in the morning, think, hey, there's some humans out there, let's go kill them and steal the little ones and bring them back?"

"Pretty much."

"That doesn't make sense. They aren't like people. They don't wake up in the morning."

"I didn't say they did. You did."

"Can't you tell me a bit more?" I asked.

He almost smiled, but not quite. "I've told you before."

"Yeah, but I still can't make sense of it. I can't understand why we have to give up on Jacob and Della. There's got to be something more you can tell me. Tell me what you've already told me, and maybe this time I can make sense of it."

"There's no sense to it," he said.

"Tell me anyway."

I was looking for any crumb I could find that would explain the odd way we lived and the reasons they took the young people and killed the older ones. Why were they still at war?

Grandfather sighed. He knew me. I would worry him until he thought his head would explode. I had heard it all before, but I kept thinking that if I heard it again and again at some point it would begin to make sense.

"Once humans ruled the machines," he said. "Used them to build and travel, but then they used them for war. The aliens came, and we used our machines to fight them. I suppose you could say we won that war, though it was disease that killed the aliens. If it hadn't, they might have won. When that war was over the machines of different tribes, countries we called them back then, fought each other over land and water and food, and in time most humans were killed by the Robo Rapids of both sides. Countries didn't matter anymore.

"There wasn't always as much desert, and where we are now, we called what we are sleeping on, concrete. Great buildings made of stone and plastic and glass were built over this concrete. There were many buildings, and they went for miles, and we called those buildings a city. Once there was an ocean that licked at its shores. But that went away, and out there the Green Place popped up and grew remarkably fast. Some say it's because there was something in the alien technology that got loose and made things grow. I don't know. But it happened. There were villages in the Green Place for awhile. We had this thing called money. Shiny pieces of metal called coins, folding bills, and we went there and bought things that we mostly didn't need."

"Why buy things you didn't need?"

"Because we could. There were things called cars. You've seen their ruins in the desert, farther out on the Flatlands. We rode around in those at a high rate of speed. My parents had a red car. I remember that clearly."

"Okay," I said, "you're right. I have heard this. And there were things called dogs and cats and you loved them as pets, but when times got hard, you ate them. Some people ate their own children."

"See," he said. "You know the story. Sometimes, I think that was a good course of action, eating the children. Usually when I'm tired and can't sleep and my granddaughter won't stop asking about things that don't matter, I think maybe it was a tremendous idea."

"Tell me about the Green Lands and the star people."

"I am envisioning you now in a large pot, floating in hot water with desert onions bobbing all around you, and me adding salt."

"Grandfather, come on. Tell me... Wait. Did you eat children?"

"Of course not. Our tribe never did, but there were those who did, and many of their descendants still roam the desert."

"I've never seen any of them," I said.

"Count your blessings. Fortunately, they are few these days. Fewer than even our tribe, and I suppose after last night we are about fifty people, and many of us are old and few young children are being born, so unless you have children, or a few of the others, our kind will vanish from the face of the earth. I'm not so sure that's a bad idea."

"What about the star people?"

Grandfather sighed. "They were aliens and they came from space. Somewhere out there they had lived amongst the stars, or they came from another dimension, jumped through some kind of rift in space and time and ended up here. That was a popular theory. They wanted our resources. The Robo Rapids were used to fight them, and then disease got the aliens. They couldn't get over our common cold."

Grandfather was right. There were no answers there.

I started crying again. It came over me like a fever, and I cried for quite some time. It was as if a hard rain inside my head had broken loose and was leaking out of my eyes. As I cried, Grandfather tried to soothe me, but pretty soon he was bellowing right along with me.

After Grandfather fell asleep, I lay on my pallet wide awake. I thought of Jacob and Della, and how much they annoyed me, and yet, how much I wanted them back. I wanted vengeance for my father and mother. I didn't want to be like the others, take it in stride and move on. I decided I was leaving and I was going to find my brother and sister and bring them back. If it was too late for them, then at least I would know. I could also quit feeling like a coward. I told myself that once I did something bold, I might not have in my head the constant reminder that I had cowered behind a small sand dune while my mother and father were killed and my brother and sister were taken away. There really wasn't anything else I could tell myself. Sometimes, to do something you are afraid of doing, you have to lie to yourself, and that's all there is to it. I lied to myself that night. I said I was brave and that I would rescue my kin, and that I had to go.

While Grandfather snored loud as camel snorts, I put a small amount of food in a bag along with a corked gourd of water and fastened them around my hips with a thick cloth belt. I placed some other goods in a larger bag and rolled them up inside my cloak and made a pack of it by tying it on both ends with a rope and slinging it across my neck and shoulder. I was wearing sturdy clothes and rabbit-skin boots, and I had another cloak wrapped around me. I had my bag of stones and my sling strapped to my waist. I carried my walking stick. It was thick and heavy and almost as tall as me and was knobbed on top. I was as ready as I was going to get.

By the time morning cracked open and let the light in, I was well into the desert. I had considered taking one of the camels, but decided it was best not to, as the tribe would need it more than I would.

It was hard to think that Grandfather would wake up and find me gone and worry about me, but I couldn't let that stop my mission.

I trudged on.

After a few days my food was mostly gone and my water was one drink from being all over with. I was so hungry I was starting to imagine the dunes of sand were piles of fruit. In the distance, just as I swigged that last bit of water, I saw what I thought might be an encampment of nomads, or a mirage.

I squatted down and spent some time staring at it. I couldn't make the place out clearly, but it looked to be a series of tents at first, but in time I wasn't so sure what it was. I was certain of only one thing. It was not a mirage.

I wondered if there were people there, and if they were friendly, or perhaps the tribe Grandfather told me about; the ones who ate people. I would certainly make a stringy meal.

Squatting down in the desert, I thought about things. I feared going into that camp, but I also feared dying of thirst. The important thing was they would have water and perhaps could spare enough to fill my gourd. Or they could eat me. Right then, either seemed acceptable. In that moment I wished I had not left the tribe. Wished I had stayed with them and started the great circle, and at night read from the books Grandfather had. Read again of Moby Dick and foaming seas and great heroics, of philosophers who talked about things that didn't really matter. Instead, here I was, wandering the desert, sleeping wrapped up in a cloak, my teeth full of sand, not to mention my buttcrack, my throat parched and my belly rumbling.

And there was another problem. I picked them up out of the corner of my eye.

Four wild dogs, hungry, growling, slinking toward me.

Pulling my sling into play, opening my bag of stones, I placed one in my shooter, pulled it back and aimed between the V of it and let loose. There was a yelp, and one of the beasts jumped straight up and ran away. That was good, though actually, I had been aiming at a different one. I was an indifferent shooter.

The others rushed forward. I reloaded, shot again, missed. When I fired the next time, I was on target. It was a solid shot and I could hear the brute's head crack like a lighting strike. He had been as close as ten feet away, which may have accounted for my accuracy.

The beast went down and didn't get up. The remaining two took a hint and ran away. I watched until they were out of sight. The up side was I hadn't been eaten and I had a meal of wild dog at my disposal.

Or I thought I did. The beast I had wounded got up then, and began to slink off. It staggered as it went. I chased it down with my walking stick and beat it in the head until it was dead. I dragged it by its back legs across the sand towards what I thought might be a small tent village. I would go there with a smile on my face and an offering of still warm, wild dog.

—

There were no tents and no people, but there was a cluster of trees and some greenery that had grown up high and close together around a small trickle of water that came up from the earth and filled a muddy hole. There was sour, red fruit that grew from some of the bushes. I could see birds had been pecking at it, so I decided it was not poisonous. I made a fire with my flint and steel and some of the limbs I broke off trees. I skinned and gutted the dog, ate the heart and liver raw, and cooked the meat. Cooked dog is not as good as I had been led to believe by some old timers who claimed it was the meat of the gods. It was stringy and sour to me. I ate enough to not be hungry, and leaned into the water and licked at its source, trying not to stir the mud too much. It was still a muddy drink.

I rested there a night and a day, exhausted, eating more of the wild dog and the fruit, and filling my gourd with muddy water for the trip onward. I started out when it was night, studying the position of the waning moon for direction, before abandoning the oasis, and continuing my mission.

Finally I came to that part of the desert where the garbage floated; the remains of crashed alien airships. Whatever the ships had been made of the material defied gravity, but didn't leave the planet. The debris floated over the desert night and day. It moved when the wind moved it and never touched the ground. It glowed in the sun and shimmered in the moonlight. The pieces were all the colors of the rainbow and colors I couldn't put a name to.

I had observed the great line of drifting fragments from a distance before, but now I was close enough to touch them. The pieces were all manner of sizes and went on for miles. According to Grandfather, the saucers were shot down and broken open by Robo Rapids. The ship fragments lifted off the ground and inexplicably drifted about, and had floated about ever since.

We had won the war with the aliens, but then humans fought amongst themselves, and finally the metal monsters killed their human controllers with reverse energy surges that Grandfather said made the drivers inside the machines jump and crackle, smoke and pop. And then the machines were in control, powered by who knows what, but with only one guiding impulse left. Kill humans.

I strolled between the slow, swirling parts, and then in the distance I saw a great heap of metal. It glowed in the soft moonlight. The pieces were not alien, because they didn't float, and as I went forward I saw they were piles of Robo Rapid machines. The great heads had been pulled off and stacked into a mound of metal skulls. This gave me pause at first, but from the way the bodies lay, leaning this way and that, feet poking to the sky, I knew they were harmless. It looked like a carrion pile but without the smell.

I used my walking stick to help me forward, as the sand was starting to churn as the wind picked up. Sometimes that sand could blow so hard it could grate your eyes out. Grandfather had known it to happen. The fragments of the alien ships were swirling faster, darting past me, almost smacking me a few times.

My only thought was to reach that pile of wrecked machines and find a place to tuck myself in before the wind grew so bad and the sand blew so hard that I would be knocked down and covered, possibly with my eyes scratched out.

Arriving at that heap of metal, I saw there was a crack through which I could slip, and slip I did. It was dark in there, and with the sand blowing, darker yet. I moved farther in, hoping I hadn't trapped myself, that the sand wouldn't seal my exit. At the center of the heap there was a large opening, and overhead the metal pieces were fastened tightly together.

I had flint and steel to make a fire, but I only had a bit of kindling in my bag. That was for starting a blaze, not maintaining it, so there was no use bothering. It had become so dark by then I couldn't see my hand in front of my face. I could hear sand scraping outside against the pile like claws.

Sensing movement in the dark, I cocked my walking stick over my shoulder, ready to swing. I couldn't see anything other than darkness, but I knew something was scuttling about, and then there was a spot of fire, and a shape behind the flame. A human face, the skin dark as night. A voice said, "Who are you? This is my place."

"A traveler," I said.

The fire went out, and then I sensed someone standing next to me. A voice said, "Would you like fire, something to eat?"

Desert people can be very cautious and unfriendly to outsiders, so I was surprised, and not entirely trusting, yet, I lowered my walking stick and leaned on it.

"If you would be so kind," I said.

"Kindness has nothing to do with it. I am bored and the last of my kind."

"Aren't I of your kind?"

There was a small flare of light next to me, and the dark face appeared and leaned forward as the light glowed. I saw the light was from a small stick with fire on its tip. "You are of my kind, but you are not of my tribe."

"If what you said is true," I said. "You are your tribe."

"Good point," said the voice, and then the fire swept away from me and moved low. Flames snapped up from the floor of the metal cave and brightness jumped about. In front of me, squatting on his haunches, still holding what he had used to light a pile of dry wood was a young man.

"Thank you for the fire," I said.

"Would you like a bite of sand rabbit?" he said. "I have eaten most of it, but there's still a leg left."

"That would be nice."

Moving quickly, his light moving with him, he came back with a bone from which hung ragged chunks of meat. "It was cooked yesterday," he said. "But I think it's fine. Cold, of course. I could warm it."

"That's all right," I said.

He gave me the meat and I sniffed it. Okay. Not too bad. I ate. A bit gritty, but it tasted fine.

I checked out my host, but didn't sniff him the way I had the rabbit meat. I thought that would be too much, but he did have an odor, more sweet than sour. I could see him better in the firelight. He was small and moved like a sand rat, had a bushy head of dark hair and wore a single garment that fit over his head and hung loose to his knees.

"How long have you lived here?" I asked. "Did your tribe live here?"

"No," he said.

The stick with the fire had gone out, but now he was sitting closer to the driftwood fire, and I was sitting nearer to him.

"My name is Nim. My tribe roamed the desert until the Robo Rapids did them in. I was told once, when my father was alive, that this was where the remains of the blasted ones were heaped."

"Blasted ones?"

"By the aliens, during the war. Maybe by other Robo Rapids in the wars that followed."

"I have never seen a dead Robo Rapid before. I guess dead is the right term."

"You remember a lot of the old days?" he asked.

"No more than you. My grandfather remembers. He tells me many tales. My mother and father too. Or they did. They're dead now."

Mentioning them caused me to have a catch in my throat.

"The Robo Rapids?" he asked.

"They took my brother and sister. I am going to try and get them back. Hopeless, I suppose."

"Very likely," he said, "but it hasn't come the ritual yet."

"What ritual?"

Nim shook sand out of a couple of cups and poured me a cup of water from a skin bag, and then poured a cup for himself, said, "The Robo Rapids live off blood and spite, my mother once said."

"The Robo Rapids have become more than machines," I said. "They have chosen the faults of humans."

"I think they are what they were meant to be. Killers. They can think, but it's small thinking. They wanted to become the masters. That much they figured out without programming. That's what my grandparents did. They programmed the machines, programmed them for war."

"Robo Rapids won't have much to master if they keep killing us."

"That's what I mean about the ritual," Nim said. "You see, they don't understand exactly."

"Understand what?"

"Human sacrifice."

"They sacrifice humans?"

"Are your ears stopped up?"

"No, it's just, well, I don't get that."

"Neither do they. They do it because we did it. They learned from us. They learned about war, and they learned from old movies that were made about such things."

"I know about movies," I said. "I've never seen one, but Grandfather has told me about them. He has told me stories from the movies. I know one about a rabbit."

Nim did not appear open to hearing my movie story about a rabbit, so I cleared my throat and waited.

"I don't have the movies here," Nim said. "But there's a place I can watch them. I'll show you sometime."

"Actual movies?"

"That's right. I might have the one about a rabbit there. I might have more than one about rabbits. I don't know. It's a big collection."

"I would like that, but I won't be staying long. What do movies have to do with the Robo Rapids?"

"War movies and movies of violence. There's one about the Aztec sacrificing captives for religious purposes. They've seen it, and have it at the ready, or at least part of it. It's the one they mimic. The human idea of programming them with that stuff was to saturate their wires, batteries and computer codes, stuff their nooks and crannies with violence. They were, after all, machines designed for war. Unlike people, they can't watch and evaluate in the same way. To them, what they see is reality because they don't have a family to raise them, to guide them, to let them understand that violence is merely an emotion to be explored, not practiced literally. They see it and they do it."

"If humans taught it to them, and we did, we are no better than their worse acts. Grandfather told me that."

"He sounds wise."

"I think he is," I said, "but he is not brave. None of my tribe is brave. Some of the other tribes call us the Rabbit Clan. That isn't meant as a compliment. Tell me about the Robo Rapid ritual?"

"When the moon wanes they sacrifice prisoners. They think it brings the moon back. Something to do with that movie I was talking about, the way they are programmed."

"There are only a couple of days until the moon goes away," I said. "How far are they from us?"

"Walking, they are four or five days."

"I need to leave now. I have to try and make it there before the ritual."

Nim shook his head. "If you ran all the way and never rested, you would not make it in time before the ritual. There's a lot of desert out there. If there's another storm, like this one, without a tent, supplies, you wouldn't make it. There's scorpions as well."

"I can stomp those."

"That might require a bit of work. They're the size of a Robo Rapid."

"That does change matters."

"They live in the desert near the jungle. They have their territory, same as humans, and they rarely leave it. Next problem is the jungle itself."

"The Green Place?"

He nodded. "And then you have to make your way through the jungle, and if you don't know the trails, even if you could get there in time, it's an unlikely rescue."

"So my kin will be sacrificed, and there's nothing I can do to stop it?"

"Not the way you're going about it," Nim said. "Maybe not any way you go about it."

"But there's another way?"

"Rest for now," Nim said. "Build your strength, digest that bit of food. Tomorrow morning, first light, I will show you how to get there faster, but for now, trust me and rest. You'll need all the stamina you can muster. And think it over. It's hardly worth you going. They are big and they are many and you are one and you are small."

"But I'm spry," I said. "And you are willing to help."

"Only up to a point," Nim said.

———

I was exhausted and it was comfortable inside the pile of machines. The wind howled in a pleasant way around the stack of metal, and no sooner had I laid out my cloak, covered myself with the other half, I drifted down into a deep sleep.

I awoke refreshed. I stood up and moved about, pushing another pile of wood onto the dying fire.

Nim said, "Good. You slept a few hours."

I looked up to the sound of the voice. I couldn't see Nim, but there was a pile of metal legs and arms that made a kind of staircase.

"Come up," he said.

At the top of the pile was an enormous Robo Rapid head. That's where Nim's voice was coming from. I climbed up there. Nim was sitting in an old chair inside the head, looking out through the strip of glass that served as the Robo Rapid's one eye. The sun was starting to come up.

"I figured out how they worked," he said. "There was a cap the driver wore. It allowed the rider to send messages into the Robo Rapid, and it responded as best as it was able. That's how the rider drove it. He willed it. There were manual controls as well, but in time they weren't used much, and that's how I think the machines overrode the riders. I give the Robo Rapids that much credit as far as thinking goes, but it wouldn't surprise me if some human wasn't trying to override the system to his or her benefit, and that didn't work out. Instead it gave the Robo Rapids control. Backfired."

"All I care about is how I can get where I want to go at a faster pace."

"Fast toward death," he said.

"That is certainly a possibility."

Nim thought for a moment, said, "I will lead you where they are, and then I leave you on your own. I've seen all I want to see of murder and sacrifice."

Outside in the fresh morning light, we walked about the stack of machine parts. The sand storm of the night before had left a fine silt in the air, and the early light gave it an odd, greenish glow.

Floating in the air, about ten feet off the ground, was a large piece of metal. It was shaped somewhat like the boats I had seen in the books Grandfather had. It was a piece of alien space ship. There was a long rope tied to it, and on the ground end of the rope was a heavy and jagged piece of metal partially buried in the sand.

"That's the anchor," Nim said. "It holds it in place."

Nim was great at stating the obvious.

He led me over to a stack of metal arranged in such a way that it made a great series of steps. Nim scampered up them, and I followed. At the top Nim reached out and took hold of the rope attached to the craft, and tugged on it. The floating scrap of alien metal glided toward us, light and effortless.

"There's a rope ladder inside, fastened to a metal peg in the raft."

Nim made a nimble step off the top of the pile and onto the air raft. I followed, less nimbly. The craft was about ten feet long, with a slightly lifted front and back. The sides of it curled up. Inside the raft were four long poles and a rope ladder was coiled at the back end. Attached to another peg was a coiled rope and a spare anchor. A large knife lay next to it along with a bag full of something.

"It was naturally shaped this way," Nim said. "I don't know what part of an alien ship it was, but it makes a wonderful air boat." He pointed at the poles. "Those fasten together. I'll show you what I mean."

The raft wobbled slightly as Nim moved toward the poles. The four poles were made of metal, and Nim fastened them together to create two poles about twenty feet long.

"One is for you, and one is for me. The spare anchor is if the first one gets snagged and I have to cut it away. I can usually work it loose, though. I've had a lot of practice. The raft, no matter how much you put in it, doesn't change its air level. It's amazing. I saw this piece, thought about it, got hold of it when it floated by the Robo Rapid heap. I've had it ever since. I use it to travel about. You know, I haven't asked your name?"

"Sheann," I said.

"It's good to meet you, Sheann. I hope ours is not a short acquaintance. In that bag I've got some water, a few pieces of dried fruit. If you got to pee, don't do it in here. If you got to do the other, sure don't do it in here. We can stop and climb down, take care of that business, then climb back up."

"Got you," I said. "Don't pee or shit in the raft."

"Actually, you might want to go now. I don't like to stop once I start floating. And we have a long way to go."

———

I gathered my sleeping cloak and cudgel, and we climbed back onto the raft.

Nim pulled up the anchor, showed me how to utilize one of the poles, and he used the other. He sat near the front and I sat near the back. We hung our poles over opposite sides, and pushed off.

The raft went hurtling over the desert like an angry hawk. Once or twice Nim used his pole to poke another fragment of floating craft aside, and we continued on, moving much faster than I could have walked, or ran for that matter.

The sun rose upwards behind us. The air turned warmer and warmer, and finally hot. The sky was clear and blue and the lines of sand in the air had fallen to earth. From time to time, Nim would use his pole to alter our course. At first the sun was at our back, then it was to our left, and eventually it was high and centered above us.

Come late day, with the light starting to fade, we came to an oasis of palms, a much larger oasis than the one I had stopped at before. Nim, experienced and aware of our location, used his pole to change the direction of the raft until it glided toward the oasis. He came to the rear of the raft, placed the coil of rope over his shoulder, and began to swing the metal anchor fastened to it over his head with a whistling sound.

When Nim let the rope go, it sailed out and uncoiled off his shoulder. It was a thing of beauty, the way he did that. The anchor came down in the sand and began to drag, and we began to slow. I watched as the anchor made a small ditch in the earth, a ragged line with puffs of dust rising over it, and then it caught good and deep.

By the time we climbed down, not bothering with the rope ladder, using only the line attached to the anchor, the sun had mostly been swallowed and the night was a deep shade of blue. Beneath the trees we found bushes with fruit, and the water in a large pool nearby was clean and cold and tasted sweet.

Satiated, we leaned against trees and watched the stars and the partial moon rise. Soft silver light fled over the desert like a flood of water. I had only read of floods, and seen the great waters in books, but that's how it looked to me, like those photographs, deep and wet and full of shadow.

Finally, Nim spoke. "I've got no one."

"For now you have me."

"For now, and then you're gone, and you won't come back, Sheann. You won't. We could live here, under the trees by the spring. Water and fruit to eat. Animals come here to drink. There are more animals than you can imagine. We could trap them, eat them along with the fruit. It would be nice and we wouldn't be lonely."

"You mean stay here by a wet hole in the ground?"

"Is that worse than wandering the desert on a mission you can't fulfill?"

"They are my clan. I get them back, you can come live with our tribe."

Nim shook his head. "No more tribes."

⸺

Next morning we cast off from the oasis and into the sunlight that glimmered off the sand and toasted our faces and backs. I was a little sick about leaving. I thought about what Nim had said, and during the night I had seriously considered it. I had visions of living there, me and Nim, eating fruit and banging small animals in the head with sticks and cooking them up.

But there wasn't any way I could stay. Not with my family captured by the Robo Rapids. If Nim was right, and they had been spared for a ritual, I just might get there in time to save them.

The raft went faster this day, blown by a high wind. Once or twice, in the distance, I saw strange animals I couldn't identify. They were large and menacing looking.

We passed those great, black scorpions Nim told me about. They ran swiftly after us with cocked tails tipped with poison-dripping spikes. They were almost as tall as the height at which we flew. Nim guided us in such a way that we gave them a wide berth.

By midday there was a shift in the wind, and we had to fight to keep the raft flying the way we wanted it to go, but as the wind increased the view changed. Rising up in the distance was a dark line that stretched for miles. The line became a thickness of green trees.

It was the Green Lands.

The raft would not rise any higher, so at the edge of the jungle we had to anchor it, climb down, and enter the forest on foot. The trees were full of screeching birds and growling animals. I had my staff and my sling shot, but I wasn't confident of my ability to use either against anything larger than a rabbit or a wild dog. And as I said before, I'm an indifferent shot.

The trail Nim led me on was narrow and twisty. Snakes, like Grandfather told me about, slithered in our path and dangled from trees overhead. They were in a variety of colors and of extraordinary lengths and made my skin tingle. Nim paid them no mind.

He said, "It's the little ones you have to watch. A lot of them are poisonous and they can strike quickly. You get hit by one of those it's all over but the pain and the screaming. There's one kind, when it hits, you can't scream. Paralyzes you. You fall over and quit breathing, and that's it. Lost an uncle that way. Oh, and watch for the big cats. They sometimes like people for dinner. They can grab you and drag you off and crush your head so fast you won't even know you've left the trail."

The track widened as we continued, and at one point we came to where the jungle ceased and there was a great expanse of knee high grass. It was then that I saw the horror.

Stacked way high, shiny white in the dying sunlight, were piles of human skulls, empty eye holes growing darker as light slipped into shadow. Beyond the stack closest to us was another, and to the right and left of that stack were more. Stack after stack after stack. At the bottom of the pyramids of skulls were other bones. Leg bones, arm bones, rib cages, skeletal hands and feet, all precisely organized. But what really bothered me was a stack to my left where the heads were fresh with strips of flesh peeling off of them, curling up tight from the continual blazing of the sun. Black birds fluttered above the stacks and some lit on the skulls and picked flesh with their beaks.

"This is where the humans, or what's left of them, end up after the ritual," Nim said.

"You've seen the ritual?"

"I came here just as you have to rescue the last of my family. I failed, obviously."

"But you tried."

"I lost my courage. There's a place where it's done, and I came to that place, concealed and watching. I saw them do what they do, and I saw it done to my younger brother. Only a child, mind you. Terrible. This spot is where the refuse goes when it becomes too much. They want to keep their space clean of waste. They have enough skulls where they are. You'll see. Tonight the moon goes away. For the Robo Rapids everything human dies in the dark of the moon. It would be best not to see it, Sheann, because you can't stop it. Come back with me and live at the Oasis, or in the bodies of the Robo Rapids. It's less dangerous."

"You know I can't."

"I will take you where you want to go, where you can see, and do whatever it is you think you can do, but then I leave you."

"I won't think the less of you."

"It wouldn't matter if you did," he said.

———

We continued on, then, and eventually there was another clearing. In the brightening starlight I could see Robo Rapids standing tall in long rows holding wrenches and metal clubs. Nim walked directly toward them. I panicked and started to dart for the concealment of the jungle, but he grabbed my shoulder.

"These are the dead ones," he said. "Come see. I think it is their idea of a graveyard. They are their own tombstones. Look here."

Nim guided me through the legs of several of the machines, and finally he came to one and stopped. It was a big one, still blue and white, but there were patches of rust like spots on a wild dog. In its hand it clutched a large, rusted wrench.

At the back of the machine's leg, Nim grabbed a piece of metal that was dislodged, tugged gently. There was a gap in the leg, and he said, "Come inside."

Nim touched something on the wall and light climbed up the leg and into the structure above. I had heard of that kind of light, but had never experienced it. There were stairs inside the leg. He started up and I went after him. We came to where the stairs ended and walked out into a room. It was well lit, but there was a blanket over the face of the machine where the view glass was.

"I come here from time to time, during the ritual. I know what they're doing down there, but I come here because I can hide inside. I could live here all the time, I suppose. But they do come to this place now and again, with their worn out and rusted, stacking them in rows. In that way, they are thinking for themselves, I suppose. It's a sign of grief, though I think nearly all of what they do is based on programming."

"You've said that."

"I have, haven't I?"

"More than once."

"I have been reading the old manuals for the machines. This model is my favorite. It's an early one. Its manual is slightly different from the others. I've been trying to figure all the manuals for all the machines out, but this is the easiest one. I know how to turn on the lights and I can watch movies and listen to music with headphones. That way they can't hear."

Nim pointed at one of two swivel chairs near the front of the view glass. In the seats were helmets.

"Those helmets were what the riders wore to control the machines. But the machines figured out enough to reverse it, and they burned the riders' brains out.

"I know this much. Reason the machine is dead, is its battery, a big block of hard-ass plastic up there, finally lost its serious juice."

I looked up where he was pointing. Yep. A big hard-ass block of plastic was up there in the center of the Robo Rapid's head. Cables came out of the block and wound into the walls of the machine.

"It was merely shook loose. I fastened it up tight and right, but it doesn't have enough power to run very long. I can watch movies and listen to music for quite a few hours, but it won't kick the machine into motion. It seems the battery recharges itself on a low scale, but not on a big one. I let it rest, I come back, it's partially charged again. Once the ability to surge big dies, the machines are useless, and considered dead. The Robo Rapids can't figure out how to repair themselves, or give the machines the kind of energy perk they want to give them. They bring them here. But this one, like some of the others, isn't really dead, it just doesn't have enough power in its battery to operate the way it once did. Some day it won't work at all, won't even have the power for lights and music and movies. I dread that day. I enjoy coming here."

"Needs more batteries," I said.

"That's the problem, all right."

Nim went back to pointing, this time at a large square of clear plastic jutting from the wall beneath the window which was the eye of the machine.

"From what I can figure, the driver used that screen along with cameras imbedded in the machine's head to see all about. The drivers could get a view all around, could see more what was going on than just what they could see through the window. The driver could also watch movies on it during down time. Let me show you one."

"I have a more urgent situation, Nim."

"Not yet you don't. They keep the prisoners in a place that allows no opportunity to get to them unseen. Fact is, when they move them for the ritual, it is only slightly better. That will be your chance, or what chance you might have. Perhaps you should see at least part of a movie before you die."

"That's not a big mark of confidence," I said.

"There's nothing to be confident about."

Nim didn't convince me to watch a movie, but he did convince me to rest, eat and drink. I knew what he was doing. Trying to keep me away from where I wanted to go, trying to give me something to look forward to in place of putting my life on the line, hoping I'd change my mind. I appreciated it, but it wasn't going to happen. He did convince me to listen to music. He placed a helmet on my head, the headphones over my ears.

"Wait," I said, having a sudden revelation, "won't it suck my brain out or something?"

"This is merely music. It's not turned into the machines' higher functions. Listen." Nim touched something on the headphones and I could hear it. It was not the music I was used to, our tribe singing in a voice like dying dogs, beating on boxes and strumming stringed gourds, a kind of noise that made the camels bellow.

I had never heard anything so nice. As the music wormed through my head, I closed my eyes and floated away to some place I couldn't identify, and it sure felt good.

When the music ended, I lifted the helmet off my head with tears in my eyes.

"Magic," I said.

"Beethoven," he said. "Along with all the violence and war, there was beautiful music. We should have focused on feeding the Robo Rapids something beautiful instead of something ugly, and we wouldn't be living like we live, hand to mouth. Watching the movies, listening to the music, trying to figure out the Robo Rapid manuals are the only times I don't feel sad."

———

Eventually, I went down the stairs, and when I did, Nim turned out the light and came out after me, and we went out. I could sense he knew he was done with trying to persuade me to stay with him and live a life inside of a pile of machines, or out at the oasis, or up in the tall, standing one, listening to music and watching movies.

Nim led the way, resigned. We came to where there was a mountainous pile of dirt. Tall trees grew at the top of the pile, and starlight dribbled over the trees like sand.

Carefully we scrambled up. At the hill's summit we lay between trees and looked down into a bowl of earth. It was not so deep, but it was acres wide, and almost perfectly round. It had been dug out by machines of some sort, and not recently, because vines grew up its sides in thick leafy ropes. There were trees sprouting from the bowl here and there, grass grew up in occasional green twists, and there were flowers, their true colors I couldn't discern at night.

In the center of the bowl was a pyramid made of human skulls, as we had seen before, but this was a higher and wider pyramid. At the bottom of it was a great gap, and at the top was another. The gap on top opened onto a platform of skulls. All of the skulls were tightly fastened together in some manner, unlike those Nim had shown me before, which were loose.

Across from that pyramid was another even wider pyramid, but there was only one great gap. It ran from near the top to the bottom. The skull walls curled around on either side, and in the gap was a giant green wall. As I looked at the wall it began to glow. There was a brief flicker, and then there were images on the wall.

Nim, sensing that I was confused, whispered, "It's a larger version of the screen that was in that Robo Rapid. It was left behind by the programmers. It seems indestructible. I've tried to damage it and can't. See that large bolt at the bottom? That's the control for the Robo Rapids. Everything they are is programmed into that by their former human Overlords, or so I believe. I've tried destroying the screen, damaging the bolt. I've tried screwing it loose, but it's far too large for human hands and the wrenches I have. Even if I had a wrench the right size, it would be too big for me to handle, and if I could handle it, it would be too tight to turn. It was screwed in place by Robo Rapid hands, and it isn't coming out. As long as the bolt and that screen survive, the information the programmers gave the Robo Rapids will be received and interpreted by them in the manner their owners wanted. I think the Overlords used to change the bolt out from time to time, give them different programmable images. Now there are no Overlords. What was there when the Robo Rapids took over plays again and again. They copy humans in many ways, and one of those ways is making the pyramids they see on the screen, piling up dead humans the way the humans used to pile up deactivated Robo Rapids. Them gathering here, that's some kind of programmed ritual."

I paid attention to the images on the screen. The images were of people, all men, and they were moving. They appeared to be talking, but there was no sound coming out of their mouths. They wore loin cloths, headdresses and cloaks made of colorful feathers. They were climbing stone steps on a pyramid, its design not too different from the one made of skulls across from the screen.

Near the top of the pyramid, where they stopped, was an opening and a platform of stone reminiscent of the platform of skulls the Robo Rapids had built. One of the men, the one with the tallest and brightest headdress, came to stand before a block of stone.

A man was brought out by four others. They tossed him on the stone and held him to it. The man with the tall headdress raised his face and hands to the sky, one of those hands was holding a black blade of what looked like glass. Words were spoken, but still there was no sound. The hand with the knife came down, there was a spurt of blood as it entered the man's chest, and then his heart was cut free, and the man—a priest, I suppose, pulled the heart out of the man's chest, held it out, still beating, for all to see. Below the pyramid a crowd of faces lifted, stared contentedly at the man holding the heart, and then the screen went black.

"It's not real," Nim said. "It's a movie. No one dies. It's all makeup and such. But it's real to the machines. It's their religion. There's another segment that will come up shortly on the screen. It's a battle scene, these warriors going to war, banging their enemies in the head with clubs. So you see, the Robo Rapids are imitating what they see. Aztecs from a movie. Do you know who the Aztecs were?"

"Grandfather told me what he had read about them. I remember some of it."

The screen popped bright again. There were images of war this time. Men rushing against each other, swinging clubs, killing. It looked real, even if it wasn't.

And then there was a creaking sound, along with groaning and hissing and whistling. The dreaded sounds of the machines. Several of them came out of the pyramid across from the screen, walking mostly, but some were on wheels or treads.

On their big heads they wore ridiculous head bands with awkward arrangements of leaves in place of feathers. They wore cloaks raggedly stitched together from what appeared to be human skin. The cloaks were decorated with a smattering of feathers and leaves. They were carrying a half-dozen cages made of wood and metal and plastic. They hoisted them on litters supported by long poles and vines.

Through the plastic walls of the cages I could see people. In one of the cages I saw my brother and sister, their hands pressed against the plastic, their faces had collapsed in a way that made them seem much older. They were nude and filthy. They didn't see me. They were not looking up, but the sight of them both cheered and depressed me at the same time.

I watched as they were carried to the base of the pyramid.

As the moments passed the stars were not enough, and lights positioned in the pyramids and around the earthen bowl, popped on. More Robo Rapids came along a trail that cut its way through the jungle. I counted twenty-five machines, moving down the sides of the bowl and on toward its center. Counting the ones that had come out of the pyramid, that made thirty-six.

Some of them were large and some were small and a few were sad-ass ragged. One dragged a leg, another's arm hung loose to its side. A few had heads that were cocked too far to one side or leaned too far back or too far forward. Nearly all were pocked with marks from blowing sand and dents from attacks. Over the years the Robo Rapids had taken a beating in the alien wars, and then in their battles to take over the humans. Their days were numbered, but the days they had left were way too many, because right now I was looking down and seeing my brother and sister in that cage and feeling watery inside. It was no different from the night the Robo Rapids had come and I had peeked around the edge of a dune and watched my mother and father die, saw Jacob and Della stolen away. I was no more able to do anything about it now than I was then.

I understood then what Nim had said about realizing there was nothing he could do when his own family was being killed. I had certainly rated myself higher than my actual ability. I turned to say as much to Nim, but he was gone.

———

The first group of Robo Rapids, those who had come from the bottom of the pyramid, ceremoniously climbed or rolled over the skull steps, and climbed to the platform above. The skull structure trembled with their weight. Up they went, heads bent, arms outstretched as if reaching for something. When they arrived at the upper platform, out of the opening came a smaller machine on treads. It held in one of its metal hands a knife. Small in its large hand, but for me it would easily have been the size of a sword.

The knife was given to the Robo Rapid with the tallest headdress. His face plate was rectangular and red as blood and glowed as if heated by fire. Red Face stood at the edge of the platform where a stack of skulls had been made into an altar similar to the one on the screen. Out of Red Face came a loud squeak, and then a kind of humming. Down below all the Robo Rapids bent to one knee, and those that couldn't due to injuries, dipped their heads or sagged on wheels and treads.

Red Face, their priest, raised his arms high, the knife in one hand, tilted his head to the heavens. The lights in and around the bowl skipped along his blade, made it shimmer and appear momentarily to be made of smoke.

One of the cages was opened below and there were yells from the humans. Robo Rapid hands reached in and pulled them out, as easy as humans grabbing up mice. The humans screamed and wriggled in the machines' grasps, but it was a useless struggle.

The metal monsters carried their victims up the pyramid steps, making a slow ritual of it. They were placed before the altar in a line and held firm by those metal hands. They were all nude, and stood trembling in the cool moonlight. The first in line, a young boy, was pushed forward. Red Face grabbed him and lifted him onto the altar.

The smaller machines on either side grabbed the boy's arms and feet and Red Face brought the knife down. Blood gushed up and turned bright in the glow of the lights in the bowl. The blood seemed to fall in slow-motion droplets as it splashed onto Red Face's metal body. It ran in rivulets down the steps made of skulls.

Red Face, using metal fingers like tweezers, reached into the poor child's wrecked chest and pinched out the beating heart. Red Face held it up and let the warm blood drip down onto its blood-red eye. Finally, Red Face dropped the heart. It went bouncing down the steps to the machines below. Then Red Face beheaded the body with the knife and gave the head to an assistant who tossed it like a broken bowl into a large container made of metal.

Red Face hoisted the decapitated body off the altar, flung it down the steps, sent it bouncing into the waiting Robo Rapids who fought for position and a clutch at the corpse. They easily ripped it apart. Those that managed to grab a piece of it, rubbed the bloody meat over their metal bodies and faces. More of the same followed with the screaming prisoners on the pyramid platform.

I slid down the hill away from the horrors, bent over and threw up. I began to weep silently. I was within touching distance of my brother and sister, but if I were to attempt anything at all, I would be captured and marched up the pyramid to have my heart torn out; and still my brother and sister would not be saved.

I was pondering all this when I heard a metallic screech followed by a thudding noise. I cautiously climbed back up the hill and took a peek.

It was coming down the opposite side of the hill, slipping a little, falling finally, getting up precariously. It was the great machine Nim and I had been inside of and it was moving about.

When it had managed a solid standing position, I could see through the glass that Nim was strapped into one of the rider seats and the helmet was on his head. I knew then that he had not abandoned me, but decided he could take over the machine somehow, and that was exactly what he had done. In one hand Nim's Robo Rapid still held the wrench, and in the other was something I couldn't quite make out.

Nim's machine moved like a person hit too hard in the head. All the Robo Rapids had turned toward it, including Red Face. All activity had stopped.

I knew this was my moment. Clutching my walking stick, I slid down the side of the bowl where the pyramids and Robo Rapids were, skidded in on my butt, then glanced up to see what was happening so I could judge how much time I had left, if any. I doubted Nim and his Robo Rapid could hold their attention long. One glance back and they would see me.

As I rushed toward the cages, holding a finger to my mouth to insist on silence, I opened the box with Jacob and Della in it by using my stick to push up the large latch. The gate to the cage swung open. Everyone inside, including my kin, filed out. I could see Della and Jacob wanted to come to me, but I pointed up the hill with repeated, sharp gestures, and up they all went, scrambling as silently as they could manage, attempting to make the lip of the bowl.

I moved to the next cage, gave quick attention to Nim as I used my cane to move the latch. I assumed I would be more than a little lucky if I could unlatch the other two cages before I was spotted, but I was damn sure determined to give it a try.

And then Nim's machine began to dance.

It skipped sideways, tucked its arms and jutted out its elbows, bent its knees and stepped right and then left, stepping high. I could hear music now, coming from inside his machine, piped out through a gap somewhere.

It was loud music, and quite different from any I had ever heard, harsh and heavy as lead. All the Robo Rapids watched as Nim skipped his machine across the bowl, nodded, spun, and then leaped toward the giant screen. Nim's Robo Rapid hit the earth on its metal belly, scuttled forward until it came to the great bolt beneath the giant screen. It snapped its wrench onto the bolt, and turned. The music in his Robo Rapid ceased. The bolt Nim's machine was turning snapped free. I understood what was in the machine's other hand. A new bolt.

The Robo Rapids were starting to come loose of their stupor. They moved toward Nim, swinging wrenches and clubs at his machine's body. There were clangs and clatters, but even as the blows rained down on Nim's Robo Rapid, denting it in spots, it was screwing in that bolt with ferocious speed and dexterity.

Suddenly, the air was filled with the sound of new music, and it was coming from that giant screen.

———

The hills were alive with it.

At least that's what the song the lady was singing said. I could hear her but there was nothing to see, and then the screen sputtered and spat out the vision of a beautiful woman, cleaner than anyone I had ever seen, spinning on a beautiful hill of flowers and green grass. Her voice was high and powerful, and I know no other way to say it—kind.

All the Robo Rapids began to move slowly toward the screen. Down from the pyramid came Red Face, stepping lightly, and then spinning, lost its footing and went tumbling down into a mass of clunking metal.

The lady on the screen continued to sing and twirl. The very fiber of the air filled with her voice. I felt as if I could reach out and take hold of the notes and stuff them in my mouth, and I wanted to. There was something about them that made me think they would taste sweet.

Nim's machine stood, started to spin, and all the Robo Rapids began to spin in response to the programmed bolt in the great screen. Nim had been right. Now they were reprogrammed, singing and dancing and lifting their heads to the dark place where the moon should be.

Tomorrow night the moon would be back, and from the machines designed point of view, they would have danced it back into creation.

I was going from cage to cage now, freeing the prisoners, and up the hill they fled, like a reverse flow of fleshy lava. The machines weren't trying to stop them. The prisoners were no longer a consideration. Up they went, over the hill, and away from the sound of music, while down in that bowl the machines twirled and whirled.

Nim had complete control of his machine. He danced it up the side of the bowl, slipping and sliding, but making its way. When it reached the top, it danced into the night and out of sight, surprisingly graceful, but with a clank and a rattle and a hiss of hot air.

The prisoners ran through the jungle. They ran real fast. It was all I could do to follow, so ecstatic were they to be free. They ran through briars and thickets of greenery and dangling vines. They tripped and fell and rose up again.

Where the jungle broke the escapees fell to their knees, breathing deeply, some of them throwing up. They were weak from their time in the cages, from the fear they had felt, from the horror they had seen. I was not much better.

I urged them on, not entirely certain of the permanency of the Robo Rapids' current attitude. Across the green grass we went, and into the jungle, and down a narrow trail, frightening animals as we went. Startled birds awoke and took briefly to the sky and found new nesting places, snakes slithered quickly.

It took some time, but finally we broke out of the jungle completely and onto the edge of the grass that led to the desert. We stopped there. I built a fire of scattered wood, and then pointed out the fruit. The prisoners, who were a large, smelly wad of humanity, attacked the trees and dragged the fruits from them and ate savagely. It was almost frightening to watch them eat, and that included Della and Jacob. They were famished. I was surprised they weren't dead. What had they eaten or drank during captivity?

Later my brother and sister would say they were kept in a deep pit with an open sky, and the rain came down and it filled the pit up to their ankles. They drank the water and it made them sick, but it was the way they survived. And then the machines brought fruit and shoved it over the edge of the pit, and the only way to eat was to scramble and claw for it. Many had died.

That was then, and this was now, and when they finished eating, mostly too fast, many of them threw up. They lay out on the grass, exhausted. Then came the clumping and groaning and hissing of a giant machine.

Everyone staggered to their feet, certain their escape had ended.

It was Nim's machine, its face plate glowing. It pushed through the trees, bending them back, shoving into the clearing, and then it stopped.

"It's all right," I said. "It's all right. This machine is controlled by a friend."

That reassurance didn't keep the prisoners from scattering into the jungle, a few running wildly out into the desert. Only my brother and sister remained, and there was nothing to be done for it. The machine stopped moving and the face plate went dark. Nim came out from the opening in the back of the Robo Rapid's leg.

He staggered as he came. His head had two black marks at the temples where the helmet had fit. Thin, white smoke curled up from them. I ran to him and hugged him. "That was smart," I said. "Except, has it...hurt you?"

"Stunned me a bit. Couldn't have worn it much longer. Now, every time I see something bright I want to shit. I think that'll pass. Hope so. If not, it could be awkward."

"We'll get you some dark glasses," I said. "I've seen such a thing."

My brother and sister had wadded into a knot behind me. "It's okay," I said. "This is Nim. He's a friend."

Still, they clung to me, peeking around at the man with the black burns on his temples.

"It was what you said," Nim said. "About needing more batteries. It was so simple I had totally overlooked it. I kept thinking I had to power the main battery up, but I gathered batteries from several of the other machines. It was easy and quick, and it fired them up. I fed the movie I liked, *The Sound of Music*, into the machine's storage unit, which is one of those bolts. I had my Robo Rapid unscrew the bolt and take it with us. Well, you know the rest."

"You're a hero."

"I had a big machine, and all you had was you, and you went down there and threw the latches, knowing full well you might be killed. But you did it. What I did, compared to that, was nothing."

Nim wobbled and dropped to his knees.

"Okay, I see green and blue polka dots. Does anyone else see polka dots?"

He fell forward on his face.

———

We slept inside the giant Robo Rapid, and when we awoke the next morning I was surprised that nothing had killed us, for I had dreamed of snakes and Robo Rapids, and hungry cats with a taste for human flesh.

Nim was much better. He said he wasn't seeing polka dots anymore and had lost the urge to shit himself, bright lights or no bright lights. We put together some fruit and cut some gourds loose, made water containers, and set out for where Nim and I had left the floater.

It was still there. Della and Jacob climbed up the rope rapidly, and then me and Nim. Off we sailed, in the early morning light, across the desert sand, the Green Place flowing away rapidly behind us.

In time we came to the floating debris, and in greater time we came to my tribe. They had moved back toward the desert, continuing what they knew as if nothing had happened.

It was a joyous reunion. Grandfather was so excited to see Della and Jacob, as well as myself. He started to cry and cried nearly continuously for two days straight. When we told them that the Robo Rapids were dancing, and wouldn't make war again, they praised the gods, as if we had had nothing to do with it.

I spent the next few days recounting what had happened. It was a story that the tribe never seemed to tire of.

There is not much more to tell of my adventures with the Robo Rapids, but there is this: I had become quite fond of Nim. One day, before the moon went black, we gathered our things and said our goodbyes, and sailed away on our alien raft. Not to the oasis Nim had suggested, but back to the jungles of the Green Place.

We tied the raft off at the edge of the jungle and eased our way to the great bowl where the Robo Rapids had danced. Down below there was nothing but the pyramids and the huge screen. There were a few Robo Rapids that had played out and lay stone-still on the ground.

As the night darkened, the lights in the bowl came on and the screen came on and the lady sang and the lady danced. From the far side of the bowl I heard them. It was that distinct clinking and clacking, the raw hissing of air. Robo Rapids, without headdresses now. There were only a few. They made their way down a trail and into the bowl, and as the lady sang, they spun and made noises beneath the blacked-out moon, some of them stumbling, some of them falling flat, unable to rise. Time had turned heavy and had fallen down on them at last.

We lived there on the edge of the jungle, slept up high in our alien raft. We gathered fruit and drank from sweet water, and now and again we killed an animal and ate its meat. It was a good life, an easy life.

Now and again, when the moon goes thin, we go to hear the lady sing and watch her dance, and to see the Robo Rapids come down from the hill into the automatically lit-up bowl of earth.

Each time there were fewer of them, as Nim predicted, and in time there were none that moved, just heaps of metal on the vine-covered floor of the scooped out bowl. But still we came on moonless nights to watch the bowl automatically light up and see the woman dance and hear her sing. We also watched complete movies in the machine Nim had used, out there on the edge of the jungle. I loved them. But that machine is also dying, all of its batteries going to seed. Soon the movies will be nothing more than memories stored in our heads. Even the bolt with its endless loop will eventually die. Already the lights in the bowl are starting to dim.

Sometimes we go to visit my brother and sister. Grandfather is long gone now, his bones covered over by the sand. Our tribe has grown and prospered, and there are other tribes roaming the desert free of fear of the Robo Rapids. There are tribes starting to gather on the fringes of the jungle as well, and their numbers are multiplying.

There is plenty of room, food, water, shelter, and all the things that are needed to make life a pleasure.

It is a paradise.

And yet, among the tribes there are rumors of war.

Introduction to

THE PROJECTIONIST

Lawrence Block had a cool idea for an anthology. Stories based on the art of Edward Hopper. I had seen a number of Hopper's paintings, but until the invitation to write a story based on this work was presented to me, I was unaware of just how many fine paintings he had created. I found a site where you could see them all, or at least a lot of them, and I realized I could have written a story based on any one of them.

I remembered, however, that there was a cool one of a young woman, an usherette, in a theater. It had stayed with me for years, and once I was on that site I searched for it.

I located it, studied it briefly, and the story I wanted to write was suddenly there. I love it when that happens. I love old movie and stage theaters, and I decided to use it as a jumping off point for a story about a struggling theater, a projectionist, and his attraction to the young woman hired to be an usherette.

The year the story takes place is never mentioned, but I nod toward the fifties. It's all told from the viewpoint of the projectionist, and as we discover he has a crush on this young woman, we gradually discover something else. He has an unusual past and a special mentor.

I don't want to say much more. I want the reader to discover the story. This book is chock-full of personal favorites. You kind of like all of your literary kids, but some are closer to your heart than others. This nostalgic, ultimately dark piece, is one that stays with me. I think about it from time to time as if it was written by some-one else. That's odd, and pleasurable. It came quickly, and happily.

I never felt like I was touching the keys. It seemed to arrive as if by lightning flash.

I remember when Larry read it. He emailed me and said that he was only going to read a bit, go to lunch and finish later. He said he got caught up in it and read the whole thing right then.

That's nice. Coming from one of the masters of fiction, that is one hell of a compliment. He's read and written a lot of stories, and for one to stand out even a little bit is pretty cool.

Since writing this story, my son has written a good screenplay based on it, and there is interest in me directing a film version.

Will it happen?

Hey, it's film. Who the hell knows?

But, I'll always have *The Projectionist*, and I can always look at that lovely and mysterious painting that inspired it, and feel more than a little bit satisfied.

THE
PROJECTIONIST

There's some that think I got it easy on the job, but they don't know there's more to it than plugging in the projector. You got to be there at the right time to change reels, and you got to have it set so it's seamless, so none of the movie gets stuttered, you know. You don't do that right, well, you can cause a reel to flap and there goes the movie right at the good part, or it can get hung up and the bulb will burn it. Then everyone down there starts yelling, and that's not good for business, and it's not good for you, the boss hears about it, and with the racket they make when the picture flubs, he hears all right.

I ain't had that kind of thing happen to me much, two or three times on the flapping, once I got a burn on a film, but it was messed up when we got it. Was packed in wrong and got a twist in it I couldn't see when I pulled it out. That wasn't my fault. Even the boss could see that.

Still, you got to watch it.

It ain't the same kind of hard work as digging a ditch, which I've done, on account of I didn't finish high school. Lacked a little over a year, but I had to drop out on account of some things. Not a lot of opportunities out there if you don't have that diploma.

Anyways, thought I'd go back someday, take a test, get the diploma, but I didn't. Early on, though, I'd take my little bit of earnings and go to the picture show. There was an old man, Bert, working up there, and I knew him because he knew my dad, though not in a real close way. I'd go up there and visit with him. He'd let me in free and I could see the movies from the projection booth. Bert was a really fine guy. He had done some good things for me. I think of him as my guardian angel. He gave me my career.

While I was there, when I'd seen the double feature and it was time for it to start over, he'd show me how the projection was done. So when Bert decided he was going to hang it up, live on his Social Security, I got the job. I was twenty-five. I been at it for five years since then.

One nice thing is I get to watch movies for free, though some of them, once was enough. If I ever have to see *Seven Brides for Seven Brothers* again, I may cry myself into a stupor. I don't like those singing movies much.

Even if you wasn't looking at the picture, you had to hear the words from them over and over, and if the picture was kept over a week, you could pretty much say all the stuff said in the movie like you was a walking record. I tried some of the good lines the guys said to the girls in movies, the pickup lines, but none of them worked for me.

I ain't handsome, but I'm not scary looking either, but the thing is, I'm not easy with women. I just ain't. I never learned that. My father was quite the ladies' man. Had black, curly hair and sharp features and bright blue eyes. Built up good from a lot of physical work. He made the women swoon. Once he got the one he wanted, he'd grow tired of her, same as he did with my mother, and he was ready to move on. Yeah, he had the knack for getting them in bed and taking a few dollars from them. He was everything they wanted. Until he wasn't.

He always said, "Thing about women, there's one comes of age every day and there's some that ain't of age, but they'll do. All you got to do is flatter them. They eat that shit up. Next thing you know, you got what you really want, and there's new mountains to conquer."

Dad was that kind of fellow.

Bert always said, "Guy like that who can talk a woman out of her panties pretty easy gets to thinking that's what it's all about. That there's nothing else to it. It ought not be like that. Me and Missy, we been married fifty years, and when it got so neither one of us was particularly in a hurry to see the other without drawers, we still wanted to see each other at the breakfast table."

That was Bert's advice on women in a nutshell.

Well, there was another thing. He always said, "Don't sit around trying to figure what she's thinking, cause you can't. And when it comes right down to it, she don't know what you're thinking. Just be there for one another."

Thing was, though, I never had anyone to be there for. I think it's how I carry myself. Bert always said, "Stand up, Cartwright. Quit stooping. You ain't no hunchback. Make eye contact, for Christ's sake."

I don't know why I do that, stoop, I mean, but I do. Maybe it's because I'm tall, six-six, and thin as a blade of grass. It's a thing I been trying to watch, but sometimes I feel like I got the weight of memories on my shoulders.

The other night Mr. Lowenstein hired a new usherette. She is something. He has her wear red. Always red. The inside of the theater has a lot of red. Backs of the seats are made out of some kind of red cloth. Some of the seats have gotten kind of greasy over time, young boys with their hair oil pressed into them. The curtains that pull in front of the stage, they're red. I love it when they're pulled, and then they open them so I can play the picture. I like watching them open. It gets to me, excites me in a funny way. I told Bert that once, thinking maybe he'd laugh at me, but he said, "Me too, kid."

They have clowns and jugglers and dog acts and shitty magicians and such on Saturday mornings before the cartoons. They do stuff up there on the stage and the kids go wild, yelling and throwing popcorn and candy.

Now and again, a dog decides to take a dump on the stage, or one of the clowns falls off his bike and does a gainer into the front row, or maybe a juggler misses a toss and hits himself in the head. Kids like that even better. I think people are kind of strange when you get right down to it, 'cause everything that's funny mostly has to do with being embarrassed or hurt, don't you think?

But this usherette, her name's Sally, and she makes the girls in the movies look like leftover ham and cheese. She is a real beauty. She's younger than me, maybe by six or seven years, got long blonde hair and a face as smooth as a porcelain doll. Except for red dresses the theater gives her to wear, she mostly has some pretty washed out clothes. She changes at the theater, does her makeup. When she comes out in one of those red dresses with heels on, she lights up the place like Rudolph's nose. Those dresses are provided by Mr. and Mrs. Lowenstein. Mrs. Lowenstein sews them to fit right, and believe me, they do. I don't mean to sound bad by saying it, but Sally is fitted into them so good that if she had a tan, it would break through the cloth, that's how tight they fit.

Mr. Lowenstein, he's sixty-five if he's a day, was standing with me back at the candy counter one time, and I'm getting a hotdog and a drink to take up to the projection booth. That's my lunch and dinner every day 'cause it's free. So this time, right when the theater is opening, just before noon, we see Sally come out of the dressing room across from us, same room the clowns and jugglers and dogs use. She comes out in one of those red dresses and some heels, her blonde hair bouncing on her shoulders, and she smiles at us.

I could feel my legs wilt. When she walked into the auditorium part of the theater to start work, Mr. Lowenstein said, "I think Maude maybe ought to loosen that dress a little."

I didn't say anything to that, but I was thinking, "I hope not."

The Projectionist

Every day I'm up in the booth I'm peeking out from up there at Sally. She stands over by the curtains where there are some red bulbs. Not strong light, enough so someone wants to go out to the bathroom, or up to the concession stand, they can find their way without breaking a leg.

Sally, her job is to show people to their seats, which is silly, 'cause they get to sit where they want. She's an added expense at the theater, but the way Mr. and Mrs. Lowenstein saw it, she's a draw for a lot of the teenagers. I figure some of the married men don't mind looking at her either. She is something. It got so I watched her all the time. Just sat up there and looked. Usually, I got bored, I looked down into the back row where there was a lot of boys and girls doing hand work and smacky mouth, but that always seemed like a wrong thing to do, watch them make out, and it seemed wrong that they did it in the theater. Maybe I was just jealous.

It got so I'd peek out at Sally all the time up there, since she had her that spot where she stood every night, that red bulb shining on her, making her blonde hair appear slightly red, her dress brighter yet. I'd got so caught up looking at her, that once, damn if for the first time in a long time, I forgot to change a reel and the picture got all messed up. I had to really hustle to get it going again, all them people down there moaning and complaining and stuff.

Mr. Lowenstein wasn't happy, and he gave me the talk afterward that night. I knew he was right, and I knew it didn't mean nothing. He knew flubs happen. He knew I was good at my work. But he was right. I needed to pay more attention. Still, it was hard to regret looking at Sally.

Right after this talk, things got shifted. Mrs. Lowenstein had long left the ticket stand out front, and had gone home ahead of Mr. Lowenstein. She had her own car, so it was me and him behind the concession counter, and I'm getting my free drink I got coming as part of my job, and Sally came out of the dressing room. She had on a worn, loose, flower-dotted dress, and she saw us and smiled. I like to think it was me she was smiling at. I knew I tried to stand up straight when she looked in my direction.

It was then that two men came in through one of the row of glass doors, and walked over to the stand. Now, I usually lock those doors every night, thirty minutes before the time they came in, but this time I'm messing with the drink, you see, and I hadn't locked the door yet.

After it was locked up, me and Mr. Lowenstein, and sometimes Sally, though she usually left a little ahead of us, would go out the back and Mr. Lowenstein would lock the back door. Every night he'd say, "Need a ride?" And I'd say, "No, I prefer to walk."

If Sally was there when we were, he'd ask her the same thing.

Sally, she walked too. In the other direction. I took a ride once, but Mr. Lowenstein's car stunk so heavily of cigar smoke it made me sick. Dad used to smoke cigars and they smelled just that way, cheap and lingering. That smoke got into your clothes it took more than one run through the laundry to get the stink out.

Besides, I liked to walk. I even walked home in the rain a couple of times. Mr. Lowenstein argued with me about it, but I told him I liked the rain just fine. I liked coming in out of it, all wet and cold, and then undressing and toweling off, taking a hot shower, and going to bed in my underwear. It's a simple thing, silly maybe, but I liked it.

But this time these guys came in because the door was unlocked when it should have been locked. Doesn't matter. They were the kind of guys that were going to come in eventually.

One of them was like a fireplug in a blue suit. He had a dark hat with the brim pushed back a bit, the kind of style you saw now and then, but it made him look stupid. I figure it wasn't all looks. He had that way about him that tells you he isn't exactly lying in bed at night trying to figure out how electricity works, or for that matter what makes a door swing open. The other guy, he was thinner and smoother. Had on a tan suit and a tan hat and one of his pants legs was bunched up against his ankle like he had a little gun and holster strapped there.

They came over smiling, and the tall one, he looks at Mr. Lowenstein, says, "We work for The Community Protection Board."

"The what?" Mr. Lowenstein said.

"It don't matter," said the short stout one. "All you got to do is be quiet and listen to the service we provide. We make sure you're protected, case someone wants to come in and set fire to the place, rob it, beat someone up. We make sure that don't happen."

"I got insurance," said Mr. Lowenstein. "I been here for years, and I been fine."

"No," said the tall one. "You don't have this kind of insurance. It covers a lot that yours don't. It makes sure certain things don't happen that are otherwise bound to happen."

It was then that me and Lowenstein both got it, knew what they meant.

"Way we see it, you ain't paying your share," said the tall one. "There's people on this block, all these businesses, and we got them paying as of last week, and you're all that's left. You don't pay, you'll be the only hold-out."

"Leave me out of it," Mr. Lowenstein said.

The tall one gently shook his head. "That might not be such a good idea, you know. Stuff can go wrong overnight, in a heartbeat. Nice theater like this, you don't want that. Tell you what, Mr. Jew. We're going to go away, but we'll be back next Tuesday, which gives you nearly a week to think about it. But after Tuesday, we don't get, say, one hundred dollars a week, we got to tell you that you haven't got our protection. Without it, things here are surely going to ride a little too far south."

"We'll see you then," said the stout one. "Might want to start putting a few nickels in a jar."

Sally had stopped when they came in. She was standing there listening, maybe ten feet away. The stout one turned and looked at her.

"Sure wouldn't want this little trick to get her worn-out old dress rumpled. And I'm going to tell you, girlie, what you got poured into it is one fine bon-bon."

"Don't talk about her like that," Mr. Lowenstein said.

"I talk like I like," said the stout one.

"This is your only warning about circumstances that can happen," said the tall one. "Let's not have any unpleasantness. All you got to do is pay your weekly hundred, things go swimmingly."

"That's right," said the stout one. "Swimmingly."

"Hundred dollars, that's a lot of money," said Mr. Lowenstein.

"Naw," said the stout one. "That's cheap, 'cause what could happen to this place, you, your employees, that fat wife of yours, this nice little girl, the retard there, it could cost a lot more to fix that, and there's some things could happen money can't fix."

They went out then, taking their sweet time about it. Sally came over, said, "What do they mean, Mr. Lowenstein?"

"It's a shake-down, honey," Mr. Lowenstein said. "Don't you worry about it. But tonight, I'm taking you both home."

And he did. I didn't mind. I sat in the backseat behind Sally and looked and smelled her hair through the cigar smoke.

In my little apartment that night I sat and thought about those guys, and they reminded me of my dad quite a bit. Lots of bluster, more than bullies. People who were happily mean. I worried about Mr. and Mrs. Lowenstein, and Sally, of course, and I won't lie to you. I worried about me.

Next day I went to work same as usual, and when I was getting my lunch, my hotdog to take up into the booth, Sally came over and said, "Those men last night. Are they dangerous?"

"I don't know," I said. "I think they could be."

"I need this job," she said. "I don't want to quit, but I'm a little scared."

"I hear you," I said. "I need this job too."

"You're staying?"

"Sure," I said.

"Will you kind of keep a watch on me?" she said.

That was kind of like asking a sparrow to fight a chicken hawk, but I nodded, said, "You bet."

I should have told her to take a hike on out of there and start looking for other employment, because these kinds of things can turn bad. I've seen a bit of it, that badness.

But thing was, I was too selfish. I wanted Sally around. Wanted her to be where I could see her, but another part of me thought about that and knew I might not be able to do a thing to protect her. Good intentions weren't always enough. Bert used to say the road to hell was paved with good intentions.

That night after work, as Sally was starting to walk home, I said, "How about I walk you?"

"I'm the other direction," she said.

"That's all right. I'll walk back after I get you where you need to go."

"All right," she said.

We walked and she said, "You like being a projectionist?"

"Yeah."

"Why?"

"Decent pay, free hotdogs."

She laughed.

"I like it up there in the booth. I get to see all those movies. I like movies."

"Me too."

"It's kind of weird, but I like the private part of it too. I mean, you know, I get a little lonely up there, but not too much. Now and again I've seen a picture enough I'm sick of it, or don't like it, I read some. I'm not a good reader. A book can last me a few months."

"I read magazines and books," she said. "I read *The Good Earth*."

"That's good."

"You've read it?"

"No. But it's good you have. I hear it's good."

"It was all right."

"I guess I prefer picture shows," I said. "Doesn't take as long to get a story. Hour or two and you're done. Another thing I like is being up high like that, in the booth, looking down on folks, and seeing those actors in the movies, me running the reels. It's like I own those people. Like I'm some kind of god up there, and the movies, those actors, and what they do, they don't get to do it unless I make it happen. That sounds odd, don't it?"

"A little," she said.

"I run their lives over and over every week, and then they move on, and for me they don't exist no more, but now I got new people I'm in charge of, you see. They come in canisters. I can't keep them from doing what they do, but without me, they wouldn't be doing nothing. I got to turn them on for them to actually be there."

"That's an interesting perspective," she said.

"Perspective?" I said. "I like that. Like the way you talk."

She seemed embarrassed. "It's just a word."

"Yeah, but you got some words I don't have, or don't use anyway. Don't know how. I'm always scared I'm going to say them wrong, and someone will laugh. I was afraid to say canister just then, and I know that one."

"That's okay," she said. "I can't say aficionado right. I know I say it wrong, and I don't know how it's actually said. I need to hear someone that knows."

"I don't even know what that word means," I said. "Or how you would come about working it into a sentence."

"I try a little too hard to do that," she said. "I'm taking a few courses on the weekends. They got classes like that over at the college. I've only seen the word in a textbook."

"College, huh?"

"You should sign up. It's fun."

"Costs money, though."

"It's worth it, I can get a better job I get an associate degree. I thought I might get married, but then I thought I'm too young for that. I need to do something, see something before I start wiping baby butts. Besides, the guys I've dated, none of them seem like husband material to me."

"Having a family may not be all that good anyway," I said. "It ain't always."

"I think I'd like it. I think I'd make a good wife. Not now, though. I want to live a little."

Right then I got to thinking maybe a family would be all right. Maybe I could do that with her. But it was just thinking. We passed by the drugstore on Margin Street, and I seen our reflection in the window glass. She looked like some kind of goddess, and me, well, I looked like a few sticks tied together with a hank of hair. Like I said, I don't think I got an ugly face, but I sure knew in that moment, I wasn't in her league. I saw too that the shop was closing down, and there were a couple guys and their girls coming out, arm-in-arm, and they were laughing and smiling.

I seen one of them guys look over at us, see Sally with me, and I could tell he was thinking, "How'd he manage that?" And then they turned and were gone.

We finally came to where she lived, which was a two-story brick building. It wasn't well lit up, but it was brighter than my place. At least there was a street light and a light you could see through the door glass into the hallway that led to the stairs.

"I live on the top floor," she said.

"That's good. High up."

"Oh yeah. You said you like being high up, at the theater."

"That's right."

"I look out the window at the people sometimes."

"I watch people too," I said. "It's not as good as the movies, but second or third time one plays, I start to watch people down in the seats, unless the movie is really good. Sometimes I can watch a movie every night and not get tired of it. Nothing is going to happen in it that I don't know about by then, and I like that too. I know who is who and who messes up and how it all ends. Real people. They can't do anything I can figure, not really. I like the movies 'cause I like knowing how it's going to come out."

"That's interesting," Sally said.

I wasn't sure she thought it was really all that interesting, and I wished then I'd talked about the weather, or some such, instead of how I was a god up in the projection booth. I can be such an idiot. That's what Dad always said, "You, son, are a loser and a goddamn idiot."

"All right," I said. "Well, you're here."

"Yes, I am. And thank you."

"Welcome."

We shuffled around there for a moment. She said, "Guess I'll see you tomorrow."

"Sure. I can walk you home again, you want."

"We'll see. Maybe. I mean, it depends. I'm thinking maybe I've blown it all out of proportion."

"Sure. You'll be okay."

I opened the glass door for her and she went inside. She turned at the stairs and looked back at me and smiled. I couldn't tell how real that smile was. Whatever she meant by it, it made me feel kind of small.

I smiled back.

She turned and came back. "It means someone who is a fan, who appreciates."

"How's that?"

"Aficionado," she said. "Or however it's supposed to sound."

She smiled and went back inside. I liked that smile better. I watched her through the glass door as she climbed up the stairs.

———

I showered and looked at my chest in the little medicine cabinet mirror while I dried off. The mirror was cracked, but so was my chest. It was all cracked and wrinkled from where I'd been burned.

I turned off the lights and went to bed.

Next morning I got up and went over to Bert's house. Missy was gone to do shopping, and though I would have been glad to see her normally, right then I was happy she was out.

Bert let me in and poured me some coffee and offered me some toast, and I took it. Sat at his table in their small kitchen and buttered the toast and put some of Missy's fig jam on it. They had about an acre of land out back of the house, and it had a fig tree on it, and they had a little garden out there every spring and part of the summer.

I ate the toast and drank the coffee, and we talked about nothing while I did.

When I finished eating, Bert poured me another cup of coffee, told me to come out and sit on the back porch with him. They had some comfortable chairs out there, and we sat side by side under the porch overhang.

"You want to tell me why you've really come over?" Bert said.

"There's some people come by the theater," I said. "Mooks."

"All right."

"They threatened Mr. Lowenstein, me, and Sally."

"Who's Sally?"

I told him all about her, and everything they'd said, what they looked like.

"I know who they are," he said. "But I don't know them, you understand?"

"Yeah."

"Look, kid. This isn't like in the old days. I'm seventy-four years old. Do I look like a tough guy to you?"

"You're tough enough."

"That time... That time there was no way out for you. Now, you got a way out. You quit that job and get another."

"I like it," I said.

"Yeah... All right. Yeah. I liked it too. I miss it sometimes, but I like better being home. I like being alive and being home to watch *Gunsmoke*. Me and Missy, we got it all right here. She put up with some stuff, and I don't want her to put up with any of that again."

"I hear you," I said.

"Not that I don't care, kid. Not that I don't bleed for you. But again, I'm seventy-four. I was younger then. And well, it was more immediate, and you being really young... You needed the help. You can walk away now. Or tell Lowenstein to pay the money. What I'd do. I'd pay the money."

"No," I said. "I can't."

"Your skin, kid, but I'm telling you, these guys are bad business. There's those two, and there's the three that run that place. Five I think."

"How do you know?"

"I ain't as connected as I once was, back before I started running the projector, but I still know some people and I get word from them now and then. Look, how about this? Let me ask around."

"All right," I said.

—

I showed a picture that night that I didn't watch, or even remember. I was on time with changing the reels, but I spent all my time watching Sally down there under the red light. She looked nervous, kept looking this way and that.

They said they'd be back next week, and it had only been three days, so I figured for the moment we were fine. I was figuring what to do when next week came.

After the show closed that third night, Lowenstein said, "I'm going to pay them."

"Yeah," I said.

"Yeah. I got a good business here. That's a bite every week, but those guys, I can't do nothing about them. I called the cops next day, and you know what they told me?"

"What?"

"Pay them."

"They said that?"

"Yeah, way I figure it, kid, they have the cops in their pocket. Or at least the right cops. They get money from the businesses, and the cops get a little taste."

I thought that was probably true, things I knew about people.

I walked Sally home again that night, and when I got back to my place, Bert was sitting on the steps. There was a small wooden box on the steps beside him.

"Damn, boy. I was about to give up."

"Sorry. I walked Sally home."

"Good. You got a girl. That's a good thing."

"It's not like that," I said.

"She's the one you told me about, right?"

"Yeah. But it's not like that."

"How is it?"

"Well, it's not like that. I think she wasn't scared, she wouldn't bother with me. I mean she's always nice, but, hell, you know, Bert.

There's me, and then there's this doll. Smart. She goes to night classes."

"Does she now?"

"Knows big words."

"How's she look?"

"Very nice."

"Big words and nice, that's fine, kid. You ought to try and touch base with that. You deserve it."

I looked at the box.

"Whatcha got there?"

He patted the box. "You know."

"Yeah. Guess I do."

"Asked around, these guys, they're muscling in on the territory. Giving the cops a bit of their juice. It's not like a big bunch of them. It's five guys, like I heard, way I told you. They think maybe they're going to become big bad business, and you know, they just might."

"All right," I said. "Just five."

"That's still a lot of guys."

"Certainly is. Mr. Lowenstein said he was going to pay them."

"That's good, kid. That's the best way all around. But, I got to tell you, month or two from now, it won't be one hundred dollars, it'll be two. They'll suck the place dry, then end up owning it. That's how they work. They already own the candy store on the corner. They just do a few places at a time till they got everyone in line, but they're growing. Pretty soon, all four blocks there, they'll own them. And then on from there, more blocks. Those kind of guys don't quit."

We were quiet for awhile. Bert stood up.

"I got to go back," he said. "Told Missy I'd only be gone a little while, and I've been gone a long while."

"Did she see the box?"

"No. I was careful about it. What she knows is I had some bad ways before I quit and took to the projector. She don't know about you and me and what happened. She just thinks you're a swell kid. She don't know I got the box. Remember, you don't keep it, or what's in it. You get rid of it. I don't never want to see it again. These guys, they're up the end of the street. The Career Building. Top floor."

"Why's it called that?" I asked.

"No idea. But they ain't so big time they got bodyguards or nothing. They just got themselves and some plans."

I nodded.

"Lowenstein talked to the police," I said.

"Yeah, well, I can tell you without you telling me how that worked out. Keep your head up, kid. And remember, there are other theaters and other girls in other places. Ditch the box and take a hound out of here."

He clapped me on the shoulder as he passed. I turned and watched him hobble along the street, hands in his pockets.

—

That night I lay down on the bed with my clothes on, still wearing my shoes too. I lay there with the box beside me on the bed.

I remembered how my dad liked to come in with his women when we lived together, how he'd do what he did with them with me laying there nearby, just a kid.

I remembered that it wasn't enough for him, and when they were gone, he'd touch me. He liked to touch me. He said it was all right. It didn't feel all right to me.

One time I said that. That it was not right, that it was odd, and he pushed my chest down on the stove grate and held me there. I screamed and I screamed, but in that place where we lived, no one came. No one cared.

Except Bert. Bert and Missy lived there then. He had just started at the theater, doing the projection, and I'd go up there and talk with him, and one time, he sees me bleeding through my shirt. This was the time I was burned. It scabbed and the scabs busted and bled.

That's how he knew about me. I kind of spilled it all out when he asked how I was hurt. I opened my shirt. You could see the grate marks from the stove as clear as a tattoo.

Bert knew my dad. My dad, Bert said, did some work for certain men in the neighborhood that he knew. Work that involved his fists and sometimes more than that.

I never knew what Dad did until then. I never asked and had never cared. I was happiest when he was gone and I was alone. I liked going to school just to be away from him, but like I said, I had to quit that before I finished.

I told Bert how Dad came in the night he burned me and tried to touch me, and I fought him. I was bigger by then, but I was no match. He held me down and did what he wanted, way he always did. It really hurt that time. He said it would hurt even worse if I fought him next time. Said I'd end up like Doris. That was my mother. I had suspected something bad happened to her, that she didn't just run away like he said, but right then I knew it, and I knew he was the one that did it.

He pushed me into the stove after that. He made me watch him heat it up and when it was hot, he pushed me into it. Said it was a lesson.

I didn't want to whine about what happened, but that time I was in the projection booth with Bert, I told him because I was angry. I felt like there was something wrong with me that my Dad wanted to do that to me.

"It ain't you, kid. It's him. He's the one messed up, not you."

"I'm going to kill him," I said.

"He'll turn that around on you," Bert said. "I know who he is and what he is. He's worse than I thought, but he's not someone you can handle, kid. You'll just disappear."

I cried.

Bert put his arm around me, said, "All right, kid. It's going to be okay."

———

I ended up staying with Bert, which wasn't all that far from where I lived with Dad. Bert had just moved from the apartments where we were to a place around the corner. Word got around where Bert lived and that I was with him. Dad came by with another guy, a short fellow with a shiny bald head. He wasn't the kind of guy that wore a hat. You didn't see that much then, a guy without a hat.

"I've come to pick up my son," Dad said.

Dad was standing outside the door with that bald guy. Bert was holding the door open. He had a .45 automatic in his hand, out of sight behind the door frame. There was a screen between them. I was standing back in the little dump of a living room, out of sight. From the angle I was standing I could see them in the mirror across the way against the wall.

"He don't want to go," Bert said. "He's taking him a kind of vacation."

"I'm his father. He has to go."

"Naw. He don't have to do nothing."

"I could get the police."

"Yeah, you could," Bert said. "You could do that. But, the boy, he's got a story to tell."

"That's what it is, a story."

"You think I think that?"

"I don't care what you think. Tell my son to come out."

"Not today."

"What I'm thinking, is we can come in and get him," the bald man said.

"I was thinking you might be thinking that," Bert said. "And I was thinking, you do that, it won't be such a good idea."

"They say you used to be something," the bald man said. "But now you run a projector."

"There's all sorts of people got opinions about me," Bert said. "You try and take that boy, you're able to talk later, you can form your own opinion, tell people, spread it around."

"All right," Dad said. "You keep him. For now. But he's coming home."

"You get lonely nights?" Bert said.

"It's best you watch your mouth," Dad said. "Best you watch yourself altogether."

"Unless you're going to get tough and eat your way through the screen, you ought to go on now," Bert said.

"You are setting yourself up for a world of hurt," Dad said.

"Am I?" Bert said.

"Guy like you with a nice wife, and a shitty, safe job at the picture show, that could all get stood on its head."

Bert went a little stiff.

"It's never good to threaten me," Bert said.

"What we're doing here," said the bald man, "is giving you chance to make it easy on yourself, or that threat as you call it, it'll turn into a promise."

"Why wait," Bert said, and brought the .45 around where they could see it. "Come on in."

Bert flipped the latch on the screen with the barrel of the .45.

"I'm giving you an invitation," Bert said.

"We got time," said Dad. "We got time and we got ways, and you have just stepped in the stink, mister."

"We'll see who stinks when it's all over," Bert said.

Dad and the bald man turned and walked away. I went over and stood near the door. I watched them get in a car, the bald man at the wheel. Dad looked out the side window at the house. He saw me. He smiled the way a lion smiles.

———

So later I was sleeping on the couch, and Missy and Bert were in their room, or so I thought, but I rolled over and there's Bert across the way with a wooden box, and he's taking something out of it and putting it in his coat pockets, and going out the door.

I got up and put on my clothes and went over and looked at the box. It was empty. The bottom of it was packed with cloth. Otherwise, it was empty.

Slipping out the door I went down the drive and looked around the hedges and saw Bert walking brisk-like. I waited until he was pretty far down, and then I followed.

It was a long walk and the wind was high and there was a misty kind of rain. Bert walked fast. He was a younger man then, but no kid, but still, he moved quick.

Bert came to a corner and turned, and when I turned, I didn't see him anymore. I was out of the housing part of town, and there were buildings. I stood there confused for a moment, and then I eased along, and when I got to the far side of the big building, I peeked around it. I saw Bert on one of the little porches off the building, in front of a door. He was under a light. He reached up with something and knocked the bulb out, then he took that something and stuck it in the door. I heard a snick, and a moment later, he was inside and out of sight.

I eased up to the porch, but I couldn't make myself go in. I waited there and listened, and after awhile I heard sounds like someone coughing loudly, and then there was a yell, and then that coughing sound again.

After a moment, the door pushed open and nearly knocked me off the porch. It was Bert.

"Damn, kid. What you doing here?"

"I followed you?"

"I see that."

He took the automatic and held it up and unscrewed the silencer on the end of it. He put the silencer in one coat pocket, the gun in the other.

"Come on, fast. Not running, but don't lollygag neither."

"Did you?"

"Yeah. But not your old man. He's back at the apartments. That's what the bald bastard said when I asked."

"You asked?"

"Yeah. Nicely. And when he told me, I shot him. Couple times. There was another guy there I didn't know about, came out of the toilet. I shot him too. Might as well be straight with you, kid. They're deader than snow in July. Come on, hustle a little."

Stunned is how I felt, but happy too. I mean, those guys back there, they hadn't done nothing to me, not like Dad, but they were on his side. Probably thought I was telling lies. Probably thought a stove burn was something I deserved. Lot of guys thought like that around there. Your father's word was the law. And all those guys, they believed in a strict law. You were either for them, or against them.

We came to the apartment where my dad lived, where I had lived with him. There was a hedge row that was never trimmed that led along both sides of the walk that went up to the apartment house. Inside, you had to go down the hall and make a turn to the left to get to our place.

Standing in the shadow of the hedge, Bert said, "You sure about this kid? Dead is dead. And he is your father."

"He's nothing to me, Bert. Nothing. He gets me back, he'll just kill me, and you know it. I'm nothing to him, just something to own and use and throw away. Like he did my mother. My mother was all right. I can still remember how she smelled. Then one day she wasn't there, and that's because of him. She's gone. He's here."

214

"Still, kid, he's your father."

"I'm all right with it."

Bert nodded. He took the gun and silencer out of his coat pockets and screwed the silencer into place. "You sit this one out. Go on home."

"You used to do stuff like this, didn't you, Bert?"

"All the time," he said. "I ain't proud of it. Except for tonight. These guys, your father. I'm all right with that. Maybe it'll make up for some of the other things I done."

"I'm staying with you, Bert."

"You don't want that kid."

"Yeah, I do."

We went along the walk then and when we got to the door, Bert handed me the gun. I held it while he worked the lock and got it open with a little wedge. He pried the wood loose at the door. I gave him back the gun. We were inside so quickly and silently, we might as well have been ghosts.

When we got to Dad's door, Bert started with the wedge, but I grabbed his hand. We had an extra key stuck into the side of the door frame where it was cracked. You had to be looking for it to know it was there. We kept some putty over it the color of the wood. I reached around the frame and took out the putty and pulled out the key. I unlocked the door.

I could feel him in the room. I don't know how else to say that, but I could feel him. He was sitting in a chair by the bed, smoking a cigarette, and about the time we saw him, he realized we were in the room.

"It's best you don't call out," Bert said.

Dad clicked the lamp by his chair. He was soaked in light and there was enough of it he could look out and see us. We stepped closer.

"I guess I should have known you'd come, Bert. I know who you are. I know what you've done."

"Shouldn't have threatened me," Bert said.

"Guy with me, Amos, he said you did some things some years back, for some boys he knew. He wasn't in the racket then, just on the outskirts. He said you were a kind of legend. We saw you the other day, standing in that doorway, you didn't look so legendary. Yet, here you are."

"Yep," Bert said. "Here I am."

"I'm not going to be all right, I yell or don't yell, am I?"

"Naw, you ain't."

That's when Dad grabbed at the lamp and tried to sling it at Bert, but the wire was too short and the plug didn't come out of the wall. The lamp popped out and back when the plug didn't give, rolled along the floor tumbling light, and then Dad was on his feet, in front of the chair, and he had a gun in his hand he'd pulled from the cushions.

Bert fired his automatic.

There was a streak of light and stench of gun powder and a sound like someone coughing out a wad of phlegm, and then Dad sat back down in the chair. The gun he had dangled from his finger. He was breathing heavily. He tried to lift his hand with the gun in it, but he couldn't do it. He might as well have been trying to lift a steel girder.

Bert reached over and took Dad's gun from his hand and gave it to me to hold. He set the lamp up, then. The light from it lay on Dad's face like it had weight. Dad was white. I looked at him and tried to feel something, but I didn't. I didn't feel bad for him, and I didn't feel good about it. I didn't feel nothing. Not right then.

Dad was wheezing and there was a rattling in his chest. I guess the shot got him through one of his lungs.

"We can watch him die if it'll give you pleasure, or I can finish him, kid. Your call."

I lifted the pistol in my hand and pointed it at Dad.

Bert said, "Whoa."

I paused.

"No silencer," Bert said. He traded guns with me. "He can't do nothing, like you couldn't when you was a kid. Get up close and give it to him."

I moved close and put the barrel of the pistol to his head and pulled the trigger.

The gun coughed.

———

Now I had the box with the gun and silencer in it. Those many years ago, Bert had wiped my dad's gun clean with a dish rag, and dropped it and the gun on the floor. He had kept his own gun, though, and now I was to use it and get rid of it. I think it wasn't only about safety, about not getting caught. I think it was Bert's way to say he was done from then on.

Back then, when Dad was dead, we walked out of there silently and down the street quickly. I knew and Bert knew what we had done, and that was enough. We never talked about it again. Didn't even hint such a thing had happened.

I slept well for the first time in years. I finally got my own place, and eventually I took the projectionist job. Things had been all right until those guys came around.

Now things had come full circle. It wasn't just me I was protecting now, it was Sally and the Lowensteins. Under the gun and silencer there was the wedge Bert had used to jimmy the doors way back then. I saw there was a piece of paper under that.

There were three addresses listed on it. Two apartments were listed at the same general address.

The other had a place listed outside of town, almost out in the country. It was near the railroad tracks. For all the high roller talk those guys blew out, they were just like my father had been. Living on the margins, the rest of it going for booze and women. Big time in the lies, small time in their lives, as Bert once said.

I put the gun in my front pants pocket. The grip stuck out. I covered it with my shirt and stuck the silencer in the other pocket. I put the wedge in my back pocket, where I usually carried my wallet. I wouldn't need the wallet that night.

When I walked the gun, silencer and wedge were heavy in my pockets.

The first address was not far from where I was, not far from the theater.

Outside, I started to turn down the walk, and then I stopped. A car was parked at the curb. I knew that car. A man got out.

It was Bert.

"I decided maybe I ought to come," Bert said.

—

The apartments were easy and quick. Bert took the wedge from me and opened the doors. I went in and they were in bed together, naked, two guys. I had heard of such. I shot both of them in their sleep, Bert holding a flashlight on them so I could see it was them. They weren't the two who had come to see me, but they were part of the five, Bert said. The scammers, the thugs. It was over so quick they never knew they were dead.

At the other apartment we got in easy as before, but no one was there.

That bothered me, but there was nothing for it.

We drove out to the place on the edge of town and parked in a grove of pecan trees that grew beside the road, got out and walked up to the house. There was a light on inside. There were no houses nearby, though there were a couple within earshot, dark and silent.

We went to the windows and took a peek. There was a guy sitting on the couch watching TV. We could hear him laughing at something. The voices on the TV had canned laughter with them. He wasn't one of the two that had come to the theater, but Bert said he was one of the five.

Through an open doorway we saw the two who had threatened Mr. Lowenstein step into sight. They came out of the kitchen, each carrying a beer.

We stepped back from the window.

"Alright," Bert said. "That's all five, counting these three. They're together. That's all right. You don't have to worry about rounding up the one that wasn't at the apartment. He's the one on the couch."

"You're sure?"

"I know who they are," he said. "They been around awhile. It's the ones I was told about, ones bothering the block. Until recent they just been guys walking around after other guys, now they're trying to carve some territory. This is all of them."

"What do we do?"

"Well, it's easier to kill them in their sleep when they can't fight back. But I got an old saying. You get what you get."

"Meaning?"

"Meaning there's one more than I expected, and I got to go back to the car, kid."

We went back to the car. Bert got a sawed off double-barrel shotgun out of the trunk. The stock was sawed down too. He opened it and slipped in two shells from a box in the trunk, and then he grabbed a handful of shells and stuck them in his pocket.

"Hoping I wouldn't need this. It goes boom real loud."

We walked back.

We waited out there in the bushes by the house for an hour or so, not talking, just waiting. I thought back on how it had been with Dad, me pushing that gun against his head, his eyes looking along that barrel at me. It was pretty nice. And those guys earlier that night. Didn't know them. Never talked to them, but considering they were all and of a same, I was alright with it. Maybe I was more like Dad than I wanted to be.

After a while, Bert said, "Look kid. We can come back another time when they're sleeping, maybe the other guy is back in his apartment then, splitting their numbers, or we can be bold and get it over with."

"Let's be bold."

"There's a door on either side of the living room, and if we go through the back, one of us coming out on either side, we can get them before they got time to think. Another thing, anyone else shows up, more of them there than we think, we got to finish things. Hear what I'm saying?"

I nodded.

"Don't get us in our own crossfire," Bert said. "That would be bad form, one of us shooting the other."

Slipping around back, Bert took the wedge and stuck it in the door and pulled and the door made a little popping sound. Nothing too loud. Nothing you could hear over the blare of that TV set.

Inside he went right and I went left.

Only the guy on my side saw us before we cut loose. He was the tall guy that came to the theater. He had tried to pull the gun out from under his pants leg, strapped to his ankle. He should have found a better place to keep it. I fired the silenced .45. It made that big tuberculosis cough and part of his face flew off.

That's when Bert cut down with the shotgun. One barrel, then the other. Both of those guys were dead. A lot of them was on the wall. The sound of that shotgun in the house was like two atomic bombs going off.

Bert glanced at the TV. "I hate that show, that canned laughter."

I thought for a moment he was going to shoot the TV.

We got out of there quick. Going out the back way. The canned laughed roared on the TV.

The only thing that had touched the door was the wedge, so no fingerprints to worry about.

I expected to see lights on in the houses down the way, but nothing had changed. Two shotgun blasts in the night must not have been as loud as they seemed to me. Maybe no one cared.

Bert put the shotgun on the seat between us and we drove away. He wheeled farther out of town, on down to the river. He drove down there and we pulled under the bridge, got out, wiped down the guns just for good measure, then threw them in the river, along with the wedge and the silencer.

When Bert pulled up at the curb in front of my place, I started to get out. "Hold it, Kid."

I took my hand off the door lever.

"Listen here. You and me, we got a bond. You know that."

"The closest," I said.

"That's right. But I'm going to tell you something tough, kid. Don't come around no more. It's not a good idea. I done for you what I could. More than I meant to. I got my past in that river now, and I want to leave it there. I love you, kid. I ain't mad at you or nothing, but I can't have you around. I can't think on those kind of things anymore."

"Sure, Bert."

"Don't take it hard, okay?"

"No," I said.

"It ain't personal, but its got be like that. And throw away that gun box. Good luck, kid."

I nodded. I got out. Bert drove away.

———

Next night I walked Sally to her apartment, and every night after that because she was scared. Walked her home until the day before the thugs were supposed to come around.

221

Sally and the Lowensteins were worried, but Mr. Lowenstein had put aside the money for them. He couldn't see a percentage on his side. Sally said she hated it, but was glad he was paying.

Mr. Lowenstein had read the papers, read about the murders in the apartment house and in the house outside of town, but he didn't put it together with those guys we had talked to. No way he could have. He talked about it, though, said the world was getting scary. I agreed it was.

On the last night I walked Sally, she said, "I'm not going to come back to work tomorrow. After Mr. Lowenstein pays them, I'll come back, so I won't need you to walk me for awhile. I think after he pays them, I'm going to be all right on my own."

"Okay," I said.

"I don't want to be there when they come around, even if he is paying. You understand?"

"Understood."

I stood there for a long moment with my hands in my pockets. I was glad she was safe.

"Sally, putting that ugly business aside, what do you think about you and me getting some coffee next week? You know, before work. We can even go to the movie on our day off, and for nothing."

I tried to say that last part with a smile since we see the movies all the time. Me up in the booth, her over by the seats.

She smiled back at me, but it wasn't much of smile. It was like she had borrowed it.

"That's sweet," she said. "But I got a boyfriend, and he might not like that."

"Never seen you with anyone," I said.

"We don't get out much. He comes around though."

"Does he?"

"Yeah. And you know, I got the college stuff in the mornings and work midday and nights, then I got to study. My time is tight. We get the one day off, and there's so much to do, and I got to spend some time with my boyfriend, you know?"

"Yeah. Okay. What's this boyfriend's name?"

She thought on that a little too long. "Randy."

"Randy, huh? That's his name?"

"Yes. Randy."

"Like Randolph Scott. Like that movie we showed last week. *The Tall T.* You said you liked it."

"Yeah. Like that. His name is Randolph, but everyone calls him Randy."

"All right," I said. "Well, good luck to you and Randy."

"Thanks," she said, like I had meant it. Like I thought there really was a Randy.

Sally never did come back to work after that. And of course the thugs didn't show up. Mr. Lowenstein got to keep his hundred dollars. All along the block, those businesses, they got to keep their money too. Guess someone else like those fellows could come along, but what happened to those five, it's pretty discouraging to that kind of business. They don't know what kind of gang there is that owns this block. There was just me and Bert, but they don't know that.

I like it pretty good up there in the projection booth. Sometimes I look out where Sally used to stand, but she isn't there, of course. Mr. Lowenstein never hired another girl to take her place. He decided people would come anyway.

I saw Sally around town a couple of times, both times she was with a guy, and it wasn't the same guy. I'm pretty sure neither of them were named Randy. If she saw me she didn't let on. I wonder what she'd think to know what I did for her, for all of us.

What I do now, is I show the movies and I go home. I used to walk by Bert's place every now and then. I'm not sure why. I read in the papers that his wife Missy died. I wanted to send flowers, or something, but I didn't.

Just the other day, I read Bert died.

I like my job. I like being the projectionist. I'm okay with it, being up there in the booth by myself, feeling mostly good about things like they are, but I won't kid you, sometimes I get a little lonely.

Introduction to

EVERYTHING SPARKLES IN HELL

There was a real Nat Love, but my character is an amalgam of many black westerners, from cowboys to soldiers to gunfighters to marshals.

Nat Love, however, was the impetus for several stories I wrote about a western hero with the same name, as well a novel, *Paradise Sky*, which to date is my favorite of all my novels.

The real Nat Love wrote an autobiography that is obviously a mixture of real life and dime novel adventurers in the vein of other tall tales about Buffalo Bill, Wild Bill Hickok, Jesse James, and so on. I discovered the book over thirty years ago, and was immediately engrossed. I felt driven to write a novel about Nat, or at least one inspired by him.

And I did. But not right off. It took me thirty years. Problem was, thirty years ago, no one would publish a big novel about a black cowboy. Novels about the black experience existed, but not in the epic manner I wanted to write it. My idea was more of a historical than a standard Western that Elmer Kelton used to call Powder Burners, yet, I didn't want to write a pure historical document. I wanted to write about a character that was real, and simultaneously larger than life.

Publishers in the early eighties told me "Black people don't read, and white people don't want to read about black people."

So, against my wishes I put it on the back burner. In the nineties I tried again, and this time I got a more politically correct response. "We don't know who our audience would be for a book like this?"

I was discouraged, but the idea of writing the novel wouldn't go away. Finally, I decided I would write short stories, and I wrote a couple, "Soldier'n" and "Hides and Horns", and finally a novella, *Black Hat Jack*.

It gave me a bit of peace, let me siphon off some of my desire to write about the character, and that worked briefly. A short time later, I asked my editor at Mulholland if they would be interested in such a book, and he said, "Absolutely."

Thanks, Josh Kendall, and thank you Mulholland/Little Brown. The novel became *Paradise Sky*.

I never attempted to follow Nat's autobiography, or to make my Nat Love the same person as the man who wrote the autobiography, but I wanted to capture his spirit. I named my protagonist Nat Love after him because he was the only black cowboy I knew of who had written such a book, and I wanted to honor his memory in that way. I began to research other black cowboys, and found they were not rare at all, something we had all been led to believe due to racists' accounts and the marginalizing of blacks in the west, the Western movies we saw, the standard cowboy novels we read.

In fact, about every third cowboy was black or Mexican, or American Indian. There were black desperadoes, gunslingers, soldiers (Buffalo Soldiers they were called), marshals, and so on. One of the most respected marshals in the west, and perhaps the basis for the Lone Ranger, was Bass Reeves, a black man who appears in *Paradise Sky*.

When I wrote the novel, I borrowed from the short stories I had written about Nat, but not the novella, as it was out of timeline. I really liked it, but I had created a different series of events for my hero in *Paradise Sky*, so *Black Hat Jack* and the historical events it depicts, based on the Second Battle of Adobe Walls, failed to fit in.

I tried to be as historically accurate as I could, though some small discrepancies snuck in. I attempted to correct those in the paperback edition, or at least the ones I felt were worth correcting. In some cases, I decided the story trumped the true history.

This story takes place after the events of *Paradise Sky*. It is not only Nat's story, but that of Choctaw, who appears at the end of the novel. I liked that guy and brought him back.

I also had Nat leave his actual stomping grounds, and his marshal jurisdiction, to pursue a band of killers who had fled Arkansas and made it all the way to the Rocky Mountains.

One last thing. The title, "Everything Sparkles in Hell," is a title I had originally used for my novel *The Thicket*, but my editor felt *The Thicket* was a better moniker for the tale.

I agreed with him.

But I still liked that title. It came from a phrase in *The Thicket*, and it's used here again. This time, it seemed like exactly the correct title.

I love Nat. I don't know if I'll write about him again, or not, but it was sure fun visiting with him again.

EVERYTHING
SPARKLES IN HELL

"Every dog has his day, unless there are more dogs than days."

BAT MASTERSON

I tell you right off and straight as an arrow, I wasn't expecting what happened. Judge Parker had sent me out to get a two-bit chiseler named Duncan Rakes, along with three other ruffians, but when I found Duncan he was already dead. He was the first one I found, on account at some point the other three split off from him. It was his trail that was the easiest to follow, and the way you do it, is you try to take a man separate of the others, if you can, on account of then he's just one man, but also 'cause he's less likely going to feel he's got something to prove to his pals.

I had been after Duncan for quite a few weeks, and as it turned out, winter had got to him and made him miserable. The only thing worse than tracking through the Rockies in the dead of winter with snow on the ground, is being tracked. It sets a man off his feed and makes him nervous. Winter got to him, all right, but it never got around to finishing him off. He took care of that himself. Between the forks of a dead tree he had seated himself, pulled his pistol, put it to his forehead, probably holding it with both hands, and shot his brains out.

A forty-four does a damn good job for that kind of work, and Duncan's blood, and what brains he had, were splattered all over the snow behind him, and a big chunk of his head was gone, like a watermelon someone had chopped on with a hatchet.

Way I had finally found him was his horse showed up on the trail to greet me, minus its rider. At least Duncan had been nice enough to take the saddle and bridle and such off the horse and let it go. I guess he thought the horse might start him a little family up there with a nest of foxes, or some such. Thing is, if I hadn't come along, he might as well have shot it, maybe had a big fat horse steak before blowing his brains out.

When the horse showed up I figured Duncan had met up with some wild Indians or someone who had grown tired of his ways, or didn't like his conversation. The horse was glad to see me, and easily let me put a rope on it, looping it around its nose and neck to make a bridle.

From folks I had talked to who knew Duncan, I got the idea you could tire of him quickly. Rumor was his first wife had walked off into a lake and drowned herself so she wouldn't have to hear him talk no more. I like to think that there is an exaggeration, but one never can tell. You have to trust who's telling you the story, and frankly, some of us are suspect.

The saddle and such were lying under the tree. There was a couple blankets there, and I stretched one of them out on the ground and poured some grain on top of it and roped off his horse so it could eat off of the blanket. I put a feed bag on my horse, which was a spare mount, as Satan had gotten something under a shoe, and was healing up back home with my wife spoiling him with too many carrots and sugar cubes. The horse I had, Dobbin, was all right as long as you didn't need to run fast, pull anything too heavy, and didn't need it to have horse sense, 'cause Dobbin wasn't as bright as a newborn chick. I liked to think his heart was in the right place, though. He liked to give me kisses.

I went over and looked at Duncan real good, just to make sure it was him. It looked like him in general, but that bullet had messed up his recognizable features, such as they were. Still, his nose nailed him to be who I thought he was. It was about the size of a big ole cucumber and was red spotted from too much alcohol, a bottle of which I found lying at the base of the tree. The liquor had been his companion in the deed, having made it easier for him to do what he felt he ought to do, which was shoot himself, as opposed to freezing to death.

He should have brought himself a bigger jacket and some underclothes. I had. I was cold, but okay. He was real cold and dead. You got to think ahead, be you a bandit, or a marshal like me.

Come right down to it, I guess in the end, Duncan had been a good judge of character.

Now there were three left.

———

I looked him over a little more, and saw that he had been cut up bad across the body, and there was a big chunk out of his shoulder. I hadn't noticed that at first because he was so damn bloody, but I saw then an animal had been at him, and that began to change my view on why he had ended up under the tree, though I hadn't got all the answers to that yet.

Looking around a little more, I saw too that there was a blood trail where he had walked to the tree and shot himself. He had to be one tough hombre to have done that. Not far up from that blood trail I saw huge tracks. Bear tracks, and not the little tracks I was used to seeing in Arkansas. This wasn't any black bear, it was a grizzly, and an oversized one at that, though I gave thought to sunlight spreading the tracks a mite, making them look larger.

Down a slope I found something else, the corpse of a grizzly bear cub. It had been shot, and there was a swath of blood where it had been dragged. I looked it over, and I looked the ground over. In the swath of blood I could see the little bear tracks, and then I saw another splash of blood on the snow along with more of those big bear tracks, and I figured that to be where Duncan got hit up by the grizzly. It was now clear to me that he hadn't just been cold, he'd been dreadfully wounded and had finished himself off. Had probably drank the whisky before the cub showed up, after he unsaddled his horse. I got it in my head too the horse had run off from him, and he had gone after it, found the cub, shot it because that's just the kind of guy Duncan was. What really surprised me, though, was why the bear that had mauled him hadn't followed him to the tree and made a meal of him.

I trudged through the snow, back to the horses and Duncan's body, put the saddle on his horse, and led it after me, trying to follow a trail that would lead me back to where the four had split up, but I wasn't all that good at it when the weather was this bad. I could tell obvious tracks, but they might have split up days before and far from where Duncan was now.

Before night, I threw me up a tarp, tied it to a tree, and made a kind of tent out of it and built a small fire just inside of it, which is something you got to be careful about, wanting enough heat to matter, but not so much you burn you and the tent down.

Guess it must have been about daybreak when I got up, still wearing my boots, having changed my socks before bedtime and taken off my jacket to climb into my bed roll.

I pushed the front of the tent open wide so I could see clearly, then I pulled my jacket on, took my Winchester with the loop cock, and slipped out of the tent and made my way down the hill a bit, and fetched up behind a tree and watched the daylight break clean over the trees and the snow. Breathing the air was like swallowing broken glass.

I was a long way from Arkansas, and well out of my jurisdiction, but I had sworn to myself that I'd bring those four killers in, dead or alive. They were some of the worst there was. I was damn sure armed for it. I had my Winchester, and on my hip I carried a Colt .44 converted pistol, and a LeMat, which was kind of rare, in a shoulder holster. The LeMat shot nine rounds, and with another trigger you could fire off a shotgun shell that was tucked in a barrel under the one for the regular ammunition.

I took one last deep breath and drew in the beauty of the mountains, went back to the tent and squatted down and started me a fresh fire, which took some work, due to how wet with snow all the wood was, but I found enough dry under heaps of dead brush. I started up a pot of coffee. I got out the frying pan, the lard and the dried meat, and was about to cook, when I saw a man come into sight, riding toward my tent on a big horse. He was bundled up tight in a thick fur jacket and a fur hat with ear flaps. He was leaning forward in the saddle, grinning in my direction. As he came close, I touched my rifle, which I had handily propped against a log.

"Why Nat," he yelled out, "you left a trail even you could follow."

"Choctaw," I said, stood up and went smiling toward him.

Choctaw was bean pole thin, even though he could eat a hog out of house and home, and maybe embarrass it some. He had a nest of wild hair on his head, touched here and there with lint, and his skin was dark and a bit red looking, like chocolate rubbed over with strawberry jelly.

On top of that nest of hair he wore that ear-flap hat that seemed destined to be blown away, but was probably pinned up there. Choctaw was part Choctaw Indian and part colored. He wasn't a marshal, but he was a tracker that Judge Parker kept on retainer, and he could track a fish fart underwater and could tell you how much the fish weighed and who its friends were.

Some said he was the greatest tracker the West had ever seen, but I figure they wasn't counting on a lot of pure blood Indians who'd been taught to chase a deer across the countryside from the time they rolled out of their mamas, hitting the ground running.

"You ate yet?" I said, as he dismounted and I took hold of the reins.

"I always say no," he said. And this was true. As I said, he was an eater.

I tied Choctaw's horse off with mine and Duncan's, and we ducked under the tent. I gave him my spare cup and he poured his own coffee, using a neckerchief he pulled from his coat pocket as a pot holder.

He sipped the hot coffee as easily as if it were cold creek water. I put some meat in my frying pan along with a clump of lard, and started frying.

"You a long way off where you're supposed to be," Choctaw said.

"So are you."

"I got on your trail a few days after you set out. I was bored, thought you might want some company."

"What if I didn't?"

"Then I had a long trip home. But that's all right. I ain't really got nothing to do, and unlike you, I don't have a fine woman or kids to go back to. I don't even have a dog."

"You got a horse."

"I do at that, and he's a hell of a horse. Might not run as fast as some, but he's got the endurance for the mountains. Damn. This sure is pretty country. I was out here in seventy-one, and had kind of forgotten how it was, with that big sky and the trees, and this goddamn snow. I forgot how much I hate snow."

"We have snow at home," I said.

"Yeah, but not like this."

"Can you track in snow?"

"You mean besides someone just leaving big ole footprints in it? You mean when snow fills them prints and the wind is blowing, and you're so cold you'd sell your left nut for a cord of firewood? The answer is yes. And frankly, with them four being as bad as they are, I thought you might need my help, considering you ain't the tracker I am, or most anyone is."

"I'm not that bad."

"Alright, there's some worse."

I laughed at him. "It's sure good to see you Chocktaw. But, to clear things up, there's just three now. Duncan killed himself. He's back over there behind some trees. I tracked him, in my lesser way, figured out he had split up from the others, something that would have been obvious to you, and I found his dead ass under a tree. He's still there. Looks to me a bear has been at him."

"Then I'll tell you it's good I came along. You're going to need me to find your three men, 'cause tonight, the weather is going to be a lot worse and the snow is really going to blow."

"How do you know?"

"The clouds, the way the wind feels, the way the mountain feels."

"I can recognize a snow cloud," I said, "but feel a mountain? You can feel a mountain?"

"Easy as I can feel a woman's touch. I can read weather good. You ain't really bad yourself, but some of us have certain skills others don't, and I tell you, tonight the weather is going to be a sparkling hell, and hell ain't always hot, and it ain't always ugly. Truth is, my old grandad used to say, hell is misleading. It suckers you along, 'cause you see, everything sparkles in hell, and what seems pretty and inviting, can turn bad and infernal. So, I've come along to save your black ass."

"That's mighty white of you," I said, and we both laughed.

We had our coffee and breakfast, such as it was, and then on horseback we rode over to where I had found Duncan's body. I had intent to bury him. It was too damn far to pack him on a horse back to Arkansas, and yesterday I had been too trail tuckered to bury him. Judge Parker would take my word I found him, or any of the others I caught or had to kill, so I didn't need the body. I had built a reputation of honesty with Parker, and besides, I was out of my jurisdiction and I'd have to tell Parker that. Thing that didn't change, however, was these four needed to be brought in, alive if possible, but if they pushed the situation with an intent to kill me, then I'd have no choice but to fight back. Course, one was taken care of, and now there were three.

They had robbed the Fort Smith General Store back in Arkansas, shot it up, and killed the owner of it, who was kind of an asshole, but they'd also killed a woman and a child and punctured some cans of peaches in a crossfire with the colored clean-up boy, who was about thirteen. He had gotten hold of a gun from behind the counter, tried to stop them, and had paid with his life. Robbers ended up with thirty-five dollars split four ways, and had each taken a bottle of sarsaparilla and some peanut candy. It wasn't even good candy.

Well, there we were looking down on that dead man again, and during last night, something had chewed off one of his hands, and from the tracks we both knew it was a wolf.

I got the little short shovel out of the pack on Dobbin, and used it to start digging a grave while Choctaw went to look the place over, going in the direction where I had seen the body of the bear cub.

The snow was packed and the ground was hard and rocky and it was really hard to dig. I thought about just leaving Duncan lying against the tree, but finally got the grave deep enough to put him in, though it was shallow. I packed the dirt back over him, and pulled a pretty heavy log over the mound without causing myself a hernia, then sat down on it and Duncan, and took a breather.

That's when Choctaw showed back up.

"Tracks and blood tell quite a story," he said.

"That right?"

"Oh, yeah."

"Are you going to tell it to me."

"Want to hear it?"

"Quit teasing."

He came and sat down on the log beside me.

"What happened here is Duncan messed up. I don't know when he split up with his pals, but he decided to find a place to put up for the night, that tree where we found him. He was unsaddling his horse when he got distracted. I think his horse broke off from him, and he went after it."

"That was my thinking," I said.

"You got that part right. Duncan come across that cub and shot it. Maybe for food, or maybe just because he could. Anyway, he killed that little bear, but mama bear was nearby, and oh, son, she's a big one. I ain't never seen tracks that big, on male or female."

"I thought the sun made them look bigger than they was."

"Nope. That there is one big bear. She's what some call an outgrowth, meaning some kind of curiosity or such. She's got a thousand pounds on her easy, and I'd guess her head to be two feet across."

"Bullshit," I said.

"Let's hope we don't get the chance to measure it, but that's how big I think she is. Those tracks are big and they are deep, and there are a few where you can see her standing with her feet apart, and they are wide apart. Rest of the time the back feet sort of step where the front feet go."

"That would make the tracks seem bigger," I said.

Choctaw nodded. "Would, but I know how to take that into account, Nat. This is one big ole bear. Thing is, Duncan probably was going to skin out that little bear and mama come for him, and he run, and she caught up with him, swatted him around a bit. I tried to figure why she didn't finish him, and then the winding back of the tracks told me. She went back to check on her baby, see if he was alive."

"Goddamn, that's sad."

"It is. Sadder to me than Duncan's death. That bastard wasn't worth the dynamite it would take to blow him up, but that little bear wasn't doing a thing. It wasn't like Duncan was protecting himself none and I doubt he was starving. He was just mean. I think that mama bear was so grieved, she didn't come back for him right away, and then he managed to drink some whisky and shoot himself."

"Surprised mama bear didn't eat him," I said.

"She wasn't hungry, Nat, she was angry, broken-hearted."

"You can read that in the sign?"

"Naw, I can read that in my heart."

"I want to dig Duncan up now and shoot him a couple of times," I said.

"I hear you, and it's tempting. Thing is, we might want to move on pretty quick. Once that big ole bear gets over dealing with the upfront grief, she might decide to play out a grudge on anything human."

"Bears do that?"

"People do it, and so do bears. I heard stories about a black bear doing just such a thing, losing a cub to a man and taking it hard, as you'd expect a mother to do. But that wasn't no grizzly. Still, she was a bedevilment for a month or so, killing one man and a bunch of small livestock, sheep and hogs, not eating them, just killing them. She went crazy. Finally, she was shot and killed."

"All right, then, let's not be around in case the grizzly comes back," I said.

"Them are my same sentiments."

Me and Choctaw packed up the camp and got on the hunt for them other three, me leading Duncan's horse by a long rope I had fastened around its nose and looped over its neck. Choctaw picked up their sign pretty quick. It was wooded where we were, but there was a trail through the trees, though you had to watch for limbs hanging down, and we had to stay in the middle of the trail to keep from getting scraped off our horses by the tree trunks.

Choctaw pointed. "See the snow is yellow there? That's piss. I can smell it."

"They stopped to pee, or a horse did?"

"No. That there is bear pee."

"You know how different pees smell?"

"I know it's pee by the smell, and I know it's a bear because you can see where that tree is all scratched up from it scraping its claws on it. It's under that big fir tree, and the snow didn't cover it, on account of that, and that's why we can still see and smell it. Also I know that the bear killed a horse."

"How the hell could you know that?"

"Cause the horse's foot is sticking up out of the snow over there."

Here's the thing. I had seen that hoof, but had thought it was a stick, 'cause I wasn't expecting no horse under the snow.

"Got to set your mind different on what you see, Nat. Notice where those limbs over there have been bent. And their height. Either something very tall came through, or men on horseback. Nothing would be that tall other than men on horseback, and you can see how them limbs got bent back all along the trail there."

Now, this was something I always looked for, 'cause as I said, I can track a little, but the bending Choctaw was talking about was so small, I wouldn't have noticed it, even if I was looking. He showed me where some pine needles had been scraped off and had gone into the snow, and you could only see the ends of them. They were green, not rusty-looking, so that meant they was recently knocked loose, as a pine needle on a live tree stays green year-round.

"That bear caught up with them, two or three days ago. You can tell it's been that long by the blood dried on that there tree."

I leaned out of the saddle a little to look at the tree he was pointing at. He was riding to the left of me, so to have noticed the blood meant he had the eyes of an eagle. But sure enough, there was a splash of blood against the trunk, almost blended into the wood, it having turned the dark color it does in time.

"There's a lot more to it, Nat, but I figure giving you a lesson might take a year or two, so we'll just stay after them. And by the way, there are only two now."

"Because of the horse? The horse might have got killed, but there's nothing says the man did. He could be double riding."

"See between the trees there, off in the shadows?"

I looked.

"Damn," I said.

There was dried blood in the snow up a rise between a nestle of trees, and a body was under one of them, or pieces of it was, and there was a bunch of clothes ripped up.

I rode over there for a closer look, Choctaw following, the both of us pushing limbs out of our faces, me leading Duncan's horse. I handed the rope for Duncan's horse to Choctaw, got down off my horse and sunk up near to my knees in the snow. Even I could figure that the big limbs over us in that spot had kept a lot of snow off the body, leaving it to be seen days later. The blood in the snow was crusty, like a dried booger. Still, way he was tucked up in the shadows of those trees, had Choctaw not pointed him out, I would most likely have missed him.

The body had been ripped and bit on and chewed, and there were piles of bear dung here and there, or what I assumed was bear dung. I knew I could rule out an elephant. The man's head was free of the body and was lying near the base of a tree, and it was rolled in such a way that the eyes were looking at me, or at least the hollows where the eyes had been. Birds, most likely had gone for them.

"That there is Jimmy Horn, ain't it?" Choctaw said. "He was still on his horse, leaning forward with his hands resting on the saddle horn."

"What's left of him, yeah."

"That bear's mad ain't worn off."

"So, the bear is between us and them?"

"Yep."

"That ain't good," I said.

"Look at it this here way. She's whittling them down for us. Thing is, though, we got to be careful we don't catch up with the bear before we catch up with them."

"The cub wasn't killed by these men, so why is she after them?"

"Because they're men. She's a man-killer now, and for the satisfaction of it. And here's a thought, Nat. We're men too. It's not like she's sorting out the good from the bad. She sees us all as belonging in the same sack."

I got my little shovel off my saddle, and Choctaw said, "That ground is going to be as hard as a widow's heart. Might as well leave him. Birds and critters and worms got to eat too, though with all this cold, the worms might be skipping meals for a while."

I thought about that, put the shovel back, climbed on my horse, took the rope for Duncan's horse from Choctaw, and we rode away from there.

Just before night we settled on a high spot between some trees for camp. I got out the tarp and we made a tent of it. We cut some brush and built a kind of barrier around the horses. It wasn't going to make them cozy, but it would cut the wind some, and the big trees overhead might keep the snow from falling on them in heaps.

During the night I heard something prowling near our camp, and I sat up for a while with my Winchester, expecting that big bear to pay us a visit, but it didn't, and after a time I quit hearing what I thought was a snuffing sound, laid myself down and went to sleep. The wind blew wild.

In the morning I seen that snow had blown through during the night, and had mounded up against our tent and had clung to the tree limbs and made the boughs heavy, so that they dipped toward the ground. Choctaw was already up and fixing breakfast, which was again some salted meat heated up, but he had some beans, and he'd added those to the pan. The coffee smelled strong and made me crave it.

Choctaw didn't have much to say that morning, on account of he had his nose in his breakfast, and he always took to eating in a silent and dedicated kind of manner. When we was finished, I scraped the frying pan out with snow and Choctaw packed it and the coffee pot away, and we got the tent folded up and started down the hill.

We had been traveling a while when we came upon a peculiar thing, someone in a tree. We could see him for some time before we got close. He was about twenty feet off the ground, nestled up between two big limbs with his legs hanging over, and neither of his feet had shoes, and in fact, they wasn't feet anymore, they was bones, all the meat being gone off of them. His throat was cut from ear to ear and some of the blood had frozen on his neck like a necklace. The rest of him was in decent enough shape for having been dead awhile. His head was nodded forward and his eyes was gone, and there was a feather in his long hair.

"Blackfoot," Choctaw said. "He's a little off his people's spot. Been dead a few days, about as many days as them killers is ahead of us. He come across the bear. See them scrapes on the tree."

"He climbed up there to get away from it," I said.

"Yeah, and he died up there cause the bear wouldn't go away. Far as that mama bear was concerned, he was a man, and she didn't like men none, not after what they done to her baby, so this one got between her and the ones we're after. He climbed up that tree, and she wouldn't let him down. You see them wallows? She was here a good time."

"Why didn't she climb up there and get him?"

"Grizzly ain't like a black bear, they ain't much of a climber. Bear probably surprised him, killed his horse, and the Indian made for the tree. Horse is probably under the snow around here, we took the trouble to look. Blackfoot was going to wait that ole bear out, but she waited him out. Weather was killing him, so he shortened his problem, cut his own throat. Knife is dropped down under the snow, like his moccasins. A dying man will kick something furious. He kicked himself right out of his moccasins. Wonder he didn't fall off that limb. Birds got to his feet, and his eyes, of course."

"That's a hell of a way to go."

"That took some guts, is what. Having to choose between cutting his own throat or slowly freezing to death or being eaten on by a bear, he went for the throat cutting. I don't know I could have done such a thing. I'd have just frozen."

"That is one hell of a bear," I said.

"Reckon it is."

It was a bit later in the day when we caught up with the tracks of our outlaws, them having been lost even to Choctaw for a while, but we followed what we thought was the easiest and most likely path for them to take, an ole deer run, and as we started down the mountain, we could see both the tracks of their horses, and the huge, deep tracks of that bear where the snow was thin.

"That bear ain't no quitter," I said.

"Naw, she ain't."

We came to a slope covered in snow. We rode along the edge of it, and looking off to my right, I could see the snow was thick and fluffy on the ground, and at the bottom of the slope there was a long patch of ice about thirty feet across. I had no idea how far it ran in either direction, but since it was an iced over creek, it could have gone on for miles. The ice down there looked thick and the sunlight on it made it shiny. We rode on until the iced over creek was out of sight.

—

The days blowed by and we kept at it, going down the mountain side, not all the way to the bottom, but to where it leveled out some. Choctaw said he wasn't seeing the bear's tracks anymore, so it looked like she might actually have finally played her anger out.

"On the other hand," he said, "she may not be taking the same trail we are."

Where the land broke flat for a space, we could see smoke coming up from behind some trees, and the snow down there had been heated by the sun, so there wasn't as much of it, and what was there wasn't deep.

We got down off our horses and tied them and Duncan's mount up within a patch of trees, then we scooted down to the tree line and took a peek at where the smoke was coming from.

It was a cabin, and there was a long shed built off to one side of it. The shed was partly open at the front, though a lot of dried limbs and some fresh brush had been knitted together with some rope or leather, and had been put up in front of it to block the horses from the wind. You could look through gaps in the limbs and see them stirring around in there. There was smoke coming out of a crude chimney built of rock, and there was a lot of firewood leaned up against the end of the wind break. But the thing caught my attention was there was five horses in there.

"That's a lot of horses for a little cabin like that," I said.

"Looks like our fellas are here," Choctaw said.

"Maybe it's someone else, and our men ain't in there."

"They're in there," Choctaw said, "'cause I tracked them here. They're in there, and so are some others, probably them that live there."

"Let's study on this a bit," I said.

—

We went back and got our horses and brought them down and tied them off in a place where they was out of sight from the cabin, but closer, a place where there was enough trees to block the wind a bit and hide us. Me and Choctaw had an early cold supper of jerky, wrapped blankets around us, and sat on our ground cloths. The chill came right through the waxed cloths and our ass-shined pants. Snow was blowing again, and coming down like shit in a Kansas cow lot.

That cabin was starting to look mighty good down there, and I was wanting to get inside. It was either that or go up the hill well out of sight of the cabin and pitch a camp to even better shield ourselves from the wind and the cold. Frankly, pitching a camp in the cold dark wasn't all that appealing, and I wasn't sure how warm even a well-pitched camp would be in a couple hours; the wind had certainly turned vicious. Blocks of ice would have wanted a blanket in that cold.

"Them boys know you, Choctaw?"

"I know them on sight, but I don't think they know me, though they might have seen me around. Can't say for sure."

"Well, I guess it could be the same for me, but a colored man ain't exactly someone they would pay much attention to, unless I was arresting them, and the only one of the bunch knowed me personal like was Duncan, on account of I had hauled him in a couple of times on minor warrants, was even responsible for him doing a short stretch in prison. But he's bear-kilt, so he ain't a worry."

"Thanks for pointing that out. I was the one explained that to you."

"So you was," I said.

"Another thing, I'm part colored too."

"But lighter skinned than me."

"Only the bottom of a coal mine is black as you."

"Proud of it, too."

"What are you thinking, Nat? You got that look."

"That my black ass is cold and I want some fire, maybe some cooked food, and that cabin looks a hell of a lot cozier than here. And in short time, come nightfall, it's going to look like heaven on a buttered biscuit."

"The inside of a dead dog's ass is cozier than here," Choctaw said. "As for heaven, I don't know. My ole mother-in-law claimed she was going to heaven, and I don't much cotton to her company, though I wouldn't mind a biscuit or two, buttered or dry."

"Didn't know you was married."

"Was is the right word. Wife moved on, and I was glad of it. What was I thinking, though, is I'm cold. And that damn bear is out there somewhere."

Being bone-cold and bear-worried was why we decided to do what we did, the situation making our thinking a little desperate.

——

It wasn't much of a plan, but it was a plan. We rode down there and stopped in front of the cabin as the red sun dropped along with the temperature. Snow-fat clouds could be seen above the tree line, and they looked purple in the dying light. The wind was starting to snap. We didn't find some real shelter soon, we was going to be icicles come morning, if it took that long.

We got down off our horses and led them and the spare one to the shed. We carefully pulled back the covering of thatched limbs and such, and put our horses in there with the others, not stirring them too much, though there now being eight of them made the fit a little tight. Thankfully, it was a big shed. We decided to leave our rifles on our saddles, and just keep our pistols for close work.

By that time, the sun had set completely and the world was dark, but the light inside the cabin glowed warm through the wax paper covering the two windows and stuck out over the snow through the cracks in the door.

I snuck up near the door, which was made of thick slats. There were gaps between the slats, and you could hear the men inside talking. I took a stealthy step closer and put my eye to one of them openings.

There was our two men. I recognized them from having seen them around Fort Smith. There was a man's body on the floor, half his head missing, the blood around it looking like a pool of dried molasses in the flickering light from the fireplace. There was a big black Dutch oven sitting on the coals, and I could smell meat cooking, and it was such a pleasant smell, my stomach growled softly, like a kitten about to lick at some fresh poured cream.

I put my eye against another crack to give me a different angle on things, and I could see a slim, dark-haired woman in a calico dress sitting on a chunk of log by the fireplace, and a boy, who I figured was nine or ten, was standing next to her, his arm around her. They both looked frightened, and from time to time the boy would look down at the body. Firelight hopped around on their faces, and I could see they had been crying, and that told me a lot of the story.

247

This was where that little family was staying when them two come up. They had killed the man of the house, and now the woman and the child was all that was left of the former occupants. Our two men were sitting in chairs at a plank table near the fireplace that had an axe leaning against it, and on the wall, hung on some fat nails was three pairs of snowshoes.

Those two killers would look over at the woman from time to time, and they was practically licking their lips over her. I knew what that was going to lead to.

I checked to see if anyone else was in the cabin by switching to another crack in the door where I could see in the other direction. On that side was an indoor well with a rock curbing, and a low-built bed with a pile of blankets on it and a couple of pillows. There was a roll of blankets stuffed under the bed. The light inside was coming not only from the fireplace, but from some candles placed about the cabin, and some large kerosene lanterns on the bed side of the room. I could feel heat from the fireplace seeping through the gaps in the door and it felt mighty good.

The one called Keb Rutten, a fat, two-chinned, no-neck fellow, was looking at the woman the hardest, as he was facing that way, a plump hand resting on the hilt of his holstered revolver, his tongue licking out now and again, like a snake tasting the air. The other, a skinny man with a beak nose that made him look like a big chicken, would turn from time to time and look at her. One of his eyes was white from having been injured at some time in his shitty life. That there was Turnip Farner. He was a sneaky turd, had stabbed many a man with a thin, long-bladed knife he kept tucked up his sleeve. He was wearing a gun too, on his left side, and if memory served me, he wore one on each hip, though the way he sat I couldn't see his other hip to note if a gun was there.

"We could cut cards for her," said Turnip.

"Wish we could race our horses for her," said Keb. "That would be best."

"That's stupid," said Turnip. "Ain't doing no racing out there, not in this weather."

"I know that. Think I don't know that? I was just talking."

"Yeah, well, best you're just talking," Turnip said, "that nag of yours couldn't make a decent mile unless it was in the back of a freight wagon."

I eased away from the door and back to Choctaw. I whispered to him what I had heard, and then we backed off farther and considered on things.

"First thing we got to do is see if there's a back door," he said.

We slipped around back and found there was one. We needed to know where that was, just in case one of us went through the front, the other the back, or the men made a break for it that way.

Easing back into a row of trees we come up with some ideas.

"I'll stay at the back door," he said. "One of them comes out, I'll yell for him to hold his hands up. After I shoot him a couple times."

"I'll go to the front and knock."

"Oh, that there will turn out well, dontcha know?"

"I could try and kick the door in. Planks or not, it looks sturdy enough to cause some trouble, with real hinges and such, and there's a bar across it. Back door might be the same."

"Yeah, it might. Maybe it's best we both go through the front door."

I nodded. "I'll knock, and you stand off to the side with a pistol ready."

Back around front, Choctaw drawed his gun and stood to the side and I, bold as a drunk preacher, knocked on the door.

A moment passed, and then there was an eye at one of the cracks, looking out at me. It was the skinny man, as I could see part of him where the crack widened, and of course it was his good eye pressed to the gap.

"Who are you?" he said.

"Nat," I said. "My horse died on me. Seen your smoke, and I'm cold. I can chop firewood and such for you, just for a bite."

"Who is it?" I heard Keb say.

"A cold nigger," Keb said. "Says he's hungry and will chop wood to eat."

"A nigger, and he come to the front door? He's gonna get a lot colder."

"I can go to the back door," I said.

"You can go to hell, is what you can do," said Turnip.

"Little cold for hell out here," I said.

"Are you being smart, boy?" Turnip said.

"I'm being cold, is what I'm being."

"You go on away," said Turnip.

Then Keb called out, "Can you dig a grave, boy?"

"Why would I dig a grave?"

"Might be digging your own, but it's for a fellow died in here. We need to get him out, he'll be stinking up the place soon."

"I could dig it for a meal, but I ain't got no shovel."

"We got a shovel."

"Give it to me," I said.

"Why don't you give him the shovel, Turnip," said Keb.

"Yeah, I can give him the shovel."

I heard the bar on the door move, and I knew what he planned to give me wasn't no shovel.

I pulled the LeMat and stuck it against the crack with the shot-gun shell trigger ready, and before he could jerk the door open and shoot me, I fired through the crack and the wood around it shattered and some of the pellets and wood from the shot bounced back into me, but not with any real zip. I heard Turnip yell and stumble back.

"Go," Choctaw said.

I rammed against the un-barred door, and it sprung open. I had the drop on Keb, who had made a move to pull his pistol. I had fired my shotgun load, but I had nine other rounds I could use on him. I said, "Go on, pull that pistol."

Choctaw come in behind me right smart-like, and stood there with his gun drawn, pointing it at Turnip who had fallen down and then got up and was leaning against the far wall. He was holding his middle, but wasn't leaking any blood, just a few sprinkles.

"You're right spry for being belly-shot," Choctaw said to him.

I went over with my pistol drawn and took both Turnip's and Keb's guns, along with Turnip's sleeve knife, and tossed them outside in the snow. Turnip had indeed been armed with a pistol on either hip. I closed the door and barred it.

"That snow ain't good for them pistols," Keb said.

"I've heard such," I said.

—

Keb said, "What kind of goddamn gun is that?"

"LeMat," I said. "Nine rounds and a shotgun load."

I said this as I was pushing into the pistol another shotgun shell. I let the used one drop on the floor.

I went over and looked at Turnip, who was still leaning and holding is belly.

"I feel like I been punched," he said.

"Wood caught most of it," I said, as he eased a bent-up whisky-leaking flask out from under his shirt. That was why he was still alive. There were red marks on his belly, a little blood and some buried pellets, but the flask and the door planks had taken most of the shot.

"You might be the luckiest son-of-a-bitch that ever lived," I said.

"I don't feel all that lucky," Turnip said.

"Well, whatever luck you've had, it ends tonight," Choctaw said.

The woman and the child hadn't said a word. They was looking at us like they had traded two horrid desperadoes for another pair deserving of equal caution.

"Miss," I said, "you and your little boy are safe with us. I'm Nat Love, a U.S. Marshal, and this is my friend and tracker, Choctaw."

"Ma'am," Choctaw said, and touched his hat brim.

"But you're niggers," she said.

"A simple thank you will do," I said.

"They let you have a badge?" the boy said.

"Yes," I said. "And it even has a pin on the back so it'll go on my shirt."

I peeled back my coat and showed them the badge on my shirt.

"Now I've seen everything," the lady said.

"Again, thank you is nice enough," I said.

This time the lady reddened.

"Thank you," the lady said, and the boy said the same right after her.

———

"Well, boys," I said, "come daylight you're on your horses and heading back to Arkansas."

"You might even make it all the way back, you're congenial," Choctaw said.

"Congenial?" Turnip said.

"Not my fault you ain't got no education," Choctaw said.

"Just learned that word, didn't you?" I said.

"Yeah," Choctaw said.

I laughed and looked at the woman and the boy.

"I was wondering about what's in that pot cooking there," I said.

"It's rabbit," said the boy.

"Yeah?" I said. "I like rabbit."

"It's got some potatoes in there, and they're mostly good," the woman said. "We had to dig out some rot spots."

"Done that many a time," I said. "Ma'am. Considering me and Choctaw here are kind of watching these boys, do you mind fixing us all up a plate. I'm so hungry I'm starting to see cornbread trying to crawl up the wall."

"I got some cold cornbread and three plates and the rest is bowls," she said. "I got enough spoons and forks, though."

"Bowls are fine," I said. "Don't pass out any knives, however. And I think we might ought to move your poor husband to the outside before we break bread."

"That ain't my husband," she said. "My husband, Benny, done died earlier this year from some kind of sickness, and this fellow just come up today and offered to cut some wood for a meal, and that was cooking when these two showed up. I invited them in to eat, and they killed that fella right off. Fat one took the axe there and hit him in the head with it while he was piling wood into the fireplace. Truth is, I don't know none of these men, dead or alive."

One thing for sure, the lady wasn't a school teacher.

"All right, then," I said. "Turnip, you and Keb get his feet, and carry him out. Choctaw will go first, and I'll follow up. Don't get squirrelly or you'll make us have to dig you boys holes."

"If we bother," Choctaw said.

They carried the poor man who had just stopped by to cut firewood for a meal outside, and we had them tote him off a goodly distance from the cabin. I went back to the shed where my horse was, and got my little shovel and brought it back, threw it in the snow at Turnip's feet, said, "You two take turns."

They did just that, and finally the hole was dug, though it was a mite shallow. They put the poor axe-kilt fella in the hole, and then we started back to the cabin.

As we was about to go inside, I heard what I thought was something snorting. Choctaw hustled them two indoors, and I stood out there in front of the open door with one hand holding the shovel, the other resting on the butt of my LeMat. I saw a shadow move through the trees at a casual rate, and that damn shadow was bulkier and taller than a horse. The little curlies on the back of my neck stood up like wire. I watched as the shadow moved into the trees and out of sight. I shook a little with a chill that wasn't from the cold, and went inside and closed the door and put the bar across it.

"That door used to have some filling in it," said the boy. "It was dried mud, but it worked good for a long time. Papa put it in there."

I looked over at him and his mama. She had a big rag and was trying to wipe up the blood on the floor, which was a big job, considering how much there was of it, and it being dried. The floor was made of slats of wood, and there were gaps in it, and she sloshed some water from a bucket on it and some of the blood turned soft and ran through the cracks.

I got a blanket off the bed and hung it over a couple nails on either side of the door, and that heavy blanket helped cut the cold blowing in through the cracks and the hole I had made with the LeMat.

We made Keb and Turnip sit against the wall with their legs sticking out. Choctaw took the filled food bowls from the lady, who told us her name was Mrs. Jones, and he gave them to them two, and then we pulled the table to the other side of the little cabin and me and him had our meal there, while the woman and the boy ate sitting on the rock fireplace front. It was pretty comfortable, even taking into account the dried blood from the dead man, the fact that two killers were sitting on the floor, and there was a bear outside about the size of a milk wagon.

"I seen the bear," I said, while we were eating. "Just before we come inside."

"Oh, hell," Turnip said, setting his already empty bowl aside. "She's a big one for a sow. She caught up with Thompson and tore his horse up, and then she tore him up."

"Hadn't been that bear was working on him, we wouldn't have got out of there," Keb said.

"You didn't stay to help, did you?" Choctaw said.

"If we had, we'd have been kilt too. Wasn't nothing we could do for him. He was done for right off. I tell you, that bear stood up, she was fifteen feet tall and as wide as the gates to hell."

"She ain't that big," Choctaw said.

"Well, she seemed it," Keb said.

"You'll soon get to measure them hell gates, is the way I see it," Choctaw said. "They're gonna hang you two like curtains."

"Don't be so sure, half-nigger," Keb said. "Every dog has its day."

I smiled. "To say what Bat Masterson said to me once, every dog has his day, unless there are more dogs than days. So, I was you, I wouldn't count on you two dogs having that day."

"I don't know what that means," Keb said.

"I'm not sure either," Choctaw said, "but I like the sound of it."

Well, we was all out of small talk by then, and me and Choctaw decided we'd take turns sleeping, the other watching them two. We left the kerosene lamps burning, but blew out the candles. Choctaw went out and got our bedding and laid out our bed rolls. Choctaw took to his right away. The woman settled in on the bed by the well, and the boy rolled out a thick pallet on the floor, covered up, and went to sleep as if nothing had happened that night that was out of order.

I sat at the table with the LeMat on the table, and my hand on the trigger that would set off a fresh shotgun shell.

After a bit, Keb and Turnip drifted off. Turnip fell over on the floor, while Keb kept his back to the wall, snoring like a bull at rut.

I listened to the wind outside, and sometimes I thought I heard something else, that damn snuffling sound that a bear can make. But I could never be certain. I figured it might have actually been the wind, or even my imagination. But right then I was wishing I hadn't left my Winchester on my horse.

After what I figured to be a few hours, I shook Choctaw awake, and was preparing to get some sleep, but not before I went out and took the saddles off our horses and made them more comfortable. We hadn't gotten to that yet, and it was long overdue. I also learned there was an outhouse out back, and I thought I might stop there before I came back in.

I told Choctaw what I was doing, put my coat on, as I had taken it off during my watch, and went outside and started making my way to the outhouse. It was clear now, and the moon was bright and the snow was almost blinding in the moonlight.

I was watching myself pretty careful, on account of I knew that bear was around there, and I feared not only for myself, but for the horses. I looked this way and that, put my hand on the butt of the Colt and kept moving.

After I finished at the outhouse, nervous as a long tailed cat in a room full of rocking chairs, I took the barrier in front of the shed down, saw all the horses was all right. I fed them all some of the grain that was in a lid-covered barrel in the shed, and when I finished scooping that out, and seeing they was taken care of, I pulled my Winchester loose, closed up the front of the shed, and started back to the house.

I was about twenty feet from the door, but slogging on account of the snow, which had thickened due to a heavy downfall of the stuff while we was in the cabin. I was starting to anticipate the warmth and the pallet Choctaw had made, when I heard a cracking sound. I jerked my head around and seen that big ole bear coming down from the tree-line, running damn fast, faster than I had expected a beast like that to run.

And though in that moment I only took note of that bear briefly, I can tell you now, these many years later, I have never seen a bear that big. I had glimpse of her before, but now that she was out from under the trees and the shadows, I could see her damn good there in the moonlight. I didn't know nature made them that big, especially a female, but I will swear on a stack of bibles, which is easy for me as I'm a non-believer, but I swear that bear, had it stood on its hind paws, would most likely have topped twelve feet and weighed a thousand pounds. Keb wasn't far off.

I might also add that bear could run as fast as a locomotive on a downgrade, but fortunately for me, I was close enough to the door to rush inside, close it and bar it, pull the blanket in place, (as if that mattered) just as that bear hit it the way a boulder would have if it were rolling downhill.

"Goddamn," Chocktaw said. "What was that?"

I cocked the Winchester, backed up, said, "About a thousand pounds or so of bear, I reckon."

That's when the bear roared and I heard it moving away from the door, snuffling and growling, padding around the cabin, circling it out of frustration.

Now Turnip and Keb was awake, and they was hearing the bear too.

"You ought to give us guns," Turnip said. "We might need them."

"Might need them," I said, "but ain't going to have them."

Now the bear was roaring, and we could feel it hitting against the back of the cabin, probably raising up on its hind legs and slamming its front paws against it.

"Don't let it eat us, Marshal," the boy said. He had woke up, as his mother had, and they was sitting on the end of the bed, arms around each other.

The bear went on pounding on the rear cabin wall for a time, then she was moving back around to the front door, and she wasn't making any point to be stealthy.

The front door was the weak point. There was the two windows, of course, just covered with wax paper, but they were too small for the bear to come through them.

I guess Choctaw, like all of us, had turned his attention to the sounds of that bear, 'cause that was when Keb, moving fast for a fat man, leaped up and dove for the axe against the fireplace.

Choctaw wasn't as distracted as he seemed. He yelled, lifted his revolver and shot Keb between the eyes.

Keb dropped the axe and fell back against the side of the fireplace, his hand flared out and went up against the hot stones closest to the fire and the flesh on his plump mitt sizzled.

His brain must have still had some life in it, cause the hand flapped back against his chest and he lay there with his mouth open, wiggled slightly, then quit.

"You're next, fool," Choctaw said to Turnip, then turned slightly toward the woman and child, said, "Excuse me, ma'am, for shooting a gun indoors."

She nodded, and the boy sat there frozen, staring across the room at the little dark hole in Keb's forehead.

That's when the bear slammed against the front door and the wood slats cracked.

———

I fired a couple of quick shots from my Winchester through the blanket over the door, knocking it loose and onto the floor. That bear let out with a squeal, rustled away, crunching snow underfoot. She didn't move far, though, as I could still hear her snorting out there.

"Hit it?" Choctaw said.

"You heard it squeal," I said. "I hit it all right."

I sidled up close to the front door and peeked out through a gap that had been widened by my shotgun blast and the weight of that bear. I didn't see her, but I could hear her out there, growling low down in her belly like someone was heating up a boiler.

I picked the blanket off the floor and hung it in place again, because it made some difference in the warmth.

The woman and the child had risen from the bed and had moved near the window on that side, the woman against the wall, the boy in front of her, her arms wrapped around him.

"Is it gone?" she said.

"Can't say for sure," I said. "But you'll want to get away from that window."

And then the wax paper over the window ripped and a paw I could have sat in swiped through the gap and caught the widow upside the head and knocked her across the room. Her body went rolling up against the well curbing.

The boy was still in his exact spot, it had all happened so fast. He turned, and there was the bear, forcing her head through the window, snapping her teeth at him. She would have had him too, had Choctaw not leaped across the room and grabbed the back of the boy's overalls and jerked him to safety.

I pumped a couple of shots at the bear with the Winchester, and I swear, one of my bullets bounced off that beast's thick head and went clattering onto the floor. The second may have hit it. I couldn't be sure right at that moment. But the shots were enough to drive it away.

I eased over to the window and looked out. I could see dark drops on the snow, but no bear.

"I know I hit it," I said, "but it was about like sticking it with a needle. Annoyed it more than hurt it, I think."

"Can you see it?" Turnip said.

He was pressed against the far wall so tight, he could have been one of the logs.

"No," I said. "She's moved out of sight."

"Did you see that head?" Choctaw said. "That is one big bear."

The boy started crying.

I went over and looked at his mother, but the bear had swatted her so hard, her head was at an angle that didn't cause me to question her being dead. I got a blanket off the bed and covered her up and went over and put my arm around the boy's shoulders. He was sobbing something awful by then.

All of a sudden, he broke loose and grabbed my Winchester, which I had leaned against the wall next to me, and made a run for the door.

Chasing after him, I caught him quickly and snatched the Winchester from him.

"You ain't got no chance against that," I said.

"I'm going to kill it," he said. "I'm going to do it. You can't stop me."

To prove his point, he turned and charged at the door. He didn't have no kind of weapon, not even a pocket knife, but he was crazy mad.

I snatched him back again, wheeled him around, and socked him on the jaw pretty hard. He crumpled to the floor. I picked him up and laid him out on the bed and got the covers over him.

I looked at Turnip, just to make sure he hadn't tried to get feisty during the distraction, and he hadn't. He was still tight against the wall.

"You got to watch after me," Turnip said. "I'm your prisoner, and you got to take me back alive."

"Who says," Choctaw said. "This here place is piling up with bodies. What's one more?"

———

After a while, the boy was sitting up in bed, wide awake, crying and shaking, a big bruise on his jaw where I'd socked him. Choctaw walked him from the bed and set him near the fire and put one of the blankets from the bed around him, gave him a pat on the head.

I patched over the window by hanging another blanket over it. That wasn't any protection against the bear, but it was protection against the wind, and there was just something about having that gap covered that made me feel better. That cabin was simple on supplies, but it had a lot of blankets, and that turned out to be a good thing, because it was really cold, now that we had let the fire burn down.

There was a bit of wood inside, but the bulk of it was outside in a stack against the cabin. I decided I'd go out and get some of it. It was a decision I would have hesitated on until morning, had my breath not been blowing out in clouds.

"I'll go," Choctaw said.

"No, you won't. I'm the Marshal."

"You're not my boss," he said.

"Still, I'm going."

I carried the Winchester with me along with a lantern, and went out and had Choctaw close and bar the door. I crunched through the snow, looked first in one direction, then the other, paused to look behind me. I had the Winchester in my right hand, the lantern in my left. I was ready to drop that lantern if need be, and start firing my Winchester. I figured with the moon as bright as it was, I'd see that bear coming, and before I saw it, I hoped to hear it, but though a bear can be a noisy critter, if it decides to be stealthy, it can be.

As I neared the shed, I saw one of the horses lying in the snow, coloring it with its blood. When I got closer, the barrier was down, and all the horses were gone, except that dead one. There was blood inside the shed. I could see it in the lantern light.

I blew out the lantern and left it by the side of the shed, gathered up some wood, and trudged back to the cabin, my Winchester on top of the pile. Mama bear didn't come down out of the woods to eat me.

I knocked on the door and Choctaw let me in. I dropped the wood against the wall near the fireplace.

"The horses are gone," I said. "One of them, not mine or yours, is dead, maybe all of them. Can't say. They probably run off in the timber there. I don't know if the bear got them or what."

"Now if that don't cut all," Choctaw said. "I didn't hear a thing."

"It's like it's planning," I said. "Do bears plan?"

"I can't see them organizing a picnic, but I think they might plan a simple thing or two, like sneaking up on them horses and knocking the barrier down. I don't know that she knew it was putting us on foot, though, but I guess it's possible. Damn, she done that quiet. I didn't hear a thing."

"Me neither," I said.

"Oh shit," Turnip said. "Shit, shit, shit."

"The boy," Choctaw said. "Cut that talk."

"Hell, he don't know shit from wild honey," Turnip said. "Look at him."

The boy was sitting on the rock facing around the fireplace, the blanket pulled tight around him, rocking back and forth, his eyes glazed over. His mother's body was just a couple feet away from him.

"Still," Choctaw said, "watch your goddamn mouth."

"I'm going to go back and get the lantern," I said.

"We got enough lanterns and candles, leave it," Choctaw said.

"Reckon you're right," I said.

"Why the hell would you go out there again for a lantern?"

"I have no earthly idea," I said.

"What now?" Turnip said. "What now?"

"First," Choctaw said, "you shut up."

"We can't stay here," I said, "we got to get Turnip back to be hung."

"Damn you," Turnip said.

"I told you to shut up," Choctaw said.

"Morning, we can go out and look for the horses," I said.

"Guess that's all we can do," Choctaw said.

I put some wood on the fire and fanned it with my hat. When it was going good, I stretched out on the bed and covered up and slept while Choctaw took watch.

—

The next morning felt warmer than the day before, but that may have been due to me feeling a bit more positive in the daylight. Still, it was wise not to fool one's self into thinking the world had grown hospitable.

I did a bit of a scout outside, carrying my Winchester at ready. Over by the corral I could see that during the night the dead horse had been chewed on, but not by that bear. She wasn't killing to eat, she was killing for revenge. From the tracks around the body I knew wolves had come out of the woods to dine on what the bear had left them.

The horse tracks of the other mounts were clear as well, and they had bolted across the clearing and into the woods. They could have been caught there by the bear, could have wandered off, or could be well on their way home, a trek they were unlikely to make, it being so damn far, and them being accustomed, as they were, to being housed and fed.

There wasn't nothing for it but to head out home on foot, or find some place where we might get a horse, though that would be some distance from where we were now. The other alternative, maybe even the smarter one, was to hole up in the cabin for some months until the weather was good.

—

Back inside, I explained the situation to Choctaw. The boy had ended up in the bed and was asleep. Turnip was eating a breakfast of pickled eggs that the woman and her boy kept in a wide mouthed jar full of brine. He looked unhappy about it, sitting there with an egg balanced on a spoon.

I took out my knife and speared me one of the pickled eggs, said to Choctaw. "We can stay here until spring, when things warm up and the trail is more passable without a horse. There's some food here and the game is thick, so we could do that. Or, we could start out on foot, see if we can veer off and find someplace where people live and have horses. We got three pairs of snowshoes, and there's four of us, so we need to make us a make-do pair."

"Y'all go on and leave me here," Turnip said. "I'll just slow you down."

"We leave you here," Choctaw said, "it'll be the same way your pal Keb and that poor woman will be left here. That what you're looking for, Turnip?"

"Don't believe it is," Turnip said.

"Then shut up. And who named you Turnip anyway?"

Turnip didn't answer, consigning the revelation to eternal mystery.

I thought on things a minute, said, "I think we got to see if we can make another pair of snowshoes, figure out how to carry as much food as we can from the cabin, and then we got to start out. We prepare today, and go on tomorrow, starting bright and early."

We spent that day digging graves for the Keb and the boy's mother, and even went to the trouble to say some words over the boy's mother, if not the dead jackass Keb. The words were kind of hollow, me not thinking the dead went anywhere but to dust, but it seemed to make the boy feel better. I just kind of made it all up, saying it in a preacher like manner and pretending my words were from the bible, which I had read from when I was a child, the reading of it being my cure from religion.

I then spent time making a pair of snowshoes from green wood and pieces of rope from the shed. They weren't the best snowshoes that could be made, but they was probably the best I could make.

The boy's folks had horse packs, so we had the boy fill them with provisions and such, to keep him busy at something and his mind off what had happened to his mama. It seemed to help a mite.

It was still daylight when we had those chores done, and on one of my trips outside to pee in the snow, as the outhouse didn't seem necessary for such a relief, as I was walking back to the cabin, coming out of the tree line were three horses, Dobbin and Choctaw's mount being two of them, and one a little sorrel horse that was merely following the other two. As for the others, I have no idea to this day what became of them.

I carefully went into the shed and poured grain in some large pans there, and the horses heard it, and they trotted over to eat. They had most likely forgotten about the bear, as horses are some of the dumbest animals on earth, though I rush in here to say that Satan, back home, wasn't a dummy, and he had the bravery of a wild stallion. He was the sort that would have tried to kick and bite that ole bear to death, and if the bear got away, he might have formed a posse to hunt it down.

I gently put the barrier up again in front of the horses, and though it had been knocked loose, it wasn't hard to fix. When that was done, I went back to the cabin. When I come inside, Choctaw looked at me.

"What you grinning about?"

"Might not need them snowshoes," I said, "three of the horses come back."

We started out the next morning at the crack of dawn, the sun bleeding through the trees, red and gooey like a stepped-on pomegranate. We saddled up the horses, loading our snowshoes and goods on them, and feeling a mite more hopeful than the day before.

The boy rode on the back of Choctaw's horse, Choctaw in front, and I gave Turnip the small horse to ride, and rode Dobbin. I had tied

Turnip's hands good, fastened them to the saddle horn. I had taken his boots, and wrapped his feet in blanket rags so they was warm. That way he might not have the urge to run off in the snow, as his blanket-wrapped feet would have grown wet quick and he would have had about as much chance of surviving out there without boots as a plucked duck with one leg.

Anytime we stopped, I gave him his boots back, and once he was on his horse, I pulled them off and gave him the dry rags to wrap his feet again.

The first day went off smooth, and so did the night. We camped among some trees overlooking a valley, and the moon lay on the valley and the mountains beyond. The snow gleamed beautifully and shone white as flour gravy on the peaks across the way that were heaped up like mounds of mashed potatoes. The air was crisp in the lungs, but not painful as before. It tasted sweet and made you feel, that at least for that moment, you were as fresh as a new-born baby.

I was beginning to think that all we had to do was stay steady and make the trip, that the worst was behind us, and that we would get Turnip to Judge Parker, tell the judge about the others, then figure on finding someone to take care of the boy.

The boy was, as you would expect, down in the dumps, and said little. He had lost his father, seen men killed in his own cabin, and then seen his mother swatted down by a vengeful bear. I did learn one thing from him, though. His name was Peter, but his mama called him Pete.

Me and Choctaw, worn to the bone, made a warm camp and tied Turnip up good, so we could both sleep, having faith in our knots, which was a confidence well warranted, for as morning cracked some light on us, we found he was still bound and as irritable as ever.

We had a quick breakfast of pickled eggs and no coffee, as it was too damp for a fire, then we loaded up our horses and started out again, this time with Pete sitting behind me instead of behind Choctaw. I had a rope fastened to the saddle horn, and it led back to Turnip and his bound wrists. He rode without reins, the horse he was on following mine easily, and behind him, just in case Turnip decided to do something stupid, was Choctaw.

The sun was warm when we were out from under the trees, but when we rode in shade, it was quite cold. We came upon the rise with the iced creek below, the place I had admired before. Trees had grown heavy with snow since we was there last, and a couple of small ones had broken down beneath the weight, and had fallen and were lying near the icy creek. We paused there to take in the beauty of the place, and give time for our horses to blow a little. To our right was a higher rise than we was on, and there were trees there, and the snow looked deep around and between them.

As I sat on Dobbin, my gloved hands resting on the saddle horn, I saw coming through the trees a great tumbling snow-coated boulder, and of course I felt a sense of panic, on account of it was rolling right toward us, and rolling fast.

Before I could do a thing, that boulder was on us, and it wasn't rolling after all, and it wasn't no boulder, it was that damn grizzly bear, running like it had a lit pitch-coated stick stuck up its butt.

———

The bear hit my horse and me, but I didn't get clawed or bit. I got knocked, and so did Pete. I went rolling down the hill, and Dobbin sort of bounced on his side, and bounded over me like he was made of nothing. Since he was certainly made of something, I was lucky he bounced like that.

The bear tumbled after him, and Dobbin caused Turnip, who was bound to the saddle horn, to get jerked up like a rag in a high wind, and to smash into me as I was trying to stand. Turnip hit me so hard I thought I was dead. My breath went away and things went black, and for some reason I had a vision of hot cornbread on a platter, then I had a vision of being eaten by a bear, and the next thing I knowed I was on the icy creek and had come awake, and I wasn't exactly spry.

Dobbin was in the middle of the ice, and he was as dead as a pledge of chastity. His whole right side, including my saddle, was ripped like an open change purse. Dobbin's guts was pushed out between him and the cut in the saddle, and the guts steamed in the frosty air. I could smell his insides, a stink of shit and oats and blood. I was glad he was dead, lest he suffer any; it had at least been quick. Thing was, though, my Winchester was on my saddle still, stuck in its sheath.

I saw that Pete had rolled out on the ice too, and was near Turnip and Dobbin. The bear had tumbled over Dobbin, and was scrambling to get her feet under her, but the ice kept slipping her down on her belly.

Turnip, his hounds still bound, was trying to get up, but one of his legs wasn't working, and there was a bone punching through his pants like he had been shot with an arrow. He was screaming so loud I felt like my butthole was going to turn inside out.

I didn't have no choice. I pulled the Colt with one hand, my LeMatt with the other, and started out on the ice.

"Don't do it," I heard Choctaw yell, and I looked up to see him pulling out his rifle from his saddle sheath, pointing it at the bear.

Course, now the boy had stood up, and the only thing between him and the bear was Dobbin. Way he was in front of the bear, I figured Choctaw didn't have a clear shot.

I slipped on the ice, hit my knee, got up, went on out, Choctaw yelling from up where he was, "All y'all, lay down."

But the boy wasn't hearing it. He was trying desperately to run, but that kept causing him to fall, and instead of staying down, he kept trying to get up. Turnip was still screaming, and the ice-slipping bear was puffing like she had a bellows working inside of her.

I carefully worked my way toward the boy. As far as I was concerned, Turnip, at least for the moment, was on his own. I stepped in such a way I wasn't slipping, but the thing was the bear had climbed on Dobbin's corpse, and I could see the way she was coiled she was about to leap, and if she did, she was going to land on Pete like a ton of Missouri brick.

That's when there was a loud cracking sound, and I seen the ice beneath Dobbin and the bear split, and I could see water in the crack, and then it widened and away went Dobbin, taking that she-bear with him into the drink.

———

The bear came up and clawed at the ice in front of it, but that chipped away, her claws not being good for grabbing hold of something that slick.

I holstered my pistols, grabbed the boy and slung him up on my shoulders, which made me a might heavier on that thin ice than I wanted to be. I started back toward solid snow-covered ground, but I hadn't gone but a few steps when I heard the ice snap again, and looked back to see a thin crack, spreading out from where the bear was treading water, heading toward us. I quit looking, and kept going.

Turnip was yelling for help and had managed to get loose of the ropes on his wrist before Dobbin went under, but the ice had widened, dropping him into the water, and there wasn't a thing I could do for him right then. I had to get the boy to safety.

I hadn't no more than got to the snow bank, then I heard a sound like lightning snapping across the sky.

I slung the boy off my shoulder just as Choctaw fired from up on the hill.

I glanced back. If Choctaw hit the bear, I couldn't tell it. It was preoccupied with scrambling to safety, but the ice around it had gone away and now there was just water. Turnip was trying to swim out, but was drifting back toward the bear, his leg causing him paddle problems.

Choctaw fired again, but the bullet hit the water near the bear, and then Turnip floated right into the beast. There was a flurry of water, flesh, blood, and fur, and then Turnip's head was in the bear's jaws and the bear was shaking him back and forth like a dog taking down a rabbit. Turnip's head snapped free and his body went sailing out into the water amidst a spray of blood. The bear spat Turnip's head out like a rotten potato.

I was trudging up the snow bank now, and I saw Choctaw, still on his horse, lift his rifle again.

I yelled out, "No, Choctaw. Don't."

The look he gave me was at first confused, but slowly he lowered the rifle.

I got up close to Choctaw, where he sat on his horse.

"Guess the water will get that ole bear," Choctaw said.

"Come help me."

I didn't wait for him to answer, but started back down to the creek. On the creek's edge, I got hold of one of the trees, looked out at the bear that was treading furiously, trying to swim to shore. Normally a bear is a pretty good swimmer, but that water was freezing cold and there was still patches of ice, and she couldn't quite get herself sorted.

I started pulling at the tree, and though it wasn't very big around it was heavy, and I could only move it a little.

Choctaw and Pete both came down and grabbed the tree and started pulling it so that the tip of it went out in the water.

"You're a crazy son-of-a-bitch," Choctaw said.

"Don't I know it."

The boy laughed a little.

We got the tree's end moved close to the bear, and she scrambled to it, and clung there for a moment.

"I'd like to suggest we get back up that hill," Choctaw said.

And up we went.

Turnip's horse hadn't wandered far. I grabbed up the reins, and mounted, pulled the boy up behind me. Choctaw mounted and rode up next to me. We looked down on the creek.

The bear was clawing along the tree, the bulk of its body still in the icy water, but she was making her way toward shore. A man would surely have died from getting wet like that if he couldn't get right to a fire and into a change of dry clothes, but the bear might be all right; she was built for the cold.

We decided our best bet was to move on before the bear made the shoreline, and so we rode away as quickly as the piled snow allowed.

———

We rode on through the Rockies, and the weather stayed cold. One night, when we was camped, I went out to pee, and I was letting the water fly, and when I looked up, not twenty feet from me, between two big ole trees, was that mama bear. I knew it was her, cause the firelight from the camp was flickering across her face, and it was a face I had seen a lot of over the days.

———

She studied on me for a long time. I gently packed my pecker away and put my hand on my Colt pistol, which might have been about as helpful as a sling shot.

The bear moved toward me slightly, paused, and sat down on her haunches. She turned her head and pondered me, and then she snorted, stood, turned slowly, and moved back into the trees and into the shadows and out of sight.

I never saw her again. I never even mentioned seeing her that last time to anyone, until now. I like to think she knew that I had helped her, and her sparing me was a courtesy, but to tell you the truth, who can understand a bear?

We spent a long time crossing the country, moving toward Arkansas and Fort Smith. In fact, I had a birthday on the trail, and so did the boy, or at least that's how we estimated it. Finally, on a warm day in early spring, we came riding into Fort Smith. I had been away from home for months.

The boy stayed with me and my wife, and I didn't have the heart to put him out on his own or try and find an orphanage for him. He just kept staying and we let him. He took care of our children, which was younger than him. He cut wood and helped out with all manner of chores, though he never could have been called much of a talker.

Then one morning we woke up and found he had decamped with a bunch of cold cornbread, a spare pistol and some ammunition, and like the bear, I never saw him again.